# LATE SEPTEMBER

# Late September

# Amy Mattes

**NIGHTWOOD EDITIONS**

2024

Nightwood Editions
P.O. Box 1779
Gibsons, BC VON 1VO
Canada
www.nightwoodeditions.com

COVER DESIGN: Angela Yen
TYPOGRAPHY: Carleton Wilson
COVER PHOTO: Ryan J Lane

Nightwood Editions acknowledges the support of the Canada Council for the Arts, the Government of Canada, and the Province of British Columbia through the BC Arts Council.

This book has been printed on 100% post-consumer recycled paper.
Printed and bound in Canada.

LIBRARY AND ARCHIVES CANADA CATALOGUING IN PUBLICATION

Title: Late September : a novel / Amy Mattes.
Names: Mattes, Amy, author.
Identifiers: Canadiana 2023056917X | ISBN 9780889714564 (softcover) | ISBN 9780889714571 (EPUB)
Subjects: LCGFT: Novels.
Classification: LCC PS8626.A8546 L38 2024 | DDC C813/.6—dc23

*For someone I once loved. And someone I always will.*

# Été

*I am still*
*just a girl*
*with a journal*
*pulling petals off daisies*
*which are just weeds*
*saying*
*He loves me*
*He loves me not*

✤ ✤ ✤

I hit brew on the coffee machine and untied my apron, placing it on the worn melamine counter of the diner. I walked out the front door and the bells chimed behind me. I waited for my dad, out of sight of the customers in the window. I fiddled with the one-way bus ticket folded in my pocket. I had my Discman, some mixed CDs and a clip of batteries so long it looked as if it should have been connected to a machine gun. A soundtrack, my backpack and a skateboard. It was all I needed.

After Clara died all eyes fell on me with pity and people either leaned in or leaned away, which made the perpetual silence, the revered mountains mirrored in the lake, become a damning reflection. Nothing ever changed there but the seasons.

Our drive to the station was silent. Dad gave me a solemn hug and I climbed the steps into the Greyhound without looking back. He waved to me from outside the car as the bus pulled away, humming out of town. I waited patiently to not recognize the landscape. Hours passed and we hit brown prairie lands. I saw a huge Canadian flag, red and white, rippling in the wind as a train glided by in the foreground. I felt proud, like anything could happen, like with all the beauty and vastness there might even be some to claim as my own. I rooted myself in the present and welcomed the notion of change. Silver clouds followed my reflection in the window, flashing by in fast forward. I studied my face. It was peaceful to be nestled between the past and the future. I'd never spent much time in the present. I wanted to reinvent myself where no one knew why. I couldn't be "that poor dear girl." If I was "that poor dear girl," then

Clara was "that poor dead girl." People called us that. I heard the old ladies gossiping in the church basement, "Where was that Ines child when her sister went to the water?" An indignant question I replayed in my head every day.

I sat on the Greyhound for four days and three nights. Each time I put a province behind me I meditated on new beginnings. I shifted and sank in my seat. I packed bowls of pot in my pipe at rest stops, hoping to soothe my folded spine and make room for kinder thoughts to reveal themselves. I noticed that folks who get on buses are the ones who aren't allowed on planes. Vagrants and strippers, kids with dirty clothes and dirty mouths whose mothers curse a lot. Why is it the older you get, the sadder your face becomes when you think no one is watching you?

I read Bukowski and displayed the book beside me so people could see the cover, thinking it would send a message. I knew he was a needy, lonely old man, but I wanted to emulate his zero fucks attitude. My spongy, grey brain, only twenty years old, if not consumed by drugs, pickled by alcohol or suicidal from love, was the perfect age to decide upon its own beliefs and opinions, and I wanted to cast away the cares that clung to me like the wet sheet to Clara. I had a brand new journal; blank pages with beautiful purpose, waiting for their stories. Riding the bus with reckless ambition, I was startled by the hopes I had in leaving everything I knew behind. I fell asleep often and shook with the buzz of the road. I began tensing less in the right angles of my body the farther I got from home—a town so small the road ended. No way through. The only intersection streetlight blinking a repetitive red. A vacant four-way stop. I often stared at it from the café windows while I poured crappy coffee for the same hunched-over old people, wishing I could climb up the pole and turn it off. Just a red light eternally saying *pause* and *stop* and never *go*.

The bus extinguished its air brakes at every parcel pick-up town. I woke to find fellow travellers gone for good and new people wedging their belongings into the compartments above. I clutched my bag on the spare seat. I wasn't interested in sharing the space or making small talk. I took out a scratch ticket my parents had given me in a little package to ease the bus ride boredom. It contained a discouraging reminder of how unrealistic I was being, moving somewhere I'd never been, full of people I'd never met and a language I didn't understand. Dad called us country mice. He hated cities and didn't care much for the people who lived in them, saying they were *too cramped, too coloured, too liberal.* I could hear Mom's voice say, "You're being unreasonable, Ines." I wanted to be unreasonable. We had the same argument every time. She had been born in that godforsaken town, graduated high school, married Dad, moved in with him and had two kids. She folded his laundry and made his lunch, but I wanted something different. Leaving the borders of such a safe and quiet existence was a risk she would never take. Unreasonable to her meant losing control and, well, Dad hadn't outright said "way to go" or "good job" to me since I got fourth place at a cross country running meet when my limbs were still gangly and my chest was flat. He wanted a son. As soon as my hips turned outward and my breast buds softened, he turned even further the other way. I got used to looking at the back of his head. When Clara died, he hardened like a statue. I scratched the crossword until my nails were dark with metallic shavings. I blew the remnants off the page, revealing I had only scratched one complete word, but the word was EAST. I smiled and put the ticket in my journal, grateful to be reminded that life provides signs, if I was open to receiving them. I made myself so open that I was practically inside out.

When I stepped off the bus, zombified from days of stillness, the buzz of the Montreal summer hit me like a jet engine. The air was thick and hot. A carnival of people milled about the streets. A bright white light, like a searchlight looking for stars, swung from the rooftop of a high-rise in a constant 360-degree swoop. It was nine o'clock and the twilight lent a faint blue backdrop to the clamouring activity. The streets surrounding the station were blocked off to traffic by metal gates. Volunteers were guiding the hordes of people through the crosswalks and from the backs of their neon shirts I learned I'd arrived during the famous jazz festival. I wandered into the frenzy, shouldering the huge pack on my tilted frame. I was wet with perspiration and my load made walking amongst the crowds difficult. I ducked into a falafel place on the corner, dropped my board and gear, and feasted, elated at how the radish and tzatziki flavours cooled my burning mouth. I'd been living on nicotine and wordlessness.

I was on rue Saint-Denis and everything was unfamiliar and dizzying. I had no idea which direction to go, or how to speak. I'd never been anonymous, and it flitted through me like jabs of nervous electricity. I hailed a cab to my destination, an off-campus McGill dorm that accepted tourists during the empty summer months for cheap. I had a room rented until the end of August. I had six hundred bucks and no plans but to give it my damn all to break free. My eyes darted around the busy streets and up to the shimmering high-rises. The whole way there my chest heaved with the anticipation of freedom. I wasn't going back without a fight.

The hall wasn't on campus but instead was nestled into the heart of an urban neighbourhood. It was more sterile and factory-like than I had envisioned. The red brick encased the rectangular windows in uniform patterns. It was a quiet arrival and there were very few people around. A volunteer showed me to my room after I checked in at the office. I shared a dorm with a girl from Taiwan who wore matching accessories and expensive shoes and handbags. She was in Montreal for the summer to visit her boyfriend. I showered the dankness off and unloaded my things, putting my journal and the Bukowski book into the bedside drawer. I couldn't relax. I was eager and the quiet in the dorm was unsettling. I went upstairs into the common area and met a group of university boys from Texas playing foosball. They all wore khaki shorts. They were heading to the strippers and offered to take me with them to Super Sexe, calling it the McDonald's of strip clubs. I jumped at the chance, and we piled into a cab to the club. A woman could be seen dancing in a window platform from outside in the street and inside a neon sign on the wall read COME FOR THE PUSSY, STAY FOR THE TAP RYE. We shot white tequila in plastic cups, and they talked about their girlfriends and their futures with them or without them. They bought me a lap dance and the seasoned stripper played along, flipping her hair back and motorboating my face with her oversized, hard breasts. They laughed and muttered slurs at her and didn't give her any tip money. She was unfazed and strutted away to another table, but I felt outnumbered, like I was just part of their entertainment. The confident, flexible ease of all the dancers was trance-like and I enjoyed watching the women until one of the guys clutched my thigh under the table. I pretended I needed to go to the bathroom and left.

I walked the packed street until nightfall, taking in the free music. When my courage faltered, I cabbed back to the hall. I didn't know I was supposed to bring my own bedding so I slept on the bare mattress with my T-shirts as a pillow and a towel for a blanket. There was no air conditioning in the dorm. I kept the window half-open and I heard people out in the neighbourhood. They spoke French and sometimes English as well as other languages I couldn't name. Lying there on the damp single bed, sagging contours around me, and staring up at the water stains on the ceiling, I felt like an uninvited guest. The Taiwanese tourist giggled late into the night through thin walls and the rich Texan boys clinked their Budweiser bottles on the floor above.

As I explored downtown all week, my energy was picked off and stolen, returned and reshaped. The city was boisterous and all around me. I was inspired, stirred and scared. I'd lived all my life sheltered in a small town and Montreal was everything it wasn't: captivating, cultured, sexy and corrupt. I walked along rue Sainte-Catherine, hoping to blend in. I ate in parks. I read or wrote and mostly I watched. I hung around the stairs at Place des Arts and practised some basic French from my phrase book. I bought postcards with pictures of the Forum and the Old Port, and I wrote poems on them, which I never sent to anyone and kept in my backpack until they wrinkled and tore. I bought 40 oz. Labatt 50 beers and drank them out of paper bags. I chain-smoked. I walked with my head held high, relentlessly tough on the exterior, but inside I was a soft remnant, disintegrating like my poetry. Being anonymous made me feel protected, hidden in plain sight from the things I once did, but it was also very lonely. I wanted to be seen anew.

I covered Sainte-Catherine from Atwater to Papineau on foot: past department stores, tattoo parlours, more strip clubs, boutiques, cafés and bars, through the gay village, past metro stations and bus stops. I walked for so long I'd forget to relieve myself, to drink water. My legs ached. I guess I thought a journey had to be physical.

The streets were plugged with people, they infused the whole of the streets, the volunteers with their walkie-talkies, and obvious tourists standing in everyone's way, their hands on their hips, looking around blankly. The structures and stages, everything, was enhanced by a blanket of thick, humid air that cast halos over the masses. The lights were like fireworks, glaring and sparkling. My hometown was smaller than the crowds by a longshot, so small, but so full of gossip.

I finally asked a staff member about bedding and she gave me an old sleeping bag from the lost and found. It was ripped at the seam. I lay still in it, like a cocoon, so the stuffing wouldn't come billowing out. That night I had a dream that the cancer that had been eating my grandma's lungs finally killed her. We weren't close, she always loved Clara more, but when I checked my email in the common area the next day, there was one from my mom, and I found out it was true that she had died. *Dreams don't come true*, I wrote on the inside cover of my journal. *Dreams are true*.

✤ ✤ ✤

Prince Arthur was a pedestrian-only street with decorations hanging high above the cobblestone, connecting every building with dancing ribbons. Music played from the open doors of the restaurants, and the walkways were made narrow from all the protruding outdoor tables. It was crowded, time for afternoon drinks. I sat on my skateboard against a brick wall and wrote. I wanted to be one of the diners, gorging themselves on Greek platters piled high with seafood and lamb and potatoes and rice, drinking table wine from cheap crystal. My guidebook said the Plateau was famous for its joie de vivre and Quebecers called the time before happy hour *l'heure triste*, or "sad hour," when drinks were even cheaper than usual. I sat so long writing against a building the patrons must have thought I was homeless. I walked up Saint-Laurent with my skateboard under my arm and found a deli that had pizza by the slice rotating on pans in the window. The girl behind the counter had thick dreadlocks cradled in a scarf and as she worked the till I noticed her armpits were hairy. The tip jar had a sign that read MAKING DOUGH, BUT NOT MAKING ANY DOUGH. It was alluring how aloof she was. I was taught that you had to be nice to customers or no one would eat at your restaurant, but the place was full. Reggae music thumped from staticky speakers on the patio. I dropped all my change in the tip jar, hoping she would notice the hefty reward, but she didn't meet my eye. Her tattooed knuckles went back to kneading, and I went to the counter to douse the pizza in hot sauce and parmesan cheese. Big letters on the back shelf behind the condiments spelled out LOVE. I, for one, have always been a person who thinks that actions speak louder than decorative wall phrases, in case people forget to *Live Laugh Love* or the importance of *Kindness and Family*. I rearranged the letters to say EVOL and left.

I found a bar up the street where the whole front was an open garage door, with nothing separating the sidewalk from the customers. Outside a troop of bicycles weaved around people gathered around a street performer who had painted himself to look like he was made of copper. He stood on a bucket frozen in time. A group of young people drank beer in lawn chairs on a rooftop. Their laughter made me feel alone, but I relished it. It was "sad hour" after all. I ordered a Molson Ex and a shot of Jameson. I took a cigarette out and lit it. Bending my elbows to the wooden arms of the chair and leaning forward, I took a massive drag when I heard the unmistakable sound of urethane on concrete. I looked up as a posse of skateboarders came into view. A couple of them ollied onto the sidewalk and the sound switched to a bumpy grumbling from the smooth concrete coasting. Music to my ears. It made my teeth feel loose in a way that soothed me. Copper man changed his robot pose. As they pushed down the street, I exhaled and looked up to watch. I felt a smile lift my cheeks to my ears, and one of the boys on the sidewalk smiled back from behind tufts of hair kept in place by his toque. Businessmen leaned against the brick wall, smoking together and kicking the heels of their dress shoes. Private school girls bubbled down the street in the same uniform with different backpacks. They turned heads already. The music stopped for a long time and the bartender fiddled with the dials on the stereo. A popcorn maker sputtered and hissed out a fresh batch. I stubbed out the smoke and slammed my drinks. I left money on the bar, put on my backpack and hopped on my skateboard, cruising for the first time since I'd arrived in the City of Saints. I crossed the boulevard and headed down a side street. The comfort of the board under my feet reminded me of who I was. How I moved through spaces. Where I traded emotional pain for the physical kind—for sweaty, salty bruises and burning scrapes. Those were the wounds I was proud of.

I skated along the streets lined by brick and grey stone apartments, each adorned with a front-centred spiral staircase. The doors were all painted different colours. I coasted and weaved along Mont-Royal Avenue and stopped for a croissant and an espresso at a coffee bar the size of a closet. I skated farther and farther, pushing hard and feeling alive until I came to a bench at the entrance of Parc La Fontaine. It felt like a renounced place, given over to an artist with an easel, the final touches of sunshine done in dot rendering. People strolled along the pathways of lampposts and tall fragrant trees, joined by brick-laid curving bridges, a tragically perfect scene. Two women walked together having a dramatic conversation in French. I didn't understand what they were saying, but I admired the way they moved their bodies, their hands so responsive and sensual. They were dressed better than any women I'd ever seen before. I felt inferior, witnessing the way they caressed with their words as I sat with crumbs on my lips and a fresh stain on my shirt. I sat up straighter as they passed me.

A skateboarder in an orange T-shirt and baggy sweatpants darted out of a path towards the women. His long hair flowed behind him, and his side profile looked French and debonair. I watched him pass with my heart beating fast. He picked up speed as the path grew clear and I grabbed my skateboard and split between the talking ladies, pausing to say "Excuse-moi" in my best French. I followed him until we came to an intersection at the edge of the park. He glanced back and smiled at how obvious my efforts were, then cut across the red light and, with a hard push of his board, he coasted around the corner. I waited for the light to turn green and then skated across the street around the back of a building. I was surprised to see a small skate park made up of wooden quarter pipes and pyramids fenced in an empty lot. A group of skaters sat on top of a picnic table passing around a joint. I felt embarrassed and exposed so I rolled past them and sat down on top of a bench on the other side, avoiding their looks at all costs.

Skateboarding wasn't a thing in my hometown. The roads were rough and worn and the only paved location was the new sewer service station and it was simply a curb with sparse, flat ground. A friend's older brother was into it and we begged him to let us try, but she hurt her shoulder and stopped. He and I would double down hills and laugh with our heads tilted back, our feet braking into the gravel to slow us down before we bailed. That was when a friendship with a boy was still possible. I could sit behind him with my arms around him and it didn't matter. He taught me how to ollie and when he got a new board, he gave me his old one.

I put down my bag and went into the skate park, ran up the ramp and got ready to drop in. I nestled my back foot on the tail of my board, took a deep breath and with one last look around I dropped in, rolling over the pyramid to the opposite side, where I tried to rock my front trucks over the coping. It stuck out farther than I thought and I hung up, falling backwards onto the asphalt. Lying on my back and groaning, I heard my board reel away from me—across the park, through the gate and out into the lot. I wiped away the gravel embedded in my ass. The group winced in sympathy as my board rolled right under their picnic table. The girl with them reached under to grab it and gestured for me to come over. As I got close to them, the boy I'd followed into the park offered me the joint.

"Ça va?" he said while his brown hair shook from laughter. He had a big nose, but it was attractive. I took a puff off the joint.

"Oui, urgh…ça va bien," I managed, and then coughed.

"Tu es anglophone?"

"Oui. Je suis une anglophone stupide," I said, rubbing the baby hairs at the back of my neck, finding a fresh scrape at the base. They erupted in laughter. The boys dispersed into the skate park. They rolled in with grace and style, ollieing onto the quarter pipes, their baggy pants and long T-shirts billowing. They knew every dip and bump of the layout. The boy I followed, and the girl stayed behind. She took off her hat and I realized she had thick, black dreadlocks wrapped up underneath it.

"I'm Felix and this is ma blonde, Marie-France."

"You can just call me Marie."

"Salut," I said, trying for nonchalance in French. "Je m'appelle Ines."

I stuck out my hand to shake his and he went in with a closed fist to bump mine. The result was an awkward, trailer-hitch-like greeting, but I could tell they appreciated my attempt to speak French.

"I'm pretty new to the city."

"You just moved here?"

"Yeah, last week."

"By yourself?"

"Yeah."

"You don't know anyone?" Marie asked.

"Nope."

"We don't have many girls skateboarding here, but Marie," Felix said.

"Yeah, well I'm not very good."

"We're going to go to a baseball game tonight, if you want you can come with us?"

"Unless you want to skate more," Felix added.

"Yeah, that would be great."

Felix threw the roach on the ground and smooshed it with his sneaker. The suede toecap had a hole that was peeling away. The sign of a true skateboarder.

"Well let's go," he said, skating out of the park and into the city streets. I grabbed my bag and nervously followed them. My first couple of pushes were off centre and overdrawn until I found my balance and we rolled on and weaved together, pushing for blocks and blocks in the city streets or in the bike lanes.

The Stade Olympique looked like a spaceship with a retractable roof. We paid for our tickets and I followed Felix and Marie through all the turnstiles to our cheap seats, high above the field. We bought hot dogs and beers from the vendor. Mustard stained my shirt, and I wiped my dirty fingers on my lap. It was thirty degrees outside and we were in long pants and socks and shoes, our boards tucked sideways under our feet. Skateboarding made the snot in your nose turn black and the streets settle into your pores. It was a refusal to conform. The nestled-in grit was part of the package. I relaxed into my seat and let the noise and the game take me away. I was in good company. The Expos didn't win, but we laughed when the mascot ran around, waving his arms to get the crowd excited. The beer buzz tingled, and the stadium lights danced off my tongue when I opened my mouth wide and cheered along with them. When it was over, we rode the metro together, all three of us leaning back against the advertisements on the tram, our skateboards underarm, our pants hanging over the puffy tongues of our shoes.

"How do you guys get by here?" I asked.

"I do catering on movie sets and Felix does graphic design and sells weed."

"That's cool," I said.

"Why'd you move here?" Marie asked, but I just shrugged and spun the Spitfire wheels on my board, listening to the bearings hiss and studying the coloured map of the underground. Marie took a Sharpie out of her bag and wrote her phone number on my arm.

"Call the house sometime, we'll go skate."

"This was truly the best Canada Day I've ever had."

Felix laughed hard, his hair shaking again.

"It's not Canada Day in Montreal, it's *Moving Day*." His lips curled around the words, enveloping his charming accent. At Papineau station they left, and I waved goodbye to them with excitement. The doors slid shut and I sat back in the plastic seat, smiling at nothing, thinking about the interaction, continuing to study the veins of the metro and the places I had yet to discover.

❦ ❦ ❦

I'd wanted to go inside Foufounes Électriques since the first time I'd passed it, but I was intimidated by its two-storey maze of industrial metal and graffiti. It was a staple in the music scene and Nirvana had even played there before they were famous. The patio was loud and full of boisterous patrons, but after skating home from meeting Marie and Felix the night before, I was feeling up to some boldness. I peeked around the ground floor and noticed a hot punk girl sitting alone at the end of the bar. There were multiple rooms and bars and stages, pulling all types into its vortex of misdemeanour. I went in and sat a few stools away from her, leaning my board up against the bar underneath me. Her legs were crossed and her meaty thighs were exposed above elasticated fishnet stockings. A denim skirt was tucked amongst the folds of her curves. She hauled on a cigarette and bobbed, which appeared natural in her, as if she were rocking out to some profane music no one else could hear. She looked devilish and cool. She tucked her long black hair behind her ears and caught me looking at her, stubbed out her cigarette and came over to the seat beside me, asking for a light for the next one she had ready between her fingers. She slid onto the stool thigh first as I lit her smoke. Confident women like this didn't exist in the small town I was from.

"Hi," she said. "I'm Scarlett Slayer."

"That's not your real name."

"Obviously it's not my real name." She didn't pronounce the B, only the V. She glanced down at my skateboard.

"On Wednesdays there's a mini-ramp upstairs."

"Well, I guess I know what I'll be doing on Wednesdays from now on."

"Thursdays are my usual night. Lots of goths." She rolled her eyes.

"Beer's cheap."

"Always. I'll drink to that." She raised the bottle top to her pouty lips and took a long pull. She talked a lot while we drank our beers. She grew up in Westmount, with a manicured lawn and a double garage. She hated her parents, but still went there for dinner on Sundays. Her real name was April, like the month. She'd seen Marilyn Manson in concert three times. She was into boys and girls. My face warmed and I was caught off guard and changed the subject.

"Hey, maybe you can tell me what Moving Day is?"

"You mean, like, July 1?"

"I think so, like *Canada Day*?"

"Ha! Well, here in Montreal lots of people rent flats and the leases tend to expire on July 1. Half the city moves that day each year."

"So, they don't celebrate Canada Day?"

"Nope. I mean, there's no big parades and shit. Everyone's busy. On purpose." She winked as she took another slug of her beer and gestured to the bartender for two more. "Haven't you noticed all the crap everyone's left out in the street?"

I laughed. "One man's junk…"

"Oh, there are a lot of treasures."

"Do you speak French?" I asked.

"I can speak French," she said, "but just a lick." April stuck her tongue out and pretended to lick the air. "Tabarnac," she said, "pretty much the only French I know." She nudged me.

"Why do they swear at religion anyways?" I asked, not sure the answer mattered.

"Why do we swear at bodily functions?"

We both laughed again and said body part and function swears over and over until they lost their meaning.

"Do you speak French?"

"Not even close. Dropped it in grade eight, teacher didn't like me. How do you get a job here if you can't speak French?"

She looked at me a moment like she was measuring the quality of my character. She turned her head from side to side and stiffened her lips.

"I'm a cam girl," she said in a throwaway tone.

"What's that?"

"You don't know what a cam girl is? Where is it you said you were from?"

"No. Should I?"

"Got anywhere to be?"

"Nope." I drank again letting the fizz roll down my throat, taking in as much as I could.

"You want to come for a walk?"

"Absolutely."

We finished our beers and stumbled on foot through a McDonald's drive-thru. I gazed out to the lights of the Jacques Cartier Bridge while we walked and ate our cheeseburgers and slurped large iced teas.

"What do you do here for fun?" I asked her.

"I like to dance. I like makeup. I like painting. What about you?"

"You like painting?"

"Yeah, you don't think I look like a girl who paints?"

"I don't know, not really."

"So you just haul around a skateboard or do you actually ride it?"

"I ride it! Look, the graphic's gone." I turned my board over and showed her what was left of the logo. It was a gold-lettered Bill Pepper Element promodel, but you couldn't even tell anymore.

The city lights dazzled in opportunity before me and as I took in the thick, humid air, April twirled her ice cubes around and around explaining camming to me and repeatedly offering me a job.

"The boss is a nerd, he'll look out for you. So, no worries there. No one ever touches you, but they do see you naked, or at least in lingerie. You can wear whatever you want though. You can choose to do close-ups, usually only in private chat. There are regulars who pay you more to be the only guests you talk to, otherwise you're in a chat room full of people and you're basically the host, the DJ, the counsellor, the ugh... entertainment. You get paid by the hour, but in private chat mode you get paid by the minute."

The conversation was starting to feel like a job interview.

We strolled along together in natural unison until we reached the edge of the Old Port, where the city took on a historic architecture and the width of the street shrunk and turned cobblestone.

"So, what brings you to this deviant concrete jungle?" April laughed.

"I rented a dorm at the university for the summer. Just out here being a tourist for the first time."

"Yeah, but why here?"

"I don't really know. It was the most foreign I could get."

"Your locus of control must have kicked in."

"What's that?"

"Like your internal compass telling you to go somewhere."

I nodded.

"All I know is the walls were caving in, it was time to say good-bye."

"Sayonara to your old life, girl. You want to come in? This is my stop."

April pointed to a three-storey block of cement with textured designs carved into an overhanging gable. There was a restaurant at street level that looked expensive. It was busy and only open for dinner. A waiter dressed all in black was lifting wineglasses from the fog of a jug of hot water, then polishing and inspecting them by holding them up to the light. He didn't meet our eyes.

"Come on."

"I don't know," I said, feeling suddenly sober. "Maybe another time."

"Suit yourself," April said, turning to head up the staircase.

"Wait. Can I, like, grab your number or something?"

April shifted her weight back towards me and pulled her smokes out of her mini-backpack and tore off the fold of the package. She pulled a pen out and bit the lid off with her teeth.

"If I'm going to give you my number you better call me." She talked through the pen lid and then took it out and kissed the paper leaving a burgundy lip print over the number. She hugged me hard and squealed. I pushed it deep into my pocket and watched April climb the steep stairs, her thighs rubbing against each other, shifting the tight fishnet stockings, exposing patterns left on her skin from the holes.

I flipped up my headphones and hit play, skating back to the dorm, thinking of how openly April said she was into girls, reminding me of the time my cousin took me to a house party when I was fourteen. I visited her family for a week each summer to give Mom and Dad a break from me. The first time was after I got caught shoplifting. Then after Clara died, it became routine. A man outside a liquor stop bootlegged for us in exchange for a few cigarettes. We each got a two-litre bottle of Extra7 grape-flavoured cooler. I drank the whole thing. I ended up passed out in the basement on the cement floor, licking back sugary, purple vomit. A boy tried to put his hands down my pants and my cousin came running downstairs and pushed him off of me, yelling for him to stop. I remember how he opened the buttons to my jeans and put his hands on my pubic mound, searching for the opening to my vagina, but I couldn't move. After she stopped him, I got up and returned to the party like everything—including my blackout state—was normal.

That night a fight broke out because of me. A girl was coming at me from the bedroom, yelling and clawing at me. I guess the guy was her boyfriend. At first people tried to hold her back. She had long, sculpted fingernails that were painted. She was skinny and had a nose piercing. She was wearing a black tank top and had tattoos on her wrists that were black too. Her hair was shaved on the sides and spiked into a short mohawk. She screamed at me and tried to hit me in the face. I'd never seen someone so mad, and in that moment the rage was exhilarating. I was no longer invisible. When she managed to wrestle free, she grabbed me by my hair and pulled me into the bedroom, where I dropped to my knees and begged her to stop.

"Why are you doing this?" I yelled. A crowd gathered in the doorway. "Please! I don't want to fight you."

She let me get to my feet and we stood facing each other. I was anticipating a violent smack, but instead she kissed me. She jammed her hot tongue down my throat. I enjoyed kissing her. People started to whistle and whoop. She took my hand and put it under her tank top. She wasn't wearing a bra and I could feel the metal barbells of her nipple piercings and I wanted to keep touching them and pinching the taut skin. In another violent swoop of motion, she slammed the door closed and locked it. She pulled me onto the air mattress and we made out. She tried to put her hands down my pants too, but I got scared. I got up frantically searching for my cousin to take me home. I returned to my parents that summer wanting to be more punk rock, wondering if maybe I was a lesbian. I bought a leather wallet on a chain and cut my hair short like hers, and somewhere in between the raucous music and the truth that I knew I also liked boys, skateboarding came into my life, satisfying the urge to belong to both groups. I was a hoyden, like Josephine March, but Daddy always said Clara or I would be disowned if we turned out to be gay. "It's just a phase, Darryl," I heard Mom say, but he made it known that he hated my haircut and he took away the chain. I wasn't turning out to be his little girl and so he kept buying me pink clothes in an effort to change me.

❧ ❧ ❧

A mirage of bent light made the roadway glisten. We were pushing hard and carving through the streets, in and out of traffic and on and off curbs, rolling over the lines that separated the sidewalks into squares under the cat's cradle of connective wires and the patchwork poster phone poles, held together by a million staples from year after year of parties and events and festivals. We pushed past all the shops and bars I was beginning to recognize, feeling stronger with my like-minded comrades.

Felix filmed Marie and me with his brand new VX1000 camcorder. We were rolling up and down the paved banks in an alley behind an old church. I was embarrassed and frustrated that I couldn't land a single trick. I hit some gravel trying a kickflip and it knocked me forward. I put my arm out to cushion the crash, but I buckled underneath myself and heard a regretful pop. I tried to play it cool. We rode the metro all the way back to their house before Marie convinced me we should walk up to the hospital. It wasn't painful, but a blue line appeared up my wrist and it was speckled with an angry inflammation. I was nauseous and knew it was broken. I hated hospitals, nothing good ever happened there, all people did was cling and wait to hear bad news. Marie stayed with me in the waiting room for almost seven hours. I was given some kind of painkiller and we ate ketchup chips from the machine and made jokes about the people around us. She made me feel so at ease I almost told her everything about Clara then and there, but I didn't want to scare her away. I let her tell me about herself instead. Marie-France, who only wants to be called

Marie. Says there's too many *Marie-France*s and *Marie-Eve*s and *Marie-Claire*s and *Marie-Helene*s in Quebec. She was the only Marie I'd ever met.

"How did you meet Felix?" I asked.

"We've been together since high school. We got married last summer. Just a small ceremony in my parents' yard. A few of the skaters came. We had our wedding cake on a skateboard. I still wore pants."

"Wow," I said. "That's crazy. I don't know anyone my age who is married."

When I came from the X-ray machine the doctor let her stay by my side so she could translate for me as he began to put the cast on.

"Un plâtre," she said, "the plaster, it needs to start here." She pointed at the top of my shoulder. I pulled back, thinking there was a mistake. I only knew a cast to go along the forearm. Marie shook her head apologetically. "No, no, he needs to stabilize your elbow."

He began to wrap the wet lasagna-looking sheets from my shoulder to my fingertips and I jolted my arm away again but he positioned it back and looked impatient. I let him cover me like a paper mache sculpture. When he got to my fingertips and it was time to take off my ring, Clara's ring, the one I always wore, I was hit with a sorrow I tried to hide by laughing. My eyes moved around the room, not landing on anything specific. I knew if I focused on one thing I was going to cave. The sterile room with all the instruments and objects awaiting their sadistic tasks. It stung my throat remembering the times I'd been in a hospital before. I ran my tongue along the scar in my mouth. I tasted the alkaline of blood. I pictured Clara in a morgue, her naked body in a metal, child-sized drawer. I slid the ring off my pinkie and placed it in the front pocket of my jeans next to April's phone number. I completely zoned out on the pale yellow walls as he applied the rest of the cast. My jaw tensed and I squeezed the knuckles of my free hand until I felt the pulse of my veins and my tears receded.

When Clara died everything that was hers was taken out of our room and hidden in the attic. In movies I always saw people go back into the dead person's preserved room and sit and smell their things and tilt picture frames and knock the dust off, but Dad rushed right in while I cried on my bed and everything went away. Her jewellery box with the spinning ballerina was gone too and all the clothes that were too small for me and full of meaning were put in garbage bags, never to be seen again. A purse of hers was left hanging on the back of our door and I found her ring zipped inside the front pocket. I took the ring out and stuck it on my finger and pinched the cheap clasp closed. The colours had stopped changing and it was a puddle of brown. I promised I'd wear it forever.

Once back at Marie's apartment, we ordered take-out chicken and fries from Au Coq and drank big beers and smoked cigarettes around the computer in their office. We watched the Zero video, *Misled Youth*, and Jamie Thomas's part gave me shivers. I yearned to be as brave. Felix uploaded the MiniDV footage and we watched it while Marie scratched on my cast with a pen.

"What does it say?" I asked.

"*Lâche pas.* It means *don't give up.*"

"Haven't yet." The rumours echoed in my head. *Ines Moreland tried to kill herself.*

It was the first time I saw myself on tape. Hearing my voice recorded was like meeting a stranger who had my face. Watching myself being a part of something made me giddy until I saw myself bail and a familiar insecurity rushed through my insides like cheap acidic coffee. They made me a bed on their couch, but I didn't change out of my clothes. For the rest of the night I patted the denim fabric of my jeans, obsessively making sure Clara's ring was still there until I fell asleep.

In the morning I snuck out the back door. Careful not to wake them I rounded into the street, thrust my board onto the pavement, hopping on in a natural stance, front knee slightly bent. I skated home feeling satisfied, enjoying the smell of frying bacon and the long, thin line of golden sun that held up the morning and hovered in alignment with the uniform apartment buildings of Hochelaga-Maisonneuve. The cast was heavy, but I could still carve through the streets. Pushing through the streets brought me to life. It let me be a kid. It let me be myself. It wanted nothing from me. Going home amidst the roar of wheels on pavement when the whole street was empty. Pure expression in defiance of arbitrary rules. Skateboarders use the designs of a city in ways that were never intended. Marie's phone number now adorned the top of my cast, and Felix put a sticker on it from a local skate shop. Badges of honour. I held my arm close to me like a damaged wing, but the prospect of friendship and the fresh pink of the sky had me feeling anything but broken.

꙳ ꙳ ꙳

That afternoon the adrenaline of breaking my arm wore off and it began to throb under the cast. Getting used to not extending my elbow became tricky. It weighed my shoulder down and tilted me in an unfamiliar way. I couldn't wash my hair in the shower, even wiping my ass was an awkward manoeuvre. I felt embarrassed retrieving Clara's ring from my dirty pants pocket. I placed it carefully in the drawer with my journal, thankful I could still write. I took a few of the T3s I was given, swarmed by memory of a nurse saying to me as a kid, "You need to stay on top of the pain." As though it was something that could be conquered.

I hated hospitals so much because I was attacked by the family dog at age nine. I witnessed the strength of my mother then. He ate my face while she was in the kitchen cooking Clara and me dinner. We were flopped around on the furniture watching TV. Jake was a hunting dog who came from a long line of reputable family-friendly breeders and I remember going to pick him out. There were coloured lab puppies everywhere, soft as teddy bears and clumsy, hanging about the staircase to the entrance of the log home. They were wriggling around and falling over and licking our hands and faces with sweet spittle. Dad made the final call and we left with a thick-headed black one, whom he called Jake.

They said it was an accident, but I'll never forget the sound of my face tearing in his jaws, the chesty, deep thrashing of aggression, giving me enough time locked in there to wonder if he was ever going to let me go. When Mom came running and swatting, he let go and for a minute it didn't hurt. There was a numbness I can't quite describe because it was invisible; a numbness felt in the places where my face should have been. I ran to the bathroom and that's when the gash started to leak and sputter and the pain came. Once I saw my reflection I was no longer protected from it, like staring into a bad car accident. I saw the damage. My hands went to my mouth, but a finger came out my cheek. I saw the closet door open and a washcloth was passed to me, but the red mess soaked through it like ink blots on paper. I stopped hearing. Voices were more of a pulsing or whooshing like being inside a small airplane. A towel came my way. My mother and I began moving in an instinctive tandem, knowing, putting on shoes and grabbing keys and heading out to the minivan to drive to the hospital, even though it was only two blocks away. Mom called the neighbour and she rushed over to be with Clara.

I don't remember much about arriving except that it had grown dark and I was hunched over in a waiting room not looking at anybody. I could hear again, but it seemed only one sense was working at a time. After the nurse asked me to remove the towel everyone moved faster. Everyone present, that is. Our town's only doctor was halfway through his supper at home and thought it best to finish up before he came to see me. Didn't want to get to work stitching on an empty stomach, I guess. They told me I had to travel an hour to the city for a precision job. "Better off this way," they said. "They have specialists." They wrapped and stuffed my face in gauze like a mummy and I stopped hearing again because my head was so padded, but I could still see through the slits of cloth, sirens flashing blue and red then back to darkness across my mother's face as she sat next to me in the back of the ambulance. The whole ride holding tight onto my hands, looking like petrified wood, staring off into the distance.

They loaded me onto a cot while I stared face up to the stars. Then they wheeled me past the fluorescents. I wasn't noticing the panic or the prodding, just shushing along down corridors and through heavy double push doors into rooms with shadows dressed in pale green scrubs and lots of cold metal. I remember the smell of gas and sawdust on Dad. He rushed over in his work truck so fast he didn't have time to change out of his dungarees and flannel. That smell sat in the weathered, tanned crook of his neck, even when he shaved it clean. When the needles came out to do the freezing I stared at his blue suspenders and the holes in his old shirt. Here I was feeling only dull pain in those empty spaces and then the needles shot in. The worst one bore into my skull, right between my eyes, like a sizzling knife. I screamed while hands and forearms held me to the table so I couldn't defend myself. They kept drawing up another long point to stick into the layers of tissue. I squeezed my mom's hands so hard her fingers popped from their sockets, but she didn't budge. Scream after scream, needle after needle, Daddy eventually let go of me. He tugged his hands away and patted mine in defeat, snuck off and went outside to smoke and pace under the light of the glistening car park, while Mother endured. She gripped me tighter and prayed, and tears pooled on her thighs and darkened her pants. They started working from the inside of my mouth up to my split lip, my cheek of course where the finger poked through, and then the bridge of my nose, so deep I heard them say it could have caused brain damage. The green sheet they tented over me stretched into a tight workstation, but there was just enough space on the edge that I watched a gloved hand sew me up and down, pulling the thick floss to put my lips back together like a zipper.

I don't remember how long we stayed in the hospital or when we came home. I know I spent a long time thinking about Clara home alone with that beast Jake and wondering how that must have felt for her. I wondered if she finished dinner and put the dog outside while she ate, or if she just hugged him and patted his head saying, *Everything is going to be okay*. I know I didn't go to school for a little while and seeing my reflection made me cry. Zig-zagging wire and threads knotted out of me like a monster and

I was swollen up and bruised in all kinds of purples and blues, stained with yellow from the iodine. I still went to ringette practice, but I showed up and left in my helmet so the face mask covered how gruesome I was for others.

I took all the photographic evidence and destroyed it. I lied about it, telling those who asked that a German shepherd bit me on the way to school. Not our own dog, not a Labrador. I didn't want people to think my family wasn't kind. I was nervous that people would think we were mean to animals. I used to believe that for a dog to be mean, someone had to be mean to it, but now I think that dog Jake was off from the get-go. Now I know bad things happen to good people. There are no photos of him left in our albums, save for a family portrait taken at the beach. We're all posing nicely in fall colours and out of style by today's standards. Our chins are pointed and our hands are clasped together. It's an odd thing how some memories only exist because there's a photo of it, but cameras or not, I wasn't about to forget about that dog. They kept him tied up on a pulley and Clara would chase him in her gumboots up and down the backyard, but to me his beefy body and massive drooling head was like a damn dinosaur. I was scared shitless of that dog and I admit I always wanted him to be put down, but as Daddy's prized hunting dog, it wasn't an option, though sometimes I overheard him and Mom bickering about it.

Then Jake bit our neighbour when he came waltzing into our house without knocking. We spent so much time with the kids on our street it wasn't uncommon to fetch each other without a phone call, or a pause at the entrance. Screen doors were always flapping and we'd be off riding bikes or climbing trees until we were called home. His hand was still intact, but the teeth sunk in and tore and there was blood and tears in the entryway. I wasn't there, but I saw stained droplets when I got back. After that, Jake disappeared.

I found out at Clara's funeral that Jake was "affordably euthanized," meaning Daddy took him up some logging road to the bush

and shot him with his gun and left him there. He was commiserat-
ing about death and buzzed on rum when the topic came up. He
didn't know I was hiding and listening to him and Uncle Jim from
the stairs. I'd always had a feeling, but I never asked. I don't know if
what Daddy did was appropriate, but that was his way. The fact that
he was dead now, I didn't care. He deserved it. Clara didn't.

I hated what he did to my face, but I hated him more for causing
my mother an awful sadness while she held me down as I wailed to
hell in agony like I was possessed. Daddy just couldn't stay. He was
a physically strong and capable man, but the sight of his daughter's
face torn apart was too much for him to bear. What we didn't know
at the time was that pain was just getting started in our family. Up
until then I thought that strength was dependent on how burly you
were. Mother wasn't going anywhere and I don't believe she even
considered that she might leave. I would give anything for Mom to
hold me like that again. When Clara died a year later she started
saying, "Everything happens for a reason," though I don't think she
really believed that, it just became easier to say than anything else.
When Clara died I became Jake.

❦ ❦ ❦

My fingers squeezed around the handle and the door closed behind me with a thud. I had trouble getting my feet to move. The sight of the pristine tables at the restaurant, full of glassware and polished silver for each course, reassured me that nothing bad could happen in the vicinity of such tasteful luxury. I made my way upstairs to a maze of makeshift empty bedrooms, each set up with a computer and a microphone on a stand. April appeared in the doorway pulling out her high ponytail with both elbows raised above her. She dropped them to her sides when she saw me.

"What happened to your arm?" She ran both hands down either side of the long, awkward cast.

"Oh, I fell skateboarding. It's nothing."

"You poor thing."

"I'm fine," I said. "It's not the first time I've been hurt."

April kissed the cast, leaving her trademark print, staring up at me with fierce, freshly lined cat eyes. "Look, I gotta get on screen, feel free to hang out. There's beer in the fridge."

I grabbed one and opened it with my teeth, spitting the cap into my hand and trailing behind her into a bedroom where she put on an electronicore playlist and took off her clothes. She put them in her backpack on the floor and kicked it aside, out of view of the camera. I watched from the wing as she lay on the bed in her matching black lace bra and panties. She was voluptuous, and I was transfixed by her large breasts. She caught me looking and jiggled them in her hands and raised her eyebrows. They were so unlike my own. Her long black hair fell to her waist. It would catch underneath her as she moved and bounced around the bed, so she had to pull it all from under her, then twist it over one shoulder to her front. Soon it would tangle again and the whole mystifying process would start over. There was no air conditioning, and it was hot and sweaty in the room from all the buzzing electricity. A square fan on the floor billowed the curtains with a try-hard breeze. She greeted her guests as they began logging on. "Welcome to Scarlett Slayer's Chat Room, Big Boy…Oh, hi there, Hot Carl." She had a clear code of conduct. If people were rude, she would boot them out while all her fans stuck up for her and cheered her on. It was obvious she had a following. She was in control.

"Oh, Johnny Depth, that's not nice of you to say to me, don't you agree, guys? Should I kick him out? Okay, bye." She blew a kiss and ejected the guy.

"We have a special guest tonight. She's new here, so be nice and welcome her and you might get a private show soon." She winked lusciously. April paused her chat room video and guided me to one of the free computers in an unoccupied bedroom and logged me in. "Since you didn't run away screaming, I'm going to give you the official training. It helps to watch me onscreen. What do you want your name to be?"

"I don't know."

"C'mon, you must have some idea?"

"No, I don't. I don't know." I shrugged, releasing a nervous laugh.

"Like, what about…a favourite pet name? My Little Pony? A celebrity, a movie? Anything. I mean, don't overthink it."

"I love…*Billy Madison*."

It was the first thing I thought of. I felt silly and April over-exaggerated an eye-roll and bobbed her head until it was shaking off a no-way answer. Her Tank Girl sass denying my childish humour.

"You need a fancy sounding last name then. We definitely need to step it up from Billy Madison." She lengthened the M so that it sounded like a taste. She laughed.

"Oh, I know. How about Bancroft? Totally glam."

It sounded like the name of the fine china downstairs, and I liked it. She padded back to her room and left me to watch her on the screen. I could hear her voice in two layers: one through the speakers and another, her real voice, through the plasterboard wall between us. She looked into the camera lens and told her guests she had a fetish for casts. I knew she was talking directly to me. I touched the clunky, hard cast and tried to extend my arm; it wasn't the least bit sexy.

She was taken to a private chat and a red X appeared over her video screen with a banner telling patrons she would return soon. I went to the patio to smoke, but I could hear her making grunts and moans that were intense and beautiful. She came out to the patio a few minutes later, still in her bra and underwear, planting herself in the chair and crossing her bare legs. She wiped her liner back up with her index fingers and lit a cigarette.

"Was that for real?"

"Are you serious?"

"Yes?"

She blew out a wad of air and her big lips bounced. "Of course not. No one sounds like that when they masturbate. Seriously, Ines? I mean sometimes I do finish for real here, but definitely not then." I was serious. I'd never heard anyone masturbate before.

I started working there two days later. I didn't know what I was doing. I went to a thrift store and bought some lingerie—a teddy-style nightie in cheap black lace. It was too big in the chest and puckered when I moved. I did what I guessed was sexy. I rolled thigh-high socks up and down and I pushed my small tits together in a close-up point of view. I wasn't sure how my personality came into play. The cast made typing difficult, so I had to rely more on talking and I didn't know what to say. Someone named Pufflehump asked me what my favourite position was, and I didn't even have an answer.

"*Consensual?*" I said, looking out of place. I had nothing to offer. I struggled to set up the mic to my level with one free hand while making sure my sideways body looked good and my breasts didn't dip into that hanging U-shape. A few times there was feedback and the microphone screeched. I watched my nervous body on the screen trying to perform and pose, the reflection not unlike a frightened doe when caught off guard. I wanted to be the incognito one, but these avatars with fake names started joining my room, asking me questions and telling me they were horny. My stomach turned and I blinked slow and heavy to remind myself where I was. They were all hidden, it could've been people from home, even the church. I awkwardly chain-smoked, reaching off the screen to butt in the ashtray, waiting for the shift to finish.

The chatters were nice to me, but I was apathetic. Everyone asked me what happened to my arm. I didn't have the charisma to entertain or the wisdom to counsel. Some of the other girls used toys and props and brought their own satin sheets and fuzzy blankets, but I'd never even been inside a sex shop. My first private chat customer asked me to smoke a cigarette with my toes. I liked that because he didn't even want to see my face or hear me talk. After a week I had a regular who had the funds to do a lot of private time, but all he wanted was for me to talk like Ralph Wiggum from *The Simpsons* and I didn't even have to touch myself while I did it. I would bounce on my knees and say his peppy, silly quotes and he would type all in caps *YOU'RE GUNNA MAKE ME CUM!* He tried all the other girls, but I did the voice the best. April loved amputees and casts, and this guy wanted to hear the voice of a cartoon loser. People, I was learning, got off on the craziest stuff.

I could work as little or as much as I wanted, all I had to do was put my schedule online and show up when I said I would. Pierre monitored, but never policed us. He would log on and wait for a thumbs up and wouldn't linger. Sometimes the studio was busy and the bedrooms were full. The microphones would blare and it was more competitive to get put into private chat mode. You could hear the girls teasing and taunting over one another, their keyboards clicking away. One girl in particular named Agatha Thrash was so loud and boisterous it was ridiculous, but I kept a muted screen open to spy on her room because she was so fun and alive. She was quick-witted and had straight platinum-blonde bangs, black thick-rimmed glasses and large black pupils. She was wild and would do things like hump pillows and put vibrators in her ears. She made silly sexy and it was bought up quick. She was one of the most popular girls there. She always had a new outfit or toy and she sold her dirty underwear to her customers too. She was a veteran chat girl. She made fun of her clients and they seemed to enjoy it.

Pierre took some photos of Scarlett Slayer and me embracing topless and put them on the home page in preparation for a private show we planned to do together. Customers had to buy tickets in advance. During the show I was less nervous in April's presence and we rubbed oil on ourselves and popped tubes of pink and silver glitter all over our breasts and vaginas. We made a ton of money, but the cleanup was impossible. We ended up throwing the sheets away in the back alley. We showered together after and I tried to hold my cast out of the water, but April kept wanting to touch it and even though we scrubbed ourselves raw we couldn't get the glitter to come off of us. April washed my hair for me. Her hands massaged my scalp and I was totally excited by her. I wanted to be her. I wanted her to be me. I adored that she laughed so loud with her head tilted back, and how she bit her lip ring when she was smoking, which smudged her bowed lipstick. We were in the shower for so long that the water leaked over the lip of the basin and soaked the mat and spread onto the wood floor. Our paycheques were over a thousand dollars that day. Pierre was really impressed with the money we brought in, but not with the mess. He came storming into the bathroom trying to compose himself

in front of two wet naked girls who were falling all over each other.
His short-sleeved plaid shirt was tucked neatly into his pants and
his stylish, coiffed hair didn't budge. Exasperated, he yelled, "Girls,
girls, girls! I like what you're doing, and where you're heading, but
for the love of tiny and shiny, please no more glitter and get the fuck
out of my shower already." He looked like a man who was more
passionate about computers than pussy. I could hear my parents'
disappointment in the back of my head. I had never had sex to
feel good. When I lost my virginity I was raped. It wasn't violent,
and it happened to a lot of the girls in my school. Two girls in the
grade below me lost their virginity to the same guy in the same
way. When the rumours went around, people just called us sluts.
It happened at a bush party. He led me away from the fire, into the
dark woods, close enough to the riverbank that no one would hear
us or see. He said he wanted to talk. He kissed me against a tree
and said he knew I liked him, which was true. He put his hands up
my shirt and pushed me back onto the ground, into the sticks and
dirt, and I told him "No," but he must not have heard me. I pushed
his hand away and he grabbed my wrist and held it over my head
in a way that I took to mean *This is hot, right?* He pulled my pants
down and pushed himself inside me. I said "No" again, or at least I
did in my mind, but he didn't stop so I didn't move. It was painful,
but I didn't move. When it was over, he asked me to wait there,
so we didn't have to show up back at the party together. He left
me there and I struggled to take off my pants and then my panties
and I cried when I looked at them and saw the blood. I put the
panties in my pocket and wiped the twigs off my back. I kept them
for months in a drawer at the back of my dresser. I didn't want to
wash them or wear them or throw them away. After that I went on
antidepressants. "You're sadder than a regular teenager," Mom said.
"You've been through so much and I think they're worth trying.
The counselling isn't doing it and we drive an hour each way for
your appointments."

I saw her proposed idea as an easy fix, but she was right. I didn't like the way the counsellor probed her nose down at me and treated me like a child, trying to get me to use dolls to act out Clara's death. Always trying to get me to answer where I was when Clara went to the drop-off and why I didn't do anything to stop her. I stared at her long nose hairs during all the sessions and she was too self-involved in her own animations to notice I hadn't absorbed a shred of comfort. The doctor was easier; he wrote out an illegible prescription and I walked out of the pharmacy with a bottle of pills. Mom, making sure to take me to the one in the city, because otherwise everyone at home would know I was medicated.

One day I tried snorting some of the capsules. I took the dirty underwear and I went for a walk back to the forest where it had happened. I fiddled with them in my jacket pocket and the filthy, ruddy blood disgusted me. I threw the panties in the water and watched them disappear in the roving current. The little scalloped edges folded over themselves and they were gone, pulled down into the fast-moving green. I hoped a fisherman wouldn't catch them. I got wobbly from the drugs and fell down and passed out. I lay there for a long time pretending to decompose into the earth, not really able to move. The weight in my legs not unlike when he was on top of me. I wanted worms to take my body, like they did Clara's. I wished it was me in the ground, pure and put together. Mrs. Neilson was walking her dog and found me unresponsive and called 9-1-1. I'd already come to by the time they arrived. It wasn't a suicide attempt like everyone said. I was just trying to go back in time. I woke up to the sound of the river surging past me and through me. The rhythm of that river was like my heartbeat. I would recognize the sound of it anywhere. After that I thought if I fucked people that must mean they wanted to be with me. Round after round of the same mistake, I got used up. Practically rolling in the red flags, I turned to liquor to numb myself, but that only propagated a more usable desperation. I reacted with belligerence until the next one came along and I would convince myself they were going to be different, they would still want me after. One time I snuck out and went to have sex with an older guy at his house. He asked me why I wasn't smiling. "Aren't you having fun?" he said as he turned me over so he couldn't see my face.

✤ ✤ ✤

At Place de la Paix there were drunks sleeping on the ground and it smelt like piss. The skateboarders had to watch out for dirty needles, but there was something about the way they interacted with the down-and-outs. They knew each other's names and shared the space. It was gritty and sublime. The name was fitting despite the look of it. A castaway's haven. We skated alongside the marble ledges and Marie tried to teach me how to kickflip again, but I kept dinging myself in the shins. They stung and bruised up immediately in pale blue, so we bought some tall cans and got steamies from the Pool Room and sat back in the patchy grass. I watched all the people around us coursing in movement like cattle en route to be entertained or distracted from the homeless druggies all around them. A group of skaters were filming tricks on the ledges. They gave high fives to each other and lit cigarettes and laughed. Marie knew them all and they gave her high fives too. I shyly waved.

The guy filming was handsome. He crouched down low and skated alongside the skaters until they either fell or the ledge ended and then they all gathered around him to see the footage. They were so graceful and smooth when they attempted the grinds. Marie saw me staring and I chuckled at myself. I smiled at the filmer and he grinned back at me. A rush went through my abdomen. The skaters were so carefree and connected. I felt relief, like I had merged with the city, no longer feeling like an outsider. Life moved slowly in the shade of the day. I questioned myself, was this pretending? Was I just going through the movements? I was always on the edge of being torn down if life got too good.

Marie and I lazily made our way up to Mont-Royal—the Mountain—which was really just a big hill, for the Tam-Tams, an improv hand drumming circle in the grass at its base. Looking down Saint-Laurent, I saw hip sneaker stores and cheesy, fancy restaurants I didn't have the right clothes to enter. There was a little Portuguese grocer that smelled of salt cod and a dépanneur that sold cigarettes to minors and beer after hours. From the split-level brick façades, awnings sprawled in various shades; the most famous one had brown and white stripes marking Schwartz's Deli, where there was always a lineup. The sound of the Tam-Tams carried all the way through the Plateau where people were walking up the sidewalks in droves to the monument of a giant winged angel guarded by four reclining lions. The angel had a look of anguish on her face. There were blankets draped on the grass along the base of the Mountain and cross-legged vendors were selling their wares to all the passersby: homemade soaps and pipes and blown glass gadgets, jewellery, scarves and henna tattoos or hair wraps. Jugglers, tightrope walkers and hula-hoopers were practising in small groups about the grass slopes, enjoying the late sunshine and the drumming circle. Marie and I found a clear spot amongst the treeline and sat on our skateboards.

Marie pointed down to the Plateau. "Saint-Laurent is the street that divides east from west. The further west you go, the wealthier and more Protestant Anglophone. The further east you go, the poorer and more Francophone and Catholic."

Nothing changed on either side of the road as far as I could tell, but I was learning just how much of Quebec was separated and built on religion and it made me want to hide further in the undercurrents of city life, despite the beauty of all the churches. The purpose of them riddled me with frustration and the symbols of mercy jutted out at me everywhere I looked.

"Is your family religious?" I asked.

"No, not really, you?"

"No," I lied. "How did you get so good at English?"

"I practised a lot with my older brothers. I knew life would be easier here if I was stronger with my words. Do you have any siblings?"

"No." I shook my head, not sure what to say next. Marie gave me an odd look and reached for my nose.

"Ines, there's glitter on your face."

I tried to brush it off with my hands and darted to my backpack to make sure the zipper was closed, fearful that the lingerie inside would expose my secret employment. I was scattered with relief that it wasn't. I took out two cans of beer and carefully zipped it up tight. Marie put her hands together—at first, I thought, in prayer—but then she slapped her hands against mine and began to sing, "Stella Ella Ola, Clap Clap Clap..." I sprang to life and joined her, even though my cast was awkward. "Yes!" I shouted. "Chicko Chicko Chicko Chicko Chicko Chak!" Our claps resounded against each other and sped up. "Allo. Allo. Allo. ONE...TWO...THREE... FOUR... FIVE." We both laughed and lay back in the grass.

"Oh my god, Ines, how do you know that song?"

"I can't remember," I said, but that was another easy lie. Mom taught Clara and me when we were small and we'd play it in the backseat of the car every time we drove to the cabin, trying over and over to see how fast we could get going without missing our hands. I wanted to tell her about Clara, but I wasn't ready. I opened the can and sucked off the froth. Marie passed hers back to me.

"I can't drink right now, Ines. Gotta get to work. There's a very picky actress on set and I have to be there by four with the food. Sorry."

She gave me a high five and left through the patchwork of people. I watched her meander down to the road and hop on her board, cutting across traffic, disappearing around a corner. A vapour trail split the clouds apart. I took out my journal and stared at the blank pages. All the words I ever wanted to say were within me, taking up so much space they'd try and come out at once.

People were waving fabrics and dancing all around the drum circle, kicking up a fine, brown dust. The man leading the circle looked like a conductor. His jacket had coat tails and he blasted on a huge bass drum with a felt-covered drumstick that looked like a giant match. He was barefoot and beating and beating on the drum, the rhythm growing louder. I started writing a letter to my grandma. My second counsellor, the one I liked much better, taught me it was "cathartic" and "healing" to write a letter to the person you loved when they died. I would probably burn it like I had so many letters to the dead.

I hadn't spoken with my parents since they'd emailed to tell me that my grandma was gone, no longer suffering. There wasn't going to be a service. I was sure my dad's siblings were already fighting over who got what. I tried to think of what to write to her. We shared a name, one I never liked. We both smoked cigarettes, but look how that ended. We played with bingo daubers at her house because there were no toys and nothing else to do. I remembered her giving Clara and me perfume samples, which Mom didn't like because they were easy for our little fingers to spill and she didn't want Dad to know. I tried to imagine how my father was feeling, but all that came to me were thoughts of him highlighting Bible passages and rejoicing that Clara would no longer be alone in heaven. I couldn't focus as the beating of the drums were increasingly off. The intensity echoed in my chest, knocking and jilting around all the saved-up words.

An older man came up to me. His plain white T-shirt was tucked into brown pants held up by a leather belt. He wore Birkenstocks and carried nothing with him. His grey beard had dark, tight curls. He crouched next to me in the grass and asked me the time, which I didn't have. He said I had a lot of powerful energy and asked if he could touch my hands. I gave them over and he told me we were exchanging our energy.

"Can you feel it?" He smiled thin.

"I think I do." I wanted to reassure him. I wanted to reassure myself.

He examined the lines on my hands. "You lost someone special and you are drained." He said it with soft eyes and a kind face, and I sat and listened like a sieve, letting every word pour through me and pool into the flattened grass. I did not want them inside anymore. The drumming picked up pace and felt chaotic. The rhythm was gone and the competing beats made me lose concentration and become agitated.

"It has been three years since I've encountered someone who I can exchange energy with. I can restore you." I grew afraid of the intimacy of the interaction. I focused on a few cigarette butts in the grass and a wasp that was feasting on the remnants of a littered Slurpee. The hot sun was beginning to burn my shoulders.

"I need to go." I shoved everything around me into my bag and left half running, dropping my favourite pen behind me, too afraid to stop and pick it up. My beer tipped over into the grass. My last look back, I saw him through a glaze of tears. He was standing with his palms open. The cross on the top of the Mountain looming behind him. I skated in the bike lanes down Mont-Royal, pushing as hard as I could all the way to the metro station, my foot walloping against the asphalt. My heart raced and each push let me forget about anything but going farther and faster. The drumming receded. I pushed while my front foot held me straight and my thighs ached with the thrill of the ride. I took the orange line back to the dorm, avoiding the eyes of every stranger that glanced my way. I could be swallowed up by a monster any second and no one would even know. I stared out the tram window into the fast-moving black. My lonely face distorted. I wanted to meet someone, to drink in the brilliance of a human, someone who could dismantle my lies, someone I could trust. Someone not hiding behind a screen. Someone who would see me.

＊ ＊ ＊

July ticked forward. I worked late nights at the studio after the bars closed so I could go in with a buzz and couldn't care less about who might be watching me. There were moments when I fidgeted through the performance because the unidentified users creeped me out. I was usually the only girl on from 3 to 6 a.m. though, and it felt less like a show and more like a hangout. The guests were like lonely insomniacs looking more for interaction than masturbation, or dull people in different time zones. I'd play my own music and felt more like a host than a hoe. I'd dance on the bed in my undies to Joy Division, smoke cigarettes and read erotica from an old issue of *Penthouse* that was lying around. I kicked people out like April did. When they were mean I tried not to take the hurled insults personally, especially when people said I was boring or looked sad. But if a bully came into the room and if we kicked them out enough times, they would just leave and probably go watch some real porn that didn't talk back. Those assholes were never going to take me to private chat mode anyhow and I got paid regardless. I was a wounded tomboy with a giant cast.

I basked in the job because of the company I kept. The girls were sexy and inspiring. They owned what they had and didn't worry about the rest. They were so carefree and I wanted to be too, but it never felt natural and I was eager for finality at every request. The girls encouraged me to find more outfits and try new things, but I mostly just wore the black lace teddy, or a black sports bra and cotton panties. Sometimes I wore boys' tighty-whities and knee-high sport socks or I put electrical tape Xs over my nipples. My backpack with a six-pack was never far away. My first paycheque I treated myself to a new pair of skate shoes, the éS Accel, black with a tan gum sole.

I logged on sometimes just to watch the other girls; at first for techniques, which I realized I couldn't emulate, and then just because it was a fun thing to do when your own room was empty but you wanted to stay online to make money. They were the reason I was there. I eventually gained another regular named Multiple Scorgasm. They said they were a couple who fantasized about having a real threesome, but apparently she was too shy, so a cam girl was as close as they could get. At first I thought it was alluring and the idea of them turned me on, but when they took me to private mode sometimes they just wanted to chat and I didn't know how to fill the empty air while I waited for them to type to me. *How's our little coquette doing today?* they would say, and I'd just write *LOL* and try to adjust my body and chin and remain calm even though an anxiousness sat in my throat like hard ice that I couldn't swallow, and when I did, it burned my guts because I was going against every moral code instilled in me.

My guess was they liked me because I was down to earth and not over the top, that was the only thing that set me apart from the others. I was the easygoing amateur. Maybe it was her submissiveness, but believing a curious woman was also behind the screen, and not just some pervy man, somehow made me feel safer in the role. I just didn't know what to do.

*Madison Bancroft, you're so pretty, we love your eyes, stare at the camera for us.* I would blink and twinkle at my screen and lick my lips.

*We want to send you some pictures of us, so you know who's watching you.*

"Watching" sounded so impersonal and creepy but I sent them my email address in a private message. I didn't want to disappoint, and they were paying me a lot of money.

April and I logged off early for Divers/Cité, the city's yearly queer arts festival, and met on the deck to smoke while we waited for Agatha Thrash to finish a private. She was almost always in private.

"So…how's it going?" she asked while she lit her smoke. Her makeup was sweating off her face, but it was dewy and demure. She looked excited for me to answer.

"Actually…" I said, trying to sound spirited, "I met a couple. I think. They've been taking me private almost every night."

"Oh, do tell."

"Apparently they want a threesome but she's too shy."

"Shut up!"

"They asked for my email to send me some pictures of them."

"Fuck, Ines. You didn't give it out, did you?"

"Yeah. Why?"

"Oh, honey." She said it like I was a unworthy pupil. "No. They might not even be a couple, they might be Jeffrey Dahmer. God. I should have explained this more. Are you really that fucking naive?"

I wasn't entirely sure what the word meant. "I'm sorry," I pleaded.

"You've got to change your email. Or block them from the site or something. Pierre will help you."

I felt a terrible twitch sink in my stomach, it fell slow and turned like a helicopter seed falling off of a maple tree. "Okay. I will. I'm sorry." Sinking, twirling. Dead. While I finished my cigarette, my fingers shook and I blinked slowly, a tad stunned, but not entirely surprised by my own stupidity.

"Do you think they're really a couple, April?"

"Who knows, girl, there are some seriously messed up people out there. I'm proof. Don't be *you* online, be someone, like, completely different." April overextended her words and widened her eyes. "Lie to them."

"That's all I've ever wanted," I mumbled, shrinking in further. I bit at my bottom lip, a habit I recognized from my mother, trying to will my heart to embolden.

Not wanting to lie, but to be someone else. It was the vision above me with every regretful choice I made. In those moments, I carried myself without sorrow. My arms swung when I walked with poise and I was deserving to take down the stumbling blocks that stood in my way. I wanted to move through spaces with the confidence of April.

She wore a rubber bra and matching skirt with a rainbow feather boa. She had these black plastic boots that hugged her legs all the way up past her knees. I helped her fasten on these big black wings. She was a fallen angel. I put a white T-shirt over the taped Xs and pulled my baggy blue Dickies that I wore every day over top of my boys' underwear, the waistband still hanging out. I put my skate shoes back on and put my hair up in a ponytail and dusted back the greasy fringe.

April arched an eyebrow at me. "Thanks for dressing up for the occasion." We both smiled, knowing I'd never be an overt sexual vixen like her.

When Agatha was ready, we walked from the Port into the Village and the crowds were staggering, another occasion for the streets to be blocked off. Agatha Thrash had on a plaid school-girl skirt that showed off her butt cheeks, with a tie and white thigh-high stockings and huge heels. She was good at walking in them.

Divers/Cité was exhilarating. There were expressions of gender that sheltered small-town life doesn't permit. A hint that this was real when I was growing up could have saved me in the days when Daddy threatened to kick me out for being too boyish. We waited in line for over an hour to get into a gay club called Parking, but I had a flask of whiskey in my bag and we passed it around and shared cigarettes. As soon as we were allowed in, I cut around the packed dance floor straight to the bar and ordered shots. April reached deep into her leather bra and pulled out a little baggie with three pills inside.

"Madison, this is for you," she whispered in my ear. "Agatha, this is for you." She said it in a cute voice.

"What is it?" I asked.

"Ecstasy, dummy."

I looked at the little blue-brown pill in my palm. It had a Mitsubishi logo stamped into it. I turned away from the bartender, put it on my tongue, and washed it back with the shot. I tried to say something to April about Multiple Scorgasm but she just put her hands on my shoulders and told me it was okay.

"Just don't do anything stupid. You have to protect yourself."

In the bathroom stall I read all kinds of poetry scratched onto the back of the door while trying to muscle out a decent piss. The blue paint was fresh; only the quickest graffiti criminals made it onto the wall before it was entirely covered in scribbled inquisitions. I beamed as my butt bobbed above the toilet seat. Here I was, pondering the meaning of life in the pisser of a gay Quebecois dance club, trying to see myself in the mirrors on the ceiling without falling over.

*I Love my Cunt* one corner declared. *Help Me* asked the other. I noticed something small scrawled in red ink right ahead, and I realized I was reading something worth my while. Were they song lyrics? I tried to tell my brain to tell my legs to stop shaking. My mind retaliated by sending blasts of utter confusion to all the nerve endings in my body. Why can't I piss? I'd drank enough. My stomach was bloated and pale in the bluish light of the stall. I was doing the Elvis. I returned my gaze to the poetry, only to discover that it was no longer there. The drugs were coming on fast. I had to get out. I was pretty sure there was toilet paper attached to the sole of my shoe. Maybe it was the endless coloured streamers falling from the ceiling. I looked around, trying to get my bearings. The dancing shadows were a forest of redwoods and nursing mothers and performing surly clowns, the throbbing music was the hearts of all the dancers, all beating at once, with their eyes like wildfire.

This wasn't my kind of place. I was more used to taking refuge in Metallica lyrics, partying in the woods around a pit, smashing beer bottles on rocks and pretending that the sexual power was in my favour when in reality I was as easy as a game of Xs and Os. This was out of my league, but the drugs had me thinking it didn't have to be. I could belong here. The spine-tingling ecstasy was a wonderful change from my usual bad attitude and mixed with the shots it provided a hallucinatory lightness that was just what I needed to let go.

I woke up on an unfamiliar couch with my shirt up around my neck, and my socks and pants still on. There were creases on my face from the pillow. A large tan-coloured dog was sleeping on a rug beside me. He scared me at first, but I got up and walked down the narrow hall to the half bathroom and he shook awake at my motion and then laid his head back down with a huff. The bathroom was only a toilet and a door. There was barely enough space to turn around. I could see into the bedroom and saw April and Agatha sprawled out in bed together, limbs on top of other limbs. I went back to the couch and slept again until the afternoon, when I awoke to the dog licking his taint and a cup of coffee being waved over my face.

"My real name is Lainey by the way," Agatha said, nudging me up. "April's gone, Ines, you gotta wake up." A blanket had been placed on me at some point and I nestled further into it.

I finally sat up, bringing the blankets with me. I sighed.

"Did you have a good night?"

"I think so." I tried to remember. "You danced all night. We couldn't get you to leave." Lainey laughed.

"Yeah, I had a lot of fun. Thanks for letting me crash."

"You know, April and I were talking and I'm looking for a room-mate for September. You want to move in here? I'll be busy with classes. I'm in my last year. The rent is super cheap and it's the room with the balcony."

"Fuck. I so would, really."

"Then consider it done."

Lainey curled under the covers with me and we leaned on each other and blew the steam off our cups. The dog jumped up beside her.

"This is my dog Cedric." She patted his head. "He's a good boy." Lainey smooshed his jowls up and kissed his slobbery face.

Music blared in my headphones while I walked to Solin Hall from the station. When I turned them off I still heard the thumping of bass through my sore body. My calves cramped and my eyes felt like elastics were pulling the retinas back into my skull. I got in the shower and held my broken arm in the water and cut my cast off with scissors. It was falling apart and fraying and smelled bad. I wasn't going back to the hospital to have it removed. There was glitter stuck in it up to my elbow. My arm was skinny and pale and covered in long black hairs that clung to nothing. I felt weak and depressed from the night of dancing. Good times came at a cost, but memories of the club came to me where I was fierce in my movements, where all kinds of hands touched me in the wild light, clapping to the sounds of my bravery.

❦ ❦ ❦

I opened my email on the public computer in the Solin Hall common area and there was a message that said: *FROM MADDY'S DADDY* with photos attached. I closed the window in a hurry, my chest pounding against my sternum. I felt so dumb. I caught my breath and reopened it, tilting the screen toward me and leaning in close, afraid there might be nude shots. But it was just a photo of a couple who'd hiked a mountain, an expansive canopy of green trees around them. They were older than me, but they looked like nice and normal people. They smiled with their teeth showing and had their arms wrapped around each other and both wore bandanas and sweat-repelling fabrics. I quickly typed a response and hit send.

*Sorry. I won't be able to communicate with you via email or in private chat anymore.*

They responded right away.

*We're the ones who should be sorry. We overstepped our boundaries and want to make it up to you. I'll be dropping a gift off at X20, you can pick it up whenever, no questions asked.*

X20 was a punker store on Saint-Denis. They sold Doc Martens and Chuck Taylors. I froze and every ounce of my mistake wrapped around my face until I winced through it and clicked the mouse to log out and closed the page. I ran back to my room and scurried around searching for my journal and a cigarette. How did Multiple Scorgasm know I lived in Montreal?

I didn't want to tell April what happened so I scheduled my next week of shifts for when she wasn't there. I tried to act natural but the whole debacle was making me feel queasy. My first shift

57

back was spent wishing someone would take me to a private chat so the other clients didn't have to see me struggle. A guy named Hometown Hero logged on and I hesitated at the keyboard and was sucked into rushing thoughts of who from home could find me here.

*Aren't you going to say hello?* they typed.

"Sorry, you caught me off guard," I said into the microphone, though I didn't relax back into the bed. I stood so my face was hidden and only my lower half showed.

*You're awfully quiet today.*

"You've been here before?"

*I know who you really are.*

"No, I don't think that's possible," I said into the mic. I kicked them out. A new user named Hometown Hottie logged in and called me a frigid bitch. I kicked them out too.

I couldn't bear the thought of it. The whole town could know I was getting paid to touch myself, and by the time the news reached my parents it would be so convoluted that they would hear I was starring in porn movies and doing orgies. People from home could see me lying there, pretending to be horny, flirting with customers who had their zippers open and their dicks in their hands. Anyone could be watching, while I was so explicit, ashamed and skinny and without a shred of glamour or va-va-voom, trying like hell to get it right. I stopped the camera and pulled the Saran Wrap off the keyboard and started spraying Lysol on the buttons and mouse. I heard Pierre step around the corner and come into the bedroom.

"What are you doing, Ines?" He turned the computer screen off and muted the microphone and motioned for me to join him on the edge of the bed. The way he patted the mattress was welcoming, like it wasn't the first time a girl was leaving in the middle of her set. I knew he cared, but there was nothing he could do to change my mind.

"You know this job has a high turnover rate."

I joined him on the mattress which caused us to sink deeper together. Pierre put his hand on my thigh, and I sucked in a snotty cry and stuck my face in my hands. He lifted my chin to him with his index finger like he was going to try and kiss me. I prepared myself to let him, but he didn't. He just shook his head and pushed my chin back and forth while eyeliner ran down my cheeks.

"It's unlikely that guy knew who you were. It happens to every girl. Some people enjoy watching the vulnerability and fear on your face. You just have to get over it. It's probably someone you kicked out just trying to get back at you."

I sobbed in his lap.

"What if I know them?"

"You probably don't, but so what if you do?"

"Why do the people who don't want you take better care of you than the ones who love you?" He rubbed my back and looked confused. "I'm sorry, Pierre, I can't do this."

"Take as much time as you need. Maybe talk to the others, they'll have some tips. I'll leave your profile up for now. You can come back anytime."

I broke our embrace leaving tear stains on his dress pants. I put my clothes on and stripped the bedsheets and put them in the laundry machine and packed up my bag. When I left the cam studio, the old door shook behind me. The afternoon was muted shale. A looming building on rue Saint-Paul reflected small slits of sunlight through the alley. The patterns left on the cement were little personal-sized suns. The clouds above moved along in a quiet rumble. Black iron balconies clung to the concrete buildings and there was no one around. I smoked on the front steps and thought in the silence. How could I be in a major bustling city full of tourists and festivals and then in a fake bedroom full of strangers pretending to know me and then, in an instant, all alone in the street? I couldn't even hear the distant clops of the Clydesdale carriage horses. An electric downpour began, and the smell of wet pavement rushed into my nostrils. The heavy drops plummeted onto the metal and stone and jumped into the earth. Thirsty streams began flowing down the street, taking leftover garbage and cigarette butts with them. I wept from the weight of the moment. It was beautiful and ugly, just like life. The rain poured down on me, hot and galvanic on my skin, unlike any downpour there ever was at home. I didn't run or try to escape it; I let it hit me. I wanted it to rain harder. Maybe it would cleanse me. I dropped my half-smoked cigarette carelessly and stood still in the middle of the empty street. It continued to rain as I walked back to the dorm. I cut through the freshly mowed baseball field and swallows were flying close to the ground in big circles around me. They beeped and chirped in happy communication with each other, and when their bodies glided and flapped, shots of a magnificent purple shone out from them like jewels.

The rain ceased and I watched the neighbourhood. I heard kids playing and the echo of a basketball being bounced on tarmac. The world didn't sound like a dangerous place, but everything that had been beautiful looked hard. Around me only concrete and the many shoe soles that pounded it. Bus lines, metro stops, vending machines, book bags, flying newspapers and a community garden that was hidden entirely by a cement wall. The brick building coated in an industrious slime. I wasn't going to miss the dorm but I missed the self who had first arrived. I was already back in trouble; I was still me, already letting people down.

There was something syrupy about the afternoon I moved in; time poured out slowly, thick and golden, and I felt like an ancient mosquito encased within it. Cedric shifted from one shaded corner of the hardwood to another, letting out long grunts and looking at me with both love and contempt, as though there was something I could have done about the day's heat. The heat of the day was beginning to thin and I could hear trash scraping down the street with a gusto I hadn't yet seen—the breeze felt so foreign after weeks of heavy humidity. My new room was an odd shape and small, but it had an exposed brick wall and its own balcony. I bought the futon and duvet from Lainey's old roommate for forty bucks and began again with a rush of second-hand possibility.

I think Lainey and April knew I was going to quit before I did. They possessed confidence and trust in their bodies. Witnessing other people live in full bloom while I wilted and wished hurt like hell. I felt like their pet. A failed project. They cared little for what people thought of them. I wanted to tell them the reasons for my hiatus from the studio, for them to be pleased with me, but if I told them someone from home was watching me it would bring up more questions about where I came from and why I left.

My first night at Lainey's I made her and April dinner. I chopped veggies and prepared the tomato sauce while Lainey made garlic bread and we chatted like old friends. She was from upstate New York and in her fourth year at McGill. She wanted to immigrate to Canada and be a librarian. She organized her panty drawer into four sections: cotton, lace, period and classified. She wouldn't tell me what classified meant, just raised one eyebrow and stared down her glasses at me. As I watched her prepare for the new school year, I saw a more studious and intelligent person. She was upset about a guy she had been dating; it was casual, but he still ghosted. Just stopped calling when he said he would.

"I just don't understand why people do that."

"Unfortunately, being cynical and unavailable seems to be syn-onymous with being hip." She laughed and I looked over in her direc-tion. I saw that she was deflated, and her shoulders sunk down. "But don't take love advice from me. I've never even had a real boyfriend."

"Why is it impossible for a woman to not have feelings for a man after she's had sex with him."

"Oh, I've had sex with plenty of men I never had feelings for."

Lainey laughed and April came tumbling back into the apartment with a bottle of vodka. They sat at the table and drank out of mason jars and scarfed back olives and bread and cheese with prosciutto between slugs while I finished preparing our pasta. We listened to Elliott Smith and talked about dead celebrities and singers.

"There were no hesitation marks, he was totally stabbed, not suicide at all," April argued until we agreed with her.

"I'm sorry I couldn't hack it at the studio, guys. I just—"

April talked over me with her mouth full. "Don't be silly, you're always welcome to come back, but yeah…we get it."

"It's not for everyone." Lainey laughed at her own understatement.

"I don't know how I'm going to make any money now."

"Well your rent is covered for September, so you have a bit of time."

"Ines, you should be a cook," April said. "Look at you, you're in your element."

"You think?" I was preparing pre-made pasta.

"Oh my god, totally," Lainey chimed in.

"The only French I know is fruits and vegetables," I agreed, remembering Felix and Marie's laughter when I said *pamplemousse.* I knew I couldn't get a job serving, but maybe I could cook. I did have some experience. I carried the plates over like a waitress and placed them in front of April and Lainey. I brought mine over and sat down with them.

"I'm so glad I met you guys. You've really done a lot for me." I smiled at them both, feeling like a cat that had landed on its feet. "Cheers." I raised my glass.

"Santé!" the girls said in unison and we laughed and clinked glasses and gulped straight vodka and dug in. I hadn't cooked a meal since I'd arrived in the city. I did enjoy the feeling of being back in a kitchen. I flipped my hair back and returned to talking about all of the dead musicians who didn't make it to thirty, wondering if I wouldn't make it another decade either.

The *Gazette* had an ad for a fancy Italian place on Mont-Royal and I walked in feeling excited, but the waiter scoured my résumé without taking it from my hand, laughing in a high-pitched trill. He was wearing a fedora and cleaning the espresso machine and barely looked up from his task. "Are you sure you don't mean to go across the street?" He pointed with his nose. Across the street was La Belle Province, the Quebec version of a Burger King.

"Thanks anyways." I took an alleyway to have a cigarette by myself and passed the chefs from the fancy restaurant, leaning on the walls, smoking and drinking afternoon espresso in crisp white jackets before the busy dinner shift began. The ground of the alley was glistening with black from the oils and supplies brought in and out of the delivery door. I felt jealous of them in their uniforms, sharing inside jokes and talking about the servers. Enjoying the comradery, like a secret club.

I continued through the alley and could hear faint classical music playing inside a tiny restaurant nestled into the corner of the block. A sign hung outward from a metal pole that read Au Petit Bistro. I doubted I held the class to go inside. I looked in the front window and the floors were a beautiful honey shade of wood. It was another "dinner only" venue, but it was small and simple. A well-dressed man holding a long-stemmed lighter saw me pressed up against the door. When he came over to see what I wanted, I jumped in surprise.

"Bonjour, madame. Est-ce que je peux vous aider?" He was formal but kind.

"Uh, salut. Je m'appelle Ines. Ummm, I am looking for a job."

"Tu parles Français?"

"Non, juste un petit peu." I put my index finger and thumb up unnecessarily to show him just how little and then felt stupid for it.

"Would you like to come in and see our kitchen?" He bowed and held the door for me. I showed up at the right time. He didn't even look at my resumé. I stayed for the evening as a plongeur and as I washed the dishes, I inspected the plates with trout bodies and mussel shells. After the last service I leaned on the counter, my stomach wet from the sink. They fed me leftover duck confit and asked me to come back as a daytime prep cook. I took a menu home and looked up the dishes on Lainey's computer to find out what was in them. I studied the menu in bed and said the names of the dishes out loud.

The day chef was from Paris. His name was Thierry and he did a lot of coke. He left me alone to do all of the work and would change from French to English rapidly, but was willing to show me how to do things when I had questions. I wondered if they had hired me, a grubby, clueless Anglophone because I wouldn't get in his way, or challenge his drug use or talent. He would go down to the storage cellar and sit on a flour bag, watching soccer on a little TV with an antenna, yelling. When he was upstairs with me, we spent a lot of time smoking cigarettes and drinking espresso out of tiny cups. He never mentioned my lack of knowledge on French cuisine, and I never mentioned his habit. He taught me what a *mise en place* was and how it should best be organized for the coming day's work. He had me clean the floors multiple times a day. He was meticulous about where everything went. There was such little space, it had to run like a well-oiled machine. When Thierry went downstairs, I got to control the music and I put on Tchaikovsky and Mötley Crüe, or Iron Maiden cassettes that I found in an old bucket, and cranked up the food-crusted tape player as high as it would go. I rolled up my sleeves and made crème brûlées and duck foie gras with brandy and melted butter. I cut beautiful filet mignon and formed blue cheese crusts to wrap them in. My arms were sore from whisking homemade mayonnaise. I added roux to the soups and sauces, and I stirred and sang and moved with more precision than I ever did skateboarding or camming. I threw myself into it, as though it was the job I'd always wanted. Thierry and I pretty much had the place to ourselves on the day shift. The servers didn't arrive until four, when we were getting off. Afterwards we would each drink our allotted beer per shift: a hefeweizen for him and a Boréale Rousse for me. I was growing obsessed with learning the terms and techniques of French cuisine and Thierry would help explain them to me as best he could in his broken English. By the time the bistro opened at five, we were gone.

One afternoon I was twisting my fingers around a meat grinder trying to wipe up leftover bits of one of the bistro's specialties, tartare de cheval. I felt like I was holding a muscle in my hands, feeding it through the grinder and pulling it out in dark burgundy tendrils. I'd never seen real horse meat before. Grandma used to make tourtière at Christmas and I refused to eat it. I called it "horsemeat pie" and threw my nose up at it and all her hard work. Mom was horrified by me, and I grew all the angrier because Clara loved it. I sat scowling with my arms crossed while everyone dug in. It wasn't even made with horsemeat. The memory of my irrational defiance made me sad. I didn't try the tartare because it actually *was* horsemeat, but the unexpected remembrance of Clara soured the appeal all the more. I didn't get away with being squeamish though. Thierry demanded that I try the kidneys, flambéed in sherry and butter. They reeked of some inedible urine. Thierry gawked at me as I put some in my mouth but struggled to swallow. I spat them out into the garbage and he laughed at my lack of sophistication. I just couldn't acquire the finer taste of organs, I guess. But while my palate had its limits, my appreciation for the fine art of French food continued to grow. I felt a lot of peace to be part of the morning world instead of the night life. There were families out for bike rides, and people off to their jobs or reading newspapers in café windows. I would skateboard to get coffee and a pastry and write a little bit in the coffee houses around the Plateau before I had to be at work. Under the swollen bowl of late-summer warmth, a haze of freedom filtered over my life. I began to recognize people's faces, and they began to recognize mine. I was starting to peel back the hurt. If only I'd let myself bloom.

✤ ✤ ✤

The anniversary of Clara's death was approaching and I couldn't stop thinking about the cabin and the day she died. How the sunflowers grew beyond the height of the loft that year. They drooped and bowed their heads in grief, solemnly folding in their large leaf hands. The cabin was modest and furnished the way it had been when my father's parents owned it. He bought it off them when he turned nineteen and he and my mom lived there until I came along, and we moved into town. Nothing was new and nothing matched. We brought our groceries with us when we went and came home with our backpacks full of dirty laundry. The cabin smelled musty and old like a coarsened book or a life jacket worn through the generations; it still worked perfectly, but was faded. There were rumours the lake was bottomless, and I used to dive deep down until the water was frigid and beams of sunlight shone into the dark abyss and I'd get scared or run out of breath. Clara and I spent our days catching water spiders with nets and putting them into our plastic buckets. They chased each other in a game of scatter and bump, and I couldn't tell if they did it in friendship or with menace. We lived under the sun then and had bellies pink as strawberry ice cream.

The day they pulled Clara's body onto the dock Mom made pancakes for breakfast and we had them with homemade jam. We were supposed to go for a walk around the lake. Dad was going to teach us the different varieties of trees, but I was lagging behind. I kept launching and diving off the dock, coming back up for air until I was pruned and hungry. I called to Mom to watch me dive, but every time I looked at her, she was bending to Clara, making a sandcastle. I swam back to the shore and crushed it. At the cabin I took a deck of cards and asked Clara if she wanted to play 52 Pick Up and I sprayed the deck in her face and the air and refused to explain it wasn't really a game at all, but a trick. I didn't help her clean them up. The pile stayed on the floor the whole next day until I couldn't look at it anymore and I scattered the cards under the couch.

That day, she cried and threw her ponytail bobble at my head. Mom yelled, "Be nice to your sister" and went to take a shower and Dad went out front to work on rebuilding the engine in his early seventies Jeep. They often took up separate activities while on vacation, and it seemed that Mom was always left to be in charge of us while Dad was able to putter freely and fix things around the property that may not have even needed fixing. She was always more focused on Clara.

The ambulance siren spread the first sounds of gossip, long before the details of what had happened were known. The news spread quickly throughout our small community. A death like this had everyone's pity. A neighbour helping in the search started screaming and I just knew she was gone. She was stuck in the reeds and cattails, where it was shallow and mucky, where we weren't supposed to play because it was too dense and the drop-off came early. I saw how blue and puffy she was before a sheet was draped over her by the emergency response people.

Dad shook my shoulders while I combed the sand with a stick. "Why didn't you tell us where she went?" I couldn't find an answer within the shock. It wasn't intentional. I was only searching for a moment to myself and what I got was a lifetime. Time was only before and after. I don't remember coming home without her. I only remember walking around our house with a blank stare while relatives hugged me or shooed me away. Casseroles and mini sandwiches overflowing from the fridge. The mailbox so full of cards they were falling out onto the ground. Cards from people who lived on the same street but couldn't face us and say *Sorry for your loss* in person, like Clara was a stray mitten, or spare keys. I stayed in my room a lot. I wanted my parents to knock on the door and come see if I was okay, but they never did. They put the cabin up for sale. Mom said the water was too cold to swim. She spent all her time chewing on the inside of her lip and hiding bottles of vodka around the house. One time I found one in the toilet tank.

I didn't return to school with a new outfit or brand new school supplies, no binders waiting to be marked up with fake signatures of the boys I was hoping to marry that year. I took a few months off and when I did go back I hid in the bathroom with another girl who hated her dad and would pretend she was adopted. She put coverup on my scar and we would braid each other's hair and talk about doing heists like stealing my parents' car. We never talked about what we would do once we got to where we were going. Truly, escape was so inconceivable that even our fantasies weren't worth imagining in detail. The stoic mountain peaks, glazed by the sun and doubled by the lake, were the only world we could fathom. A main-street, one-store existence. A blip on a map.

The church had held a viewing where the family could go say their goodbyes, but I didn't go. I didn't want to see my eight-year-old sister in the white dress Mom had picked out. I saw it hanging on the banister downstairs. Her hair to be curled, with matching red bows, while makeup covered her dry veins, and it was someone's job to wash the mud from her legs and pour chemicals down her throat.

We used to be a regular family. We had Super Channel and we watched family movies like *E.T.* and *The Land Before Time* on a brown and gold patterned couch that had wagons and trees on it. I knew we were a regular family because I knew other families had that couch and the matching chair too. It was a middle-class couch. Every night at dinner, one of us set the table and the other one cleared. Clara and I would fight over who got which coloured plastic cup depending on what colour Kool-Aid we were making. We had a Snoopy snow cone maker. We got Pogo Balls at Easter and new bikes for our birthdays. We put neon plastic beads in the spokes of the wheels and rode up and down our street with the neighbour kids playing kick-the-can and hide-and-go-seek. There was never a palpable silence until she was gone.

Though Clara was two years younger than me she made friends with almost anyone. She gave her tender smile away freely and hugged strangers and strange family. From birth she lit up rooms and giggled often. Her dresses stayed in place and she didn't pick out her wedgies or get her tights dirty like me. She got new outfits for special occasions instead of my stained hand-me-downs. While adults coerced me into opening my arms to hug them or nudged me to smile more often and sit up straight, she displayed a natural angelic softness that was magnetic and made people swoon. She was shiny and pretty to the tips of her nails and everyone patted her head with approval. The head I saw them cover with a sheet. I was born too early, living my first six weeks in an incubator, eating from a tube, looking like a lifeless stomach lining with sockets for eyes. No one could hold me for a while because I could break, but then they did nothing but hold me because I was cold. I used to joke that I just wanted out so badly to see the world, but I was beginning to understand that I was an issue from the start.

❦ ❦ ❦

The sky hung between light and dark. The leaves outside my balcony were brittle and pale. The sun set the way fires burn. A glowing opulent heat blasted off the buildings. I lit candles and prayed I would find my way through the loss of my sister. Even though ten years had passed there was a powerlessness, embarrassment, even, that bound itself to all my other feelings, telling them to shrink. There was a crisp restlessness as the city was transforming in the rippling heat. I sat on my wrought-iron balcony staring out onto the bustle of the evening rush on Saint-Denis: people scrambling to the metro with wine and baguettes for dinner, families to feed and people to go home to. A swoop of newspapers and flyers was tossed about by the wind from the revolving doors. I sat with my journal, a beer on the stool beside me, an open heart calling out, releasing the pent-up words, expanding my ribs. The ashtray overflowed and my hair blew all around my face. I ripped a page out of my journal and furiously wrote a note to the universe.

I wrote Clara an apology letter every anniversary and then burned it, but I was sick of the shame. If that man in the park thought I had powerful energy in me, I wanted the world to show it to me. I wished for love, for respite from myself. I asked for salvation. I rolled up my note, tied it with the black shoelace from my old shoes and left for Carré Saint-Louis. When I got there, I sat on a bench in front of the fountain and started to cry. I held the note tight. I spent a few moments eyeing the trees for one that called to me. No one paid me any mind. I gently threaded the lace around a thick branch, tied my wish with a bow and left. I wasn't destroying this letter;

the world could have it. I envisioned the string blowing loose and without a sound the page would be carried to its fate. Treasured, or trampled into the sidewalk in wrinkled, wet smithereens, laid eternally beside the flattened black spots of old gum.

When I arrived home the doorknob slipped from my fingertips and snapped back. The wind carried up the stairs and slammed the bedroom door. The candles toppled over. Wax shrapnel moulded to the sides of the patio iron, my journal and the floor. My clumsiness was disheartening. I took off my clothes and climbed into bed, crying into the pillow until I fell into a deep sleep, away from the lonely renunciation of my heart. My dream was florid and I felt peace. I was standing on a cliff looking out to an endless calm ocean. My arms were extended in Christ-like repose and I dove into the water, breaking my incandescent reflection. I dreamt about water a lot, the weight of it, after Clara died. I feel the hard rush of a dive over my face, disturbing the stillness and then I wake up, or sometimes rocky and aggravated with emotion I will be shipwrecked, or swimming against a hard current, rattled and sweaty. Rarely, I am above still waters.

When I woke it was raining, and I watched through the open door the droplets leap off the roof into puddles, a sudden dense downpour, fuelled by the clammy electricity in the air. The smell of wet, black pavement seduced me in and out of wakefulness. I got up, put on my underwear and sat in the plastic chair. I was being an exhibitionist, but I liked the curve of my breasts. I liked the way my legs were tucked into me, my knees under my chin. You couldn't see anything except the undersides of my thighs and the arc of my cotton panties. I enjoyed being half naked and alone. I suspected that it helped me in small ways, maybe if I could begin to like my own body, someone else could too.

I watched the park from the balcony. Down Saint-Denis I could see part of the sign for x20 and I panged with curiosity about what Multiple Scorgasm had picked out. Every time I walked by there, I fidgeted with my Discman or smoked and tried to look down and be busy. The paths into the labyrinth of Carré Saint-Louis were barely visible. I could see where they branched out from the fountain. The treetops, less generous, were showing signs of change, beginning to bare themselves as they swayed back and forth. Leonard Cohen wrote poetry in that park and now I suppose I had too, poetry left on a bough. An omen. Water poured from the top of the fountain. My breath showed in the air and a chilliness set into my hands. I picked at the wax on my journal. The indented callous on my middle finger from writing was sore. I pushed so hard when I wrote that it left a mark. My note to the universe had been set free. Maybe it had joined the fallen leaves, swept in the rush of rain and wind, and away it went to run its course. Taken by water, just like Clara. I looked around at the people in the park and wondered if any of them had found it. If it was tucked into a warm pocket. I wondered if my prayer had even touched the ground, or if the rain had dissolved it and it would go forever unnoticed. The dangling shoelace, the only reminder I had ever existed there, that I had ever wished for something more.

# Automne

The Mountain cross dazzles
Like a Vegas hotel sign
Impure
earth, drenched and fecund
Pockets of light
I gather and spread while the night moves
Closer
labile
My organs harvested
Take my heart

✤ ✤ ✤

The turning of the trees beckoned me to be out skating as much as possible in the remnants of days before the air grew brisk and the leaves could no longer hang on. After that it would be skating in the underground city only. I skated down to Square Berri to meet Marie. I hung back on the hill on my board and wrote while I waited, away from the core group of skaters who were there every day. I watched them, admiring the passion and creativity it took to nail a new trick. I didn't have the courage to join them. I tried to draw their pictures. When I saw Marie come out of the station, I skated down to her and together we carved through the streets to Fouf's for skate night.

Lainey was there waiting for me after her cam shift, drinking white wine in a puffy down jacket, reading a linguistics textbook alone. She was probably the only person who'd ever ordered wine there, let alone read a book. I admired how she didn't seem to consider it might be out of place. School didn't even start for a week and she was already studying. "Complete Control" by the Clash blared from the speakers. I introduced Marie and Lainey. Marie was under the impression I met her from a message board at Solin Hall. I asked Lainey beforehand not to bring up camming. I grabbed a cold Molson Ex from the bartender and lit a cigarette. I sat with Lainey and played with the tear in the knee of my jeans, watching Felix and Marie and some of the other skaters on the ramp out of the corner of my eye. When I was sober at the bar, I always felt a need to catch up to everyone else and so I drank fast as though I had something to prove. After my first I started ordering two at a time. When a solid buzz hit me, I decided it was time to skate. How was liability not a factor in allowing people to drink, smoke and skateboard simultaneously in a bar? Only in Quebec. I found solace in skating while I was drunk. I was less afraid and nothing hurt until the day after. It took me somewhere else. Marie and I were cheered on by the guys as we dropped in and practised new tricks. I was working on 50-50 grinds over and over, but I held my healing arm too near to me, to protect it, and couldn't stay balanced across the coping. I took a pretty hard bail so I looked around for Lainey and I noticed from atop the ramp that a girl was at our table rummaging in her stuff. I leapt off the ramp and scattered the crowd to get to her.

"What are you doing?"

She pointed to the other side of the room at a guy with gelled black hair and tight pants. They didn't look like the usual low-class clientele; they should have been on Crescent Street. He sped right over and got up in my face.

"What's going on here?"

"Your girlfriend was trying to steal my friend's backpack."

"No, I wasn't! I didn't take any backpack. What in the fuck are you talking about?" She was wasted and she delved deep into her throat and spat straight into my face. In my mind's eye, everything stopped. The music, the bartender, the skateboarding. Patrons pulled cigarettes from their mouths in silent slow motion, the ash clinging tightly to their ends, careful not to miss a thing. Even Joe Strummer stopped mid-chord. The hush broke when I smashed a beer bottle on the table beside me and threatened her with it.

"I was picking up her scarf." She raised her hands.

"Sure, you were."

Lainey's backpack hung off the chair, her book was poking out of the top and her scarf had fallen to the floor. The woman lunged at my neck with both hands, yelling in French. I dropped the bottle, realizing my scare tactic was stupid. I swung at her cheek. My shot was weak, and my healing arm stung with aggravation. She tackled me to the beer-soaked floor. The bouncers had us both in awkward locks in seconds. They escorted her and her friend down the stairs and out the front door. Another bouncer handed Lainey back her wallet. I could hear her yelling the entire time. I knew I saw her do it. I was set free and handed a beer and told to chill out. Bouncers usually hated me, but at Fouf's I felt like they watched out for me. They were big, smiley men with names like Bubba, stacked and thick like football players with rough and secret histories. The skateboarding resumed, the music carried on, the ashes flicked and disintegrated. The storm calmed, but I fumed. Lainey returned from the bathroom.

"Thanks, Ines," Lainey said. "I wish I was tough like that."

"No, you don't," I bit back. I flipped up my hood, slammed the beer and left.

The girl was waiting outside for me, ready to pounce. A late-night crowd was gathering outside the bar, expecting directions to an after-party or looking for someone to spend the night with. A congregation of noisy drunk people uninhibited by guilt, inspired by temptation. She jumped me again. I wasn't ready for it and she took me down quickly, landing on top of me and swinging her elbows and fists into my face. It wasn't a fair match. She swung and swung again, striking my eye. The sting of it in my ear shell-shocked me. Marie swung her skateboard down on top of the girl's back, seemingly the only force strong enough to make her stop hitting me. She fell to the ground on one side. The chaos felt so alive it was disturbing. A gentle rain had begun to fall, landing on our heads, weightless like glitter. I got to my feet. Marie asked me if I was okay. The scene was rambunctious and hostile and crowded, and amid this group of drunkards on Sainte-Catherine, I saw him looking at me. Our eyes met and the anger dropped in shards around me. He stood so far out from all the noise: his deep red hair, darker than copper, like wet, red earth, in a plain white T-shirt with an unbuttoned plaid flannel and blue jeans. His skateboard held up by one foot. Spray-painted words on the griptape: DON'T TRUST LOVE.

We stood there in front of each other, smiling under the dusting of rain. I felt propelled to move near to him. I stared into his muddy brown eyes and he put his hands to my chin and held my face, already swollen from the punches; I recoiled at his touch. My eyes were swelling too, and I watched us, as though from outside of myself, through the slits of my throbbing eyelids, the aperture of his growing larger. We tangled into each other as the crowd began to disperse.

"You're Max, right?"

"You are Ines. I have seen you skateboarding with Marie."

"I see you filming with the guys all the time. You've smiled at me before."

"Je me souviens," he said. I remember.

He took me by the hand and we left together, relieved and gritty. We skated in the street, weaving in and out of the cars on the road. The late-night traffic stopped at the lights and we passed them in a stupor, headlights bright for a moment in our faces and then diminished. The green light popped behind us and movement commenced. We passed by a corner of sex workers in latex bras, their heels higher than their hair. I stared so hard I felt perverse. I wanted to know them, their stories. I wanted them to be safe from harm. We continued east into the Village, which became obvious right away. Rainbow flags in all shapes and sizes. Max stopped me outside a doorway and we kissed. I had to rest both my hands behind me on the iron railing to keep from falling over.

"Come with me," he said. "I have an idea." I followed his lead to a fence around the side.

The next morning, he was still sleeping in his ruffled bed while I sat and wrote in my journal on the patio, looking out at the high-rises. I was remarking on my hastiness. The drunken desire to kiss this man while adrenaline coursed through me and my face swelled. The griptape on his board already telling me the future. DON'T TRUST LOVE. But he was purposeful in his approach, he singled me out, he knew who I was. Below me was the pool we had snuck into, behind the building next door. Anyone looking out their windows could have seen us. I could still smell the chlorine on my hands. I felt the sensations zooming through me as I remembered all the details. My legs were rippling shadows, warmed by the underwater light. I was up against the tiled wall of the shallow end with his face so close to my own that his wet red hair dripped into my open mouth. I swallowed the drops that fell, and we consumed each other. After, we hurried to leave and struggled to get our sneakers back on over our wet feet. Max had to lift and heave me back over the fence because I was laughing so hard from the impulsivity.

"Bon matin," he called from behind me, and when I turned to look, he was there in the frame of the door, shirtless, leaning in to kiss the crook of my neck. He was slim. Deep, defined muscles jutted out of his jeans and followed the line up to his hips. I blushed. I closed my book and tucked it into my bag. His eyes were big, doe brown, round like life preservers I was about to jump into and be saved by. I stood to meet his kisses and Max led me back to his bed. His skin was tight and pale, softened by the pool, and I kept my eyes open to watch his biceps harden as his body went tense. In turn, I felt myself relax. Afterwards I dressed slowly and he watched me with a desirable shyness and a crooked half smile. Max got up and turned on a computer at his desk.

"I've got some work I need to do today, but I'd love to take you out for dinner tonight."

"You want to see me again?" I said, pulling up my jeans and doing up the button.

"Of course I do."

I wanted to ask about his griptape but I didn't even want to say the word love out loud in case it put him off. When I left we kissed at the top of his stairs. I didn't want the suction of his upper lip to part. I breathed him in.

"Can you believe what happened last night?" I said.

"The fight, or the pool?" Max raised his eyebrow to me.

"Both."

"You okay?"

"Yeah," I said, "I'll be fine."

"How about we meet at Square Berri at seven." His lips lingered.

"See you then."

When I opened the door to our place Lainey was standing on top of the stairs.

"Where the fuck have you been? I was so fucking worried."

"I'm sorry. I met someone and …"

"Fuck that, Ines, you left me at the bar, you didn't even tell me where you were going. Don't do that."

"I'm sorry. I should have told you first. I was just caught up in everything." I hauled myself up the stairs into Lainey's arms.

"Your eye looks right messed."

"I know."

Max and I skated up avenue Laval into the Plateau together. When we got to the hill, we walked and he held my hand as I gazed at all the beautiful houses, the carvings in their doors and the trestles of their roofs. Each staircase with a different iron banister, steps that were painted, the balconies with cute bistro tables. In the windows were glimpses of large works of art and big tropical houseplants, high ceilings and old hardwood flooring that was shiny and clean. Vines grew up the front walls. Some of the ground-floor apartments had tiny backyards with tiny painted fences around them. People lived close to each other in this city, in spaces that connected them physically. On one block there was a park and kids played and their parents yelled to them. The laughter was joyous. Purple popsicles stained the kids' lips and made their fingers sticky, and they played in the dirt and got their feet grungy. The adults and kids all spoke a mix of French and English and I felt that it was special when people spoke to each other in whatever manner worked. I wanted what they had.

Max took me up Saint-Laurent to a Portuguese rotisserie called Jano. In the front window, a hot grill was covered in splayed and spitting rabbit meat. The smell of charcoal smoke and meat and spices came out into the street. We sat at a table for two in the back and ate iceberg lettuce salads with whole cherry tomatoes and waited for our grilled meat. Max and I talked about skateboarding and music. I asked him if he had any siblings and he said no, then he asked me and I said no too. Pretty blue and yellow tiles with roosters on them ran along the walls. Adorning the tables were vases with fake yellow flowers with fake dewdrops on their petals. Max took one out and put it behind my ear, and even though it smelled like dust, I left it there.

❧ ❧ ❧

Fall floated in overnight and the damp returned to make the earth rich. A bountiful decay that made the summer sovereignty dissolve in crisp air, speeding everything up. Max and I rode our skateboards down Saint-Paul into Old Montreal, dodging cracks and wet leaves on the sidewalks. We passed the cam studio and I looked up at the large windows with a secret pang of knowing what went on inside. Max was taking me to see the Notre-Dame Basilica, which looked like a cathedral out of Gotham City. Two identical spires rose high into the sky, glowing with brazen blue lights. Inside I was moved to tears. I held them back so no one would notice and it stung my throat. The church was solemn and heavy, with high wooden staves and sturdy rows of thick, uncomfortable benches. The intricate patterns on the stained glass told stories I didn't understand, and I remembered the singing of hymns that raised vibrations in the room and caused a ring of silence to sting my ears.

I never understood my family's devotion to Jesus. Walking into Clara's funeral I was corralled into the front row. When I saw the half-open casket, her little hands folded over, I turned and ran away, pushing past all the people, running to the park across the street. I hid in a tunnel slide until my aunt peeked into the bottom and crawled inside with me. She held me while I shook and cried. We stayed in the slide tunnel curled like beans, our shoes squeaking on the plastic. She coaxed me back into the church and sat at the back with her arm around me. All the faces, blurry from tears, scowled at me on their way out. People said faith helped my parents overcome the loss, that faith will cure pain, faith makes life after death bearable, but I don't think it's true. I took the shrapnel from their wounds and made it my own. I hated it the most when I heard people say that heaven must have needed her more than us, that they gained *another angel*. Those were the same people who saw the second coming of Jesus in their breakfast toast and slid my parents brochures at church for Pentecostal summer camps where people could send their teenagers to be rebaptized.

I was surrounded by bright light. Rays of endless gold penetrated my insides, and I felt an immense guilt for Clara's death. Why didn't I say where she went, why did I let her go alone? The church brought me right back to the funeral until I spotted a tourist taking a picture of her husband in the aisle. I offered to take a photo of them together and they accepted. They embraced between the narrow brick walls and then kissed and laughed. Their display made me feel a burst of love and energy. I imagined the photo, framed on a mantel in their house. They thanked me, but in truth I wanted to thank them for letting me be a witness to their moment in time, to see that love was possible, to snap out of the past without any need for fixing it.

After touring the church, we sat on a patio drinking coffee in the remaining sun of the day, our baggie hoods draped over our heads. We held hands and then our mug handles to keep warm. The sun didn't last long, but the light was perfect. Max stood up and took his camera out of his backpack. He told me not to move, but I couldn't help it, I felt awkward and turned away.

"Please," he told me. "You look so beautiful."

I tried not to laugh and have a double chin. I was never comfortable in front of a camera and I didn't like my teeth. Even though I had braces as a kid, there was still one on the bottom that shot out sideways and collected whatever I'd eaten. I knew I looked sullen, but I let him capture me. I took the camera from around his neck and turned it on him. He pretended to be a fashion model and put his hand on his hip and jutted out his long limbs, like goofy was his default. He took the camera back and we tried to take a picture with the two of us. His arm extended above us to capture both of our faces. He pulled my hoodie strings and kissed my cheek. I grinned recklessly with my teeth showing, but when he went to take the picture, the film ran out.

Every man needs something to hang on to and for Max it was his camera. It went with him everywhere. The strap hung around his neck and he knew all the buttons and curves of it. He would lift it and his fingers would glide into place. His first was a Holga from his grandparents when he turned nine. With cloudy and sunny as the only settings, it made a vignette effect, framing the subject with saturation. After that he was hooked. When he was filming skateboarding, he would coast along on his board and hover down low to get the best perspective of the skater's trick, following them with the big fisheye lens that would round everything out and make it look broad. He was a natural at it and I loved seeing what he captured. The skaters always rallied around him like he was magnetic. He had something they all wanted: he was the master, the director.

We watched some movies Max had made while we lay in his musty bed eating Cheerios right from the box. His cat Pantouf asleep behind our knees. The images slowly came into focus, set against the cityscape. The music and the images lulled me hard into that place that I'd been trying to get to know—the deep inside where nostalgia and desire met—creatively putting into perspective the feeling of longing. I thought it was magical that art could do that to a person, transport you and make you different. My longing was always present, whereas it seemed like others could put theirs away for a while. The TV light bounced off the walls. I was witnessing his process. The editing of film, while computers reverberated through dusty fans: focus, pause, delete, rewrite; the timing at which he made a song and an image collide; the beauty of connectivity; how music persuades you to feel a certain way. Max put on a movie he made that no one else had seen before. I was a special audience member. It was a time-lapse of the sun setting over city hall, where the reflection of the water below was the same as the sky above. It glowed blue and then turned to gold and there were close-up shots of flowers blooming and sidewalk angles of pedestrian feet shuffling off to their destinations. There were clips of the Saint Lawrence River showing how Montreal was an island. In parts, Super 8 footage made the movie appear grainy and older than it was.

He kept a collection of black and white skate photos in a book and I thumbed through them. Loose pictures from his childhood fell out. Max in denim overalls on a new bike, smiling bright, gripping the handlebars, Max in new hockey skates underneath a Christmas tree, and one I was sure was of his dad, sitting on a stoop wearing a bulky cardigan, a smoke dangling between chunky red sideburns. He and Max had the same dark, orb eyes.

"What's his name?" I asked, but I regretted it. I knew better than to ask people about their family members. Max grabbed the photos from my hands and fanned them about on the bed.

"He was François Labelle, but my father is no more. He died a long time ago." Max put the photos into a drawer and closed it.

"Car accident. If you're wondering."

"How old were you?"

"I was six."

"*Labelle* is such a great last name!" I changed the subject. Death talk was not on the wooing table. Make it about them, so it's not about you. I learned that one along the way.

Max laughed out a low puff. "Great and beautiful."

"How do you mean?"

"Maxim, means magnificent."

"English names definitely don't mean anything like that."

"Ines is not common though?" he said. "What is your name from?"

"It was my grandma's, but she's dead too."

Instead of rambling like a fool to try and explain, I got up to go to the bathroom. The bachelor studio was little more than the heavy sofa bed that occupied it. It sagged in the middle and when you sat on it you were sucked inside. There were computers hooked up to other computers with speakers and wires and video cassettes all over the place. Pantouf was often crawling all over them, stretching himself out for attention, letting out little meows and purrs at our touches. I had to step over piles of VHS tapes and CDs marked with Sharpie dates of famous skateboarding spots in cool cities, like LOVE Park in Philly or the Brooklyn Bridge. Those places were exotic to small-town skateboarders, places I only saw in magazines. Places Max captured and stored for safekeeping, waiting to be formulated with sound and movement, memory and longing. The ashtray spilled over with half-smoked joints mixed with tobacco. A bland dryer-lint grey filled the sky, while a shifting landscape of yellow, brown and brick backed the monotone grey. The city was swelling with a desire to freeze, purging the clouds of light and holding everything in. I was warm though, near Max. I was certain we could both feel it radiate.

Tangled in his single bed I watched him behind me in the mirror hanging on the back of the bedroom door. He was a generous lover who kissed freely places on my body I didn't know existed. I'd never been touched this way, with such assertiveness. He complimented my hip bones, which I always thought looked like a boy's. He held my breasts, which I thought were too small. I fell asleep dreaming I was in my own movie. I was in slow motion and there were black spots on the sun behind me. It was so bright that whenever I threw my head back in laughter the radiance blinded the camera screen. I was watching myself. I was at the lake. My feet were rooted in the muddy sand. I was holding a stick. A song with piano was playing far away. People began screaming and running to the water.

"Ines, comment ça va?"

I jolted out of the dream, forgetting everything, the fragments toppling.

"You were crying."

"I was? I… I'm sorry. It was just a dream. I should go."

"No…you don't have to go, it's okay," he said. "I want you to stay."

"I'm not feeling well, I'll call you tomorrow." I grabbed my shirt, pulled over the hoodie and tugged on my jeans and left. I ran until I couldn't, my feet losing traction on the wet sidewalks. Once at the door of my apartment building, I slammed myself into the foyer, dropping my keys and huddling in the corner. I wept into the arch of my knees. All I could think of was the pastor's voice, still echoing from the dream. Sometimes words are sermons: *A light from the family is gone. A voice we loved is stilled.* I shuddered from the cold and held myself together, afraid that if I let go I would fall apart.

*In late September you became the air, and I struggled to breathe.* My journal quickly filled with oscillating rants of reverie and fears I couldn't say aloud. I had to expose myself somewhere. I felt it all, left love lying around all over the place. I wished I could be subtle, could hold it in, could store it for later, could keep up the front, but I was failing. I wished to keep his constellation freckles forever in my pocket, to never have another person's toes touch against me in the morning. Max never left my mind, but I feared the moment he'd discover that I was unlovable. That my hometown blamed me for my sister's drowning, that I showed my vagina to the internet. That my parents were religious freaks. That I had been used and disposed of countless reprehensible times. *I am not worthy of this love,* I wrote. I wrote and I chewed on a sesame-crusted St-Viateur bagel, downing my coffee and rushing off to work with my backpack hanging off one shoulder, my thoughts spilling everywhere.

I rolled in the streets through Mile End, listening to the newly released AFI album on repeat, painfully called *The Art of Drowning.* I ollied up onto the sidewalk and coasted along until an image caught my eye in a bookstore window and I immediately put my foot down to brake, turned off the CD and went back. At the top of a tower of books in the centre of the red window frame was a copy of *The Lion, the Witch and the Wardrobe,* the cover exactly as I knew it to be. The castle flags waving in the distance, Aslan and the Pevensie children in fur coats. I tried the door, but it was locked. I shook at the handle and peered inside. I stared at the book display, remembering how our mother set the book down for the last time,

spine cracked, in the space between the dollhouse roof and its master bedroom where my Barbie, whose hair I had chopped off, was
lying naked on the bed with her shiny, nipple-less cone tits aimed
motionless in the air. Her blue eyes bulging in a blink-less vapid
gawk. Mom put the tiny blanket over Barbie's tanned, plastic body,
tucked her in and closed the roof. I could hear her voice like it was
hanging above me.

"You two know your father doesn't want me reading these stories to you, right?"

"If they're just stories, why does it even matter?" I was always
ready to disagree. She hid the book somewhere Dad would never
look, but it annoyed me. There was always some kind of restraint
from him that led to secrecy among us. We had to follow his
rules. He was as rigid as the wooden spoon he spanked us with.
He'd handcrafted the dollhouse for Clara and me and it spanned
the space between our twin beds. I was surprised we were even
allowed real Barbies, given their proportions and positions.
Originally the dollhouse was equipped with tiny fixtures and
accessories, but they had since been lost or abandoned and I'd
get reminders as they dwindled that I couldn't take care of my
things.

"It is my belief that when told through the eyes of children, the
hero's journey of redemption inspires good, but your father thinks
there is too much cosmology and would prefer that we read from
the Bible."

Mom always spoke with feather-tipped eloquence, her tone
never matching up to the tension held along her jaw, like it was true
labour to present to us a sense of togetherness.

I rattled the door again. There were no posted hours and it was
dark inside. I started to leave when I heard footsteps and the door
creaked open and a small lady stuck her head out and called to me,
"Mademoiselle?"

"I need to buy a book in the window."

"The store opens at eleven." She went to close the door, but I stuck my foot in it and leaned it back open.

"Please," I said, "it's really important."

"Which one?" She sighed.

"*The Lion, the Witch and the Wardrobe*. Please," I said hurriedly.

"Just a moment, dear." I let her close the door this time and I waited anxiously, shifting my weight from foot to foot and spinning my skateboard around and around by its nose.

I knew people thought our daddy was stern. I knew they called our family "Bible thumpers" because we went to church every Sunday and I liked those stories too, but I couldn't connect to the belief in God, that I should pray to him or go to hell. It seemed like Christians were always busy pushing all this forgiveness on themselves and each other, but when Clara went to the water and I never told anyone that she did, I ended up on the outside of their huddled circles, fearful of their cold glances that preached *God's wrath*.

I remembered Mother patting Clara's head as we leaned into her sides and pulled our matching long pink nightgowns over our knees and feet to keep warm. Mom pulled up the blanket around us and patted it down around our ankles like plotting earth around a flowerbed and she winked, and we released our jammies from their tangle. We knew she didn't like it when we stretched them out. Clara copied me all the time and it made me mad. I hated that our pajamas matched and she wanted to do whatever I was doing, but when Mother was reading to us I surrendered into the fantasy of Narnia and let it be. Otherwise I knew there would be no more stories and that was the last thing I wanted, even though part of me wanted to kick Clara away and stick my tongue out. We were supposed to read the whole series together. We only got through half that story before she died.

She returned with the book and passed it to me.

"You can have it, Miss."

"What? Why?" I said.

"We have many copies of this. Something tells me you need it more than I do."

"Merci, thank you," I said taking the book in my hands and smelling it and flipping through the yellowed paper. I wanted to hug her.

I remembered the chemical stench of our Toni home perms too. Mine turned out shaped like a frizzy triangle and I dreaded having to wet it in the cold winter mornings, for Mom to have to pick and yank it out with a stained towel slung around my shoulders, while Clara's hair bounced around her shoulders and the curls licked at her cheeks.

"Goodnight, Clara, Princess of Grace. Goodnight Ines, Tamer of Lions."

She would kiss us both and let us take turns touching the lamp on its brass base until it dimmed to dark and her blue shadow left the room. She never called me Princess anything. I was always the animal.

"Câlisse, Ines, you're late again." Thierry pushed an apron into my hands before I'd even put my things in the closet. He went out for a smoke and left me to prepare the mise en place. My mind was elsewhere as I started making the list from the clipboard. Thierry appeared again in the doorway to the cooler.

"We have a very full-on service this evening. Let's go." He swept his hand to hurry me along. I started scrambling around. I wanted nothing more than to go home and begin reading the book. It had to be a sign. I wasn't in the mood to be teased for my French while trying to whisk and prepare the night's menu. In the middle of our busy shift a dozen roses arrived. Thierry called to me with excitement, "Somebody likes you!" Then he snapped, "Wait! These better not be from the person you got in a fight with!" I assured him they were not. They were long stemmed and red and mixed with daisies. A mini envelope with a card inside read, *Dear Ines, may all your dreams come true. Love Max.* I blushed hard and put the card in my apron. They were expensive and cheesy, but I loved them. My dreams were nightmares that had already come true, but I knew it was a sentimental thing to say and after my shift, I skated home, greasy, carrying the flowers in my arms while leaves fell around me, feeling delighted that people for once looked at me with awe.

※ ※ ※

Marie, Felix, Max and his friend Seb and I hopped onto the metro to Pie-IX, the Olympic stadium exit. I knew about "the Pipe" before I arrived in Montreal, but I didn't know how to get there. I figured it was for locals only. A large mezzanine of concrete textures made the wheels of my skateboard echo like the trains that passed us. When we got to the entrance to the 1976 Summer Games track field, an enclosed full pipe revealed itself. It was covered with graffiti. The transitions were tight and partially open at the end, making it a concrete wave. A few other skaters were there besides us, and a stereo played, and we gathered with the others on the bouncy track ground, and I watched as, one at a time, the skateboarders did their stuff. With rock 'n' roll precision they carved hard at the vertical peak and slashed through the cement curve, their large wheels screeching into tail stalls and smith grinds. It was impressive. When it was my turn to try, I felt embarrassed because it was so hard. I could barely make a kick-turn it was so tight, but they cheered for me anyway.

When elbows had grown swollen, we sat in a semicircle at the opening, listening to Social Distortion and the Misfits and Bob Marley. Felix took out a flip phone and punched in a number that was written on the back of a goal post on the field, asking us what we wanted on our pizza. Less than an hour later a kid arrived with two large pizzas and a case of beer strapped to the back of his bike. We ate and drank on the ground, our dirty fingers grabbing at falling toppings and pulling strings of cheese off our chins. I reclined against Max, his legs stretched out on either side of me, and we shared the joint that was going around. I felt like I was being lifted to the sky, and when I turned my head to see his face, the stars looked suspended by him. That crooked smile seemed to come deep from within. He stroked the side of my face gently where the bruise was yellowing on my eye.

I told Max about a time two girls beat me up in grade ten. I was at a bush party. I dropped my pants and took a piss right where they were dancing. I was getting lippy and they came after me. One held me down while the other punched until the biggest guy at the party told them I'd had enough and peeled them off me. I was trying to tell them to stop, but they didn't. My nose gushed with blood and covered the whole front of the vest I'd borrowed from a friend. I wanted everyone to know I deserved it, so I yelled out "Thank you!" which weirded everyone out. I screamed that I was happy to taste my own blood because I deserved it. Then they all really thought I was insane. Sometimes we take our licks. Whomever I had been before still had something to get off her chest. I wanted to feel pain as punishment. Max laughed at the story and cocked his head back, he didn't believe someone as small as me could have that much anger in them.

After it grew chilly and we'd all pulled on hoodies, we cabbed to a Japanese karaoke bar to celebrate Marie's birthday. We piled onto the small couches around the tables we filled with bottles and cigarettes. While Max sang, Felix put his arm around me and leaned in.

"So you and Max are hanging out, hey?"

"Yep, I guess we are," I said.

"Huh."

"What?" I laughed into my beer.

"I dunno. Max is … an artist and you're kind of like punk rock, aren't you?"

"Does it matter what we are? Aren't you kind of like hip hop?"

"Just be careful, okay." Felix leaned forward and ashed his smoke signifying the conversation was done. Max was singing an eighties song by Opus called "Live Is Life," which basically just repeats that phrase over and over again.

"It's a wedding song in Quebec, they play it all the time," Marie said. I nodded, at first uncertain but then getting into the moment. We all sang out "Live Is Life" while jumping on the couches and thrashing around the room. We were all laughing and swaying together, crashing our bottles and drunkenly falling over. Felix stood on the table and did a Marilyn Monroe rendition of "Happy Birthday" for Marie. He had brought a cake for her in his backpack, but we had no way to cut it into proper pieces, so we dipped our hands into it and ate it out of our palms. Then the food fight began. Max had frosting on his nose, so I licked it off. The mess was considerable and when we left I felt bad for whomever had to clean it up. I didn't imagine we'd be invited back.

After the karaoke, Max and I skated to La Banquise, the Montreal landmark for the best poutines. I ordered the Galvaude: shredded turkey and peas with duck gravy on top of hot fries and local cheese curds, and a Boréale Rousse. Max and I settled into the booth for an uninterrupted feast, amber beer washing down the rich comfort food.

"The other night…" he said and I knew what was next. "You can talk to me, you know. If you want to tell me some things, I would try to understand them." His way of translating French to English was so gentle.

"Max the Magnificent!" I said, filling my mouth while a small fizzy burp escaped my nose. "I guess I've just never been very good at talking about things."

"Oui, mais… I can tell you are good at feeling them." He laughed soft and placed his freckled hand on top of mine. I pulled away and sank down into the plastic bench; my heart pooled into my stomach and liquefied, my throat closed up behind me. I had never been made such an offer. With my mouth full and not sure what to say, I nodded. Max's expression was intense. I wanted nothing more than

95

to trust him, but every past mistake told me not to. I didn't care what Felix had said. I wanted him.

"I like you a lot, Ines." My mouth was still full of food. I worked hard not to choke on it, just nodded again. He didn't wait to hear the same, and thankfully moved on to something else. "Let's go away tomorrow. Let's go somewhere."

"Where are we going to go?" I asked, chewing on the squeaky poutine cheese.

"Anywhere," Max said, smiling outrageously. "We could go any-where." And when we got up and paid, he tried to pick me up like a bride, but outside it was slippery and we were so drunk we both fell on the concrete like baby deer. We laughed so hard even the patrons inside couldn't hold it in and chuckled too.

♧ ♧ ♧

I stayed awake all night just watching him drive. As soon as we were
out of the city lights, the sky wrapped itself around the car: a dark
blanket of dancing stars, so many it was like jugs of them had been
spilled over. We left at 3 a.m. I was planning for a later start, but
Max couldn't sleep and was itching to go, so we took off in the Red
Rocket, his '91 Taurus, for a road trip to Quebec City. We talked
about aliens, we bobbed to reggae, we felt like two touching souls.
The conversation steered so smoothly we weren't even in the car
anymore—we weren't even in our bodies anymore. Max said we
were invisible love. I wasn't sure if he meant no one could see us or
if everyone could, but it didn't matter, acknowledgement was the
first step into sincerity. He asked me to twist up a joint, knowing
full well the extent of my rolling capabilities. I said I would do my
best. He said I already was. I soaked his love in so hard that I gritted
my teeth and actually heard my guard slip out the window with the
smoke.

We drove around for the early morning through the tight streets
of the upper and lower cities. There was very little happening, just
a few people stirring here and there. We had coffee in a beautiful
old-world-type café and then Max paid the attendant cash so we
could check in early to Le Château Frontenac, one of the fanciest
hotels in the province. The room was over three hundred dollars.
I was spoiled by the luxury. I wanted to dance on the bed, to use
up all the hot water and to scream excited profanities in the mirror
because it was the royal treatment and I was used to being treated
like garbage. We made love as soon as we unloaded our bags and

then I slept off the drive while he went out for a walk. I stretched
and spasmed and twisted in the cold. Even after a shower, a coffee
and a hot bowl of soup, my bones still ached. I missed Montreal's
humid air, it was exotic. Admiring our room while lying upside
down on the bed, I pictured how I'd rearrange the furniture if the
roof was the floor and the floor was the roof. How I would navi-
gate through the doorway down the high step into the living room,
which was of course just the ceiling getting higher. I wrapped my
toes up in the lengths of a starchy, white cotton sheet, wearing only
one of the socks I had on during the drive. The carnal smell of the
bed relaxed me, and I hoped it would linger till we did it again.

"Ines, c'est très chaud. Turn the heat down," Max called to me
when he got back.

The hotel was like a haunted castle, a lumbering old brick giant
with a green roof made from copper. Our leftover croque mon-
sieurs sat barely touched beside empty bowls of tomato soup. The
cheese had hardened, immortalized in a half drip. I poured another
cup of coffee from the carafe and wrapped my fingers around the
white china, trying to drink it in a sophisticated way, taking in the
steam and the smell, but it spilled over into the saucer and I had
to slurp it up from the plate and the bottom of the cup before it
landed on the crisp linens.

"Ines, what are you doing?'

"Come back to bed, Max."

He wouldn't stop going back and forth from the internet area
on the main floor. All morning he would go up and down, buying up custom Nike shoes off eBay. I got up and closed the French
doors he had opened, then returned to hang off the bed. I touched
the scars on my lip from the dog bite. I pinched it and remembered
the way it didn't hurt until I saw the blood. I twisted my lip in my
fingers thinking about how I hadn't cared that Clara had left the
cabin until I heard the neighbour scream. I ached to try again, to go
back and fix my mistake.

Max and I ordered more room service and made love on repeat. I had heard that each woman makes unique sounds during sex, and that when that soul sigh is real there's no better delight for a man than to hear it as its creator. I found my sound that weekend, and Max returned to my body to make it again and again, as if he had learned a new and complex tune on an instrument and wanted to be sure he could play it by memory.

I drew a bath and Max came in and stripped off all his clothes except for his socks, joining me in the bubbly water. I started laughing.

"What are you doing?" I said but he just lay between my legs and rubbed my thighs and then he turned on the shower and unplugged the bath. He hoisted me up against the cold wall as the hot water rushed over and between our kissing mouths. Awkwardly, he peeled off his wet socks to improve his traction and I giggled more, still covered in bubbles. It reminded me of the first time we were together, when the water was falling into my mouth from the tips of his hair and we became so entangled that we were one creature, a perfect fit. The light of the water rippling in rhythm to our grasping desires. Our eyes met and locked and I didn't look away like I always had before.

Afterwards my knees ached from the position and my heart pounded with exhaustion and the intensity of internal heat. I could hear it thumping in my head. The smoke from my cigarette mixed with my cold breath on the balcony, creating hefty plumes that I pushed away in relaxed puffs. The view encompassed the whole of the old town, and we stood there in the centre at the highest peak in the walled city. I felt like a princess in a castle. Max returned to the computer room for most of the evening, so I wrote in my journal and lounged around in the big bed in my panties, smelling the leftover desire.

On the way home, we got a flat tire.

"Max," I said, "it's not a big deal. We can just call someone to fix it."

"You don't understand, Ines, these aren't my plates. I took them off some other car. My insurance ran out and I don't have enough money now to get more, since the hotel."

"What? When did you do that? Whose plates?"

"In the middle of the night before we left. I don't know whose."

"What if we were in an accident?" I thinned my lips, holding them in my mouth so he wouldn't see how confused I was. I mean, I was irresponsible, but this was more than I'd bargained for.

A man stopped to help us at the side of the road. He had all the right tools and used his own spare. Max tried to give him what cash he had left, but he wouldn't accept it. He didn't speak English and seemed to have been brought to maturity and mellowed like wood by years of hard work and little education. The lines on his face were hard in the stern spot between his brows, but his gestures were so kind that I smiled every time he glanced in my direction. Max, elated by his assistance, decided we shouldn't rush home with luck on our side. Instead we stopped in Saint-Hyacinthe for a picnic. I bought Earl Grey teas and we filled them with Baileys.

"It's nice to see the girl pay for some things."

"Of course," I said, hating the pigeonholes of domestication, not understanding the rules set out before us. We walked a river trail and ate expensive treats like olives and honeycomb. It was a bright, brisk day and Max looked at me often and we swung our joined hands up to the sky. I couldn't shake the feeling that this was where the breakdown would happen, the beginning of the end. The hotel was the final gesture and he would be done with me.

"I have a lot of baggage, you know?"

I tried to say it lightly, but my cool deteriorated. The vulnerability swirling up my insides ready to take me by the tonsils, my inner dialogue telling me how stupid I was to bring it up, to have "the talk." Never have "the talk."

"I could help you carry it." He smiled and nudged me. Total nonchalance. I braced myself for the "let's not define what we're doing, let's just enjoy the moment" bullshit, and wondered whether this would be the last time we'd be together. I squeezed his hand harder; might as well, I had nothing to lose.

Max blocked me from walking by standing in front of me.

"I'm serious, Ines. I want to be with you."

I looked down at my hands as he held them.

"I just know how this ends."

"But this is just the beginning." Max kissed my fingers and looked into me. The walkway was cradled by flame-red maple trees and the fresh crackle of fall filled the air. I tried to relax and be present, to enjoy this happy news, because coming from him, from those eyes, it had to be real. He didn't try to impress me, he was just himself. He stood there, handsome in jeans and a white T-shirt, smelling faintly like Old Spice mixed with dirt, rugged like it was the hundredth day in a row that his sweat had mingled with fresh cotton. It felt rare to find people who weren't trying so hard. It was incredible to meet a man who didn't hide behind his deep-set eyes with arrogance or overcompensation. There was something inside him that was so boyish that I felt more youthful inside too. We were like kids playing. He took my hand. It would take a while for me to trust that I could offer him mine and it would be received, but it was always there waiting, anticipating our alignment. He liked it when his wrist was turned to the outside and my little fingers connected to his. We clamped on to each other, freckles dotting his creamy skin from his shoulders down to his nail beds. We held on.

✵ ✵ ✵

I was taking a nap on the couch when a late afternoon storm began rattling a loose pane of glass against the window frame in the kitchen. The strong winds threw the ripped screen into an outrage, and it flapped open and shut. I bolted it up and slammed it closed. Angry to be disturbed. The old window crumpled. The glass fell hard and quick, the smell of the approaching thunder hit me, or maybe it was the way the screen smelled like black dirt. Leaves blew outside and fastened onto buildings with a splat. Dead little bugs that had stuck to the corners of the window now littered the floor, and a giant fly droned its buzzing wings though its legs were crushed. I watched it die, disturbing the air frequency with buzzing. More buzzing became apparent in the apartment—the fridge, the computer—soon I could hear nothing else. Backing away from the open space where the window should've been, I was appalled at what I'd done. How easily I hurt and break things. The pane that separated me from the outside world was now in shards on the floor, and an electric downpour was making its way into the room.

I went to the stove and put on some coffee. I pulled out a chair and sat at the table and stared at the wall until the Bialetti pot stammered and spewed. A package had arrived from my parents and was sitting on the table. The card was of a Renaissance painting, a cornucopia on a table. My mom would have bought it at the hospice shop. Always up for a bargain, cards there were twenty-five cents. She still went to grief and loss groups there and was fond of all the gentle and hurting widows who volunteered their time. Death after retirement meant volunteering to sit with the grief of others,

I think because your own grief could never be mended that late in the game, if at all. It takes up so much space. That's why the elderly die of broken hearts. The card was simple: *Happy Thanksgiving, Love always, Mom and Dad.* The way she wrote, her cursive running perfectly straight across the card, curly at the tips. She was always so organized I wasn't at all surprised that it arrived early. Ticking off the boxes of how to show love to a child you resent. Tucked neatly in a shoebox was a key chain, a pair of socks, a pumpkin muffin recipe I'd never make and a small orange decorative squash. A necklace was nestled in the bottom, wrapped in tissue paper, with a Post-it Note attached that said: *This necklace belonged to your grandmother. We thought you would like to have it. The pendant is made from real Waterford crystal.* I rubbed along the chain of garnet beads. I examined the pendant, a timeless, classic oval that caused shiny fractals in the light when it moved. She wore it all the time. It would have been removed from her dead body. I added Clara's ring to the chain and put it on and held it close, then tucked it under my T-shirt. I was collecting talismans from the deceased. I wondered if it was bad luck to wear them. It was bad luck they existed at all.

The phone rang as I sat there in a daze.

"Hello," I said into the phone.

"Ines, it's Max."

I had my period and a need for solitude welled up inside me; the cramping ran down my thighs like growing pains.

"You want to get together?"

I didn't want to be the girl who said no.

"Sure."

"I'll bring a movie over."

I taped two garbage bags over the window, but rain still leaked in underneath and lifted the masking tape, making it curl away and stop working. While I waited for Max I ordered pho and drank red wine on the living room floor where I scattered my old photos all around me. I tried to organize them into an album but found myself throwing most of them away. I felt disconnected from the high school pictures I was saving. These people weren't my friends; we happened to achieve puberty together. I was now across the country. I wasn't that person anymore and there was no one who really took the time to get to know me. The window bags ruffled and bulged at every gust of wind. There were some photos of Clara and me together when we were kids. In one of them we held a fish we'd caught with a bobber, our dad behind us radiating pride. I was missing a front tooth.

The buzzer rang and I let Max up. We stood facing each other. "Entrez-vous," I said in my best French accent. We sat on the couch together and he put his hands on my thighs. I wasn't in the mood, but he went straight for the edges of my baggy sweatshirt, pulling it over my head, making my ponytail throw static, my bangs lifting with excitement and I liked that. I had no bra on, and my small breasts stood erect, swollen and tender, which Max noticed at once. Shyly, I looked at my deep navel, my black jeans, my bare toes, not knowing how to respond. Max touched the necklace from my grandmother. "C'est très beau," he said, and held my chin and brought my face to his, pressing himself against me with hot breath. He cupped my breasts in his hands. "Is it your time of the month?" I nodded yes, so taken aback that he knew, and that it didn't seem to deter his desire.

I unlocked his belt, lifting the latch and pulling it back to release it from the eyelet. I pressed hard on his top button to open his jeans. He was ready to take me, and, groping my bottom, he pushed hard into me. I pulled down his zipper and slipped my hand underneath the waistband of his boxer shorts. He bulged, and I held him all in my grip. I tried to kiss him, but he wouldn't let me. In one swift movement Max had me bent over the couch with my pants around my ankles and my underwear pulled crookedly at my thighs. He pushed me forward and thrust into my backside, taking all of my breath away so I could only gasp in discomfort. It wasn't until he moved in and out that I was able to understand what was happening. The necklace hung and bounced off my chest over the arm of the sofa. I felt nervous about the tampon string. I told myself this was good. I told myself this was what I wanted. I exhaled hard. It was all I could do for the pain. I tasted the alkaline of the wine in the cracks of my lips, smelled the cold air of the outside, watched the broken window covering wrinkle and list. When Max released me, he finished himself on my back and went and got himself a glass of water. He tossed me a tea towel from the kitchen to wipe myself off, which was awkward because I couldn't reach the dip of my spine. I stayed half bent over, tense and disoriented, holding my breath, irresolute. I would fall and smash to pieces if I exhaled. He left without turning around and went into the bedroom and lay down on my bed. I went to the bathroom, pushed play on the tapedeck. It was a melodic, building guitar solo from Lindsey Buckingham of Fleetwood Mac and I was relieved it hadn't landed on one of their more popular songs. It was dark and I felt that way too. I sat down on the toilet. My ass sore, I was surrounded by royal blue tile, and there was no soap left to clean myself. I showered for as long as I could and went to the bedroom and lay down beside Max on the futon. He opened his eyes.

"You're a good girl, Ines." And then he turned over. I pressed my tongue to the roof of my mouth to keep from crying. When I woke up Max was gone, and it was half past four. The dent in his pillow smelled like falling, and I lay in it for a long time breathing him in. I couldn't place why it seemed like his only mission that night was sex, loathing that I didn't have the guts to say no to it, even when I wanted to.

I lay there unable to fall back asleep thinking of the time my mom read my diary in high school. I know it was out of concern, but I was horrified by the blasphemy and threw the entire book into the wood stove and left the latch open to watch it disintegrate. I bawled loudly like a war cry at the invasion. I hated her then. I had to convince her that nothing in it was true. I said they were dreams that I had. One entry in particular was about a boy who stayed over without my parents knowing, how I didn't have any condoms so he convinced me we should try anal sex. I didn't have any lube either, and he told me that hair conditioner would work just as well, and so I went to the bathroom and brought back the whole bottle. I stayed in one place on all fours and waited for it to end. I didn't like it. He didn't spend the night. I know Mom was just looking for any answer that could tell her I was going to be okay and wasn't impure; instead she likely got the fright of her life. She couldn't even talk to me about birth control. I was repulsed that she knew my most intimate secrets. One I was already ashamed of. That the boy ignored me afterwards. After that night I got so tired of being disappointing that I went home from school one day while my parents were at work and pulled out a box from the dining room cabinet with a carving knife in it. It used to be my grandpa's. The handle was made from the bone of a cow. A useless heirloom, hard to part with, never used. I held it to my wrist and cried. I pressed down ready to slice. I didn't want to live, but I was so afraid to die.

Since I couldn't hurt myself I tried anything that let me escape from my problems. I got fucked up every chance I could. I got fucked by people who didn't care about me. I placed my value in their hands. Every time they left, they took a piece of me with them, and there were pieces of me deposited all over the ground, trampled on, for shame. Skateboarding was the only thing that made me feel free. At a party once I tried to break a beer bottle over my head, but it didn't break and the thud was ringing agony and I tried again, because at least I had grit and determination, but it still didn't break and I wished that it would knock me out so I would never remember the moment. Instead people grew bored and rolled their eyes and I went to the bathroom and cried because it physically hurt so much. I grew angrier until I rubbed up against every single thing in confrontation. The friends I still had at home were trying hard not to resent me. A change in scenery seemed my last chance to alter the course of my life. And here I was, less than a year later, yearning again for an escape route. Not able to admit to the hurt.

꧁ ꧁ ꧁

April wore a black velvet mask and a red one-piece fishnet suit with red patent leather heels. Her hair was in high pigtails, and she was licking a big round spiral sucker. A few jack-o'-lanterns with glowing grins and triangle eyes sat on the shelf headboard of the bed. The outfit she brought for me was lying over the desk by the computer monitor.

"I brought you a mask, some cat ears and a one-piece leotard. You'll feel hidden. It will be great. My clients haven't stopped asking about you. It will be double the payout of the glitter night."

I deliberated while April kept talking. I was muddled in my thoughts about what Max would think if he knew I was doing this, if this was cheating. The heaviness of this secret rose and fell in my stomach. I hadn't eaten all day. I didn't even have time to shower after my work shift and my pants were wet from the sink and my hair was lazily pulled back. I was so nervous.

"Come on," April said. "It's showtime."

I took a bottle of whiskey out of my bag and took a swill and passed it to April. I grabbed the clothes and started changing. I took another swill and went to the bathroom. I pulled at the fabric of the leotard, wrestling myself into it, not at all feeling like myself. I watched my face undulate in the mirror, and I felt like I was shrinking. I tied the mask on. I knew all about wearing masks.

I watched April for a few minutes before I joined her on the bed. She twisted her tendrils and mouthed all over the sucker, on her knees. She had put on some Nine Inch Nails. I took a box of Halloween candy and poured the mini chocolate bars all over the bed and crawled up to join her. I kept my back to the monitor until she awkwardly tried to position me beside her. When I saw the screen I noticed there were a lot of people popping into the chat room. April and I licked the sucker together and I saw Multiple Scorgasm's name.

*Hi Maddy, we've missed you,* they typed as I sunk. April tried to lay me down to straddle me, trying to whisper something in my ear, but I heard nothing. I pushed her back and got up and left the room, grabbed my smokes and headed out to the deck. I puffed on a quick smoke that I couldn't enjoy and went and started the shower. I wanted to wash this circus off. Part of me wanted to leave and never return and the other part of me needed to wait and have April validate my decision to vacate the show right as it started. I walked to the door of Lainey's usual bedroom, but she was in a private chat. I went and waited outside April's bedroom for a minute and then I heard her typing and laughing through the walls.

"Are you two ready for this?" she said. Multiple Scorgasm had taken her into a private chat. In that moment I felt jealous, but I couldn't put my finger on why. I took off the ears and mask and moped to the shower. It filled with so much steam I could no longer see in front of me. When I got out and dressed, I went back to April's door. There was a note taped to it that said, *Maddy meet me at 5 at Bonaventure,* with a kiss print at the bottom. I stood there listening to April putting on her show. I couldn't be sure if it was fake or real.

The roof of the metro station was curved and it echoed like an opera house amphitheatre. I chain-smoked in the vestibule while I waited for her to come up from the platform. She put so much work into the set and I let her down. I kicked at my shoes and leaned against the brick, trying to look relaxed. She came off the escalator peeling a leaf from the toe of her maroon Dr. Martens and I could tell that the people behind her got a good look up her skirt while she did it. In true Scarlett Slayer fashion, she puckered her lips and blew them a kiss. I knew she was wearing a thong under her fishnets. She linked arms with me immediately and trotted us forward and out of the waiting area like she had a plan that we were not going to be deviating from.

"You ever been here?"

"No," I said.

"I want to show you something."

We walked huddled together into the crumbling bleak streets of the industrial area. As far as I knew there was nothing happening down there, but I always loved seeing the Farine Five Roses sign blinking red and protruding into the skyline above the overpasses and brick abandoned factories. Up close the sign made me think of a stadium about to blast off fireworks for a celebration, yet it was set in a *Soylent Green*-looking slum of decrepit emptiness.

"I used to love coming here in my teens," April told me. "It was always so quiet and peaceful." We walked until we were underneath an old grain silo. Every window of the connected building was smashed out and graffiti covered every inch of the outside, save for the rust that ate at the metal. We walked around back where a piece of wood had been nailed to a door but then removed again. She motioned for me to follow her. April straightened her skirt and her camo crossbody and hunched down low under the railing of the stairs, moved the unfastened board and went inside. I took a deep breath and did the same. The floor was damp and littered with shards of glass and little burnt-out fires. We climbed the cement stairs until we were at the top of the building, where April kicked at the door bar and it opened and we went outside onto the sprawling flat roof. The evening sky was jarring after the dim shadow of the concrete inside.

"What do you think?" She spun around with her arms out. I took in the expansive view and didn't respond. I was happy to be alone with April, feeling like we were on the boundary of the horizon where blue turned to black. "I don't care that you ditched me, Ines, so let's get over that."

"Then why did you bring me here?" I shrugged.

"I told you. I love this place. Like a hundred years ago this was the busiest, most bustling borough in the whole fucking country. Imports, exports! My great-grandfather came here from Ireland and worked in some metal foundry. Could've been this building for all I know."

"Well, it's kind of a deserted dump now," I said as I kicked some brick crumbling from the wall of the doorframe.

"That's where you're wrong. That's what you see." April shook her head and poked my chest. I lit a smoke feeling suddenly anxious and not sure why. "An abandoned building with history and imperfection is far more beautiful to me than any place in Westmount. This place has changed, yeah—and so can you."

"But this place got worse…"

"It didn't get worse, it just got different. Look, I don't know what kind of ghosts are following you around, but you are an amazing, gorgeous woman. You just don't see it. Things change, people change. You need to let go. It's eating you alive." April grabbed my shoulders and pouted at me. "Fuck, Ines. What is your deal?"

"I feel ugly," I told her. "Working at the studio scares the shit out of me. I screwed up, I gave those guys my email. They like you now anyways. I'm scared someone from home—"

"Who cares about home? Those people you grew up with will never amount to anything. They peaked in high school and our clients are a bunch of gutless pigs who can't get laid. So what if you're naked on the internet? You're beautiful and young and sexy. That's not even what I'm talking about."

"Then what are you talking about?"

"You have a little rain cloud over your head and it hurts me to see you sad." She drew a halo around me. "Ever since I met you, it's been there. You're far off in the distance." April grabbed my head. I felt my body temperature rising in defense of something I couldn't pinpoint.

"Why do you like casts and amputees?"

"Cuz I'm weird and kinky and like my partners immobile. Why did you come to Montreal?" She looked right into me, unfazed by my attempt to derail her.

"Well, my little sister drowned for starters." I sat down on the ledge and looked up at April. "And it was my fault."

"How could that be your fault?"

"I was jealous of all the attention she got, I picked a fight with her and watched her leave and go down to the lake with the shovel and bucket. I didn't tell anyone where she went."

"That doesn't make it your fault."

"Try telling that to a whole fucking town. My parents pretty much ignored me after that. I was basically on my own to learn everything the hard way."

"What do you mean the hard way, honey?"

"Everything I do is a mistake. I get drunk and used."

April hauled me back to her level by my elbows. She hugged me and didn't let go. Over her shoulder I stared out through my tears at the expanse of rooftops and billboards and rolling clouds. It was beautiful there. I was thankful I wasn't alone, or I might have rolled myself right off the roof.

"I really like Max. Do you like him?"

"Sure, I mean he's not my type, but he adores you. That's what I like about him. He's gentle."

"My history with men would say: it started strong and is going to implode."

The clouds moved along and I felt like I was falling backwards. I was weak with relief to free the secret of Clara. We sat together against the ledge for a long time with our heads tilted next to each other, drinking up the air with no need for words. I clung to a memory of my ten-year-old self in a neon pink and black bathing suit. Clara had one too, though different colours, and we called them our *swiss cheese bikinis* because they were connected at the sides but had a hole cut out of the middle. I missed our silly jokes. She died wearing that bathing suit.

✤ ✤ ✤

It was packed at Village des Valeurs, everyone scrambling for a last-minute costume. It smelled awful, like old purses and welfare-worn kids' clothes, making my guts turn until I had the urge to go to the bathroom. I didn't like Halloween to begin with; bullies came out at Halloween. Bullies who smash pumpkins and egg cars and toilet-paper houses or write *murderer* on your locker. I didn't want to celebrate death, but I found some stuff to make an easy hippie costume and Lainey found a fascinator with a veil. Digging in the pet section I found a Santa outfit that was a perfect fit for Cedric.

At nine o'clock we met outside the metro in Longueuil and headed to La Ronde, where they had free spooky-themed thrill rides, provided you dressed up. We gathered in a circle of cigarette smoke and tall clinking beer bottles. Everyone was harder to decipher; their accents seemed thicker than usual, because I couldn't see their faces. Someone wearing a cardboard refrigerator box with a rectangle cut out of the front was a last-minute robot. When I heard his voice say "Salut" to me, I knew it was Seb. Wet leaves littered the top of the escalators. The buzz of a good night was catching on. Max approached me from behind and sashayed his hips into mine, turning me around to face him. The synthetic curls of my blonde afro wig crinkle-cut my view. Laughing and sweeping them aside, I saw he was dressed as a salesman in a brown suit and bowler hat tipped forward. He offered me a free sample of his goods. His briefcase had skateboard trucks with huge wheels attached to the bottom and swinging it up and open simultaneously, he reached in and grabbed me a tiny foil-wrapped parcel.

"Un champignon au chocolat," he announced, "for my queen."
A miniature business card was taped underneath it that read *Salesman Extraordinaire*.

Anyone who has said they'd try anything once has probably done it twice. We all waited until just before the roller coaster started moving to eat the chocolates. The metal *ka-chunk*-ing climb over the tracks was loud in our quiet anticipation, as we creaked in the carts to the top of the drop-off, sucking on chocolates filled with chewy, earthy psilocybin. I looked behind me and Marie and Felix gave a ready thumbs up. In front of me, Lainey's fascinator flew off as we fell, screaming in unison. A mirror at the bottom made it look like we were about to crash head on, and then suddenly we were whipped sharply to the right at the very last second.

After the roller coaster we hit the haunted house. I was afraid before I had even entered. I didn't want to follow but I didn't want to be alone. Circus music raised the hairs on my arms until they felt like individual needles pricking my skin. Inside there was a skinny hallway that was blocked by long, thick strips of meat-packing cooler plastic, and just beyond them, fake, heavy bodies wrapped in the plastic hung from hooks. We pushed our way through the beefy clinging bodies and I was disturbed to find I was thinking about Clara. I thanked the powers that be that I was not too high on the mushrooms yet. I was claustrophobic and the way through was impossible to locate. My reflection in the mirror maze showed a fat or slanted version of myself: my dark eyes black holes, my body converted into wave form. I called out for Max or Lainey, but now there was nobody there. My blood turned to ice water. I wanted to smell fresh cut grass, or the musty life jackets from the cabin, corn on the cob with butter—anything safe and familiar. I called out and no one came. I screamed until Max appeared out of nowhere, grabbing my hands and wrestling them to my sides so I couldn't flail.

"It's okay," he soothed, "it's okay, Ines. Ça va? No one is going to hurt you. You are fine."

"It's Clara, okay? My sister. She died when we were kids, I dream about it a lot." I sobbed into his too-big suit jacket. I didn't want him to see the emotional me, the me that no one could handle or wanted.

Max hugged me hard. My hands stayed stiff at my sides.

"It's okay, Ines. Your sister loves you." He kissed both my cheeks and then my dry mouth. "She tells me she doesn't blame you."

I took a step back, startled out of the tears.

Max laughed and pulled me by one hand. "Let's go," he said, yanking me behind a mirrored partition that appeared closer than it was: a hidden exit. He pushed the metal bar and we emerged out into the carnival of the park.

We walked past food vendors lined up outside the haunted house. I trailed behind him. We found Seb and Lainey eating corndogs and drinking lemonade.

"Do you want some cotton candy, Ines?" Marie asked me as she slowed to match my pace.

"No, I'm good," I told her. I was not good. I pulled off the stupid wig and carried it under my arm.

The boys lit a joint and at some unnoticed prompt they started running towards the train station for the tram. I walked behind, letting the last of my tears fall. I was trying hard to process what Max had said to me. It must have been altered in translation. Hearing the train come down the line Max yelled, "Un…deux…trois…allez!!" and threw his beer bottle against the train as it came above ground. I heard the pulverizing of glass against rusted iron and wondered if chaos always happened in slow motion. The breaking was slow, but the train was quick, and I capsized in my mind. I rolled my stoned eyes to keep a hold and lost my footing, stumbling backwards onto the landing. Lainey laughed at me and helped me up. We ran down to the last car and all piled in before the train could leave.

Housekeepers were on their way home from work in comfy white sneakers with mini shampoos in their purses, and loners scratched their heads under weird-smelling hats. I was starting to feel waves of vibrations.

"Why did you do that?" I asked Max when we sat down.

"Because it's fun!"

Max, Seb, Lainey and I switched lines at Berri and said good-night to Marie and Felix. When we got out at Sherbrooke, it had started snowing, lightly like dander. We walked through Carré Saint-Louis to our place for more drinks. The wispy snow stuck to my hair and to Max's bowler hat. He paused behind me and kissed me under the framework of the dusted trees. When I touched my lips to his, he bent me by the bow in my back, dipping me like a dancer and pressing into me seductively. I let him hold me there, our warm mouths and the cold snow on my eyelids the only sensations in that moment. It seemed as though Max knew about Clara, but I had never said a word. I put it out of my head, told myself it must've been the mushrooms and the beer, or the language barrier.

"Are you okay?" he asked.

"Yeah," I said, "I'm good."

The wind lifted the light flakes into twirls, and I had to focus intently on my steps through the park; I was starting to trip and the snowflakes were fertile. I walked like I was on an ice rink without skates. My stomach swollen from the hops and the mushrooms. I hugged myself, so comfortable in my clothes. Our commotion was reserved only for us. We stopped at the benches around the fountain and Seb stood on the ledge yelling something in French. Lainey was skipping, though her feet must've been freezing in her dainty slippers and crinoline skirt. Max was fidgeting with his lighter; a broken, crushed smoke dangled from his mouth. He looked up at me and grinned. He was standing beside the tree where I'd hung my message only a month before. A few leaves were left hanging on.

Big and yellow, they flapped in the breeze. The tiny flakes landed silently, biding their time till they covered the branches, when the last leaves would fall with the weight of snow and die.

Cedric greeted us at the apartment door, wagging his tail and tapping his paws on the tile. Once upstairs, we all plopped around on the couch. All we had to drink was a bottle of warm champagne, so Seb went to the dépanneur and came back with a case of beer wrapped in a black garbage bag.

"After eleven, you just have to name the right price," he said. I took the Santa costume from my room and started to dress Cedric with the red and white jacket and the little Santa hat with a white beard attached to the bottom. He looked ridiculous and embarrassed.

"I am so high," Lainey told us. "Why is this champagne warm?"

"You can drink cold beer," Seb responded while taking a huge slam.

"I have an idea. Lainey, change your shoes. Grab your coats."

We dashed outside with jackets and hoodies over our costumes, Cedric in the Santa outfit. We took my skateboard and once we were in the street took turns holding his leash while Cedric ran and pulled us up and down the road. He wasn't strong enough, so we took his place: each of us taking turns to run with the leash while another sat on the skateboard with Cedric in our laps. We laughed so hard, the snow covered the ground and the Santa outfit made me feel like it was Christmas morning and I was on a sleigh. Max tried to skateboard on his briefcase and fell down. If anyone was watching us they must have thought we were out of our minds. When our adventure wound down we went back home. The Chemical Brothers played from the CD player in my room. We smoked a joint and lit a few candles. The smoke skimmed the roof and landed in our clothes. I thought about what Max had said about Clara. We lay, tousled, until I snuffed out the candles. Eventually, as the day was beginning, we fell asleep in a pile on my futon.

Sometime in the morning Seb and Lainey went to her room together. It snowed throughout the night and something depressed me about waking up on November first to see wet pumpkins with their sagging faces, and the crystalized windshields of cars, and people hovering over them with gloves on, fervently scraping.

* * *

On Mont-Royal the cars that passed us carried veterans to a Remembrance Day ceremony, where they placed fake flower wreaths on memorials while trumpets played the sad call "Taps." I saw in their expressions their memories of love and loss. A moment of silence didn't feel long enough because their eyes said a lifetime. A store along the Plateau had Christmas decorations up in the window already, which I thought was offensive. Peace was with us that morning as we climbed the Mountain. Our icy breath replaced words as we hiked up the frozen trails, breaking into a warm wet sweat underneath all our winter coverings. Max laughed at me for spilling hot chocolate on my mittens and then wiping my runny nose with them. My toque fell below my eyes, and I tried to lift it up, but it kept slipping. The beauty of the sunshine glazing the snow gave the impression of sheets of light gold. Brown grass tips were reaching out from the ground towards the sky. That day I surrendered to the season's conclusive change. Inhaling took your breath away, and it pained my chest to let it out. It was relieving though, that seasons change, and you with them.

"Your hot chocolate empty?" Max said.

"Why?"

"Bon!" he replied, tackling me to the ground, giving me a playful face wash. He called it a Claude Lemieux, which made me laugh so hard I peed a bit. The snow stung against my cold, red skin. Our breath mixed when I tried to fight back. The cross on the Mountain's top rose behind Max's head and when it came into full sight I wanted to drop to my knees. I heard nothing but the echoes of a slow, sad trumpet which reminded me of a song that I had forgotten years ago but was trying to remember. The one with the piano. I lifted up the sleeve of my coat to see my watch. Everything was slowing down.

"It's almost eleven, Max, we should have a minute of silence."

"Pfft, I don't believe in this."

"It's not something to believe in," I said. "It's out of respect."

I sat up in the snow, not worried about how cold my ass was going to be. I looked out at the view of the city. It was beautiful, the way steam rose from the buildings and the sun cast silver reflections off of them, melding into the clouds. I tucked my chin into my chest and felt the cavity of prayer. Max scrambled to his feet and launched into song. He began marching like a soldier across the ground with his hand cocked to his forehead.

"They say that in the army the food is mighty fine. A bun rolled off the table and killed a friend of mine. Oh...I don't want to go to army camp. Gee, Mom, I want to go back to my stereo. Gee, Mom I wanna go ho-o-ome."

He turned and stomped his feet together and saluted me.

I shook my head, got up and walked away. He came tumbling after me, trying to be funny, but I kept walking, back down the hill. I was sad for the men who fought and the women who cried for them. War captivated me and knowing that others felt immense grief made mine more tolerable.

We slipped into the blue vinyl booth at Dusty's, our menus open and the Beatles playing on the stereo. *Happiness is a warm gun*...I ordered coffee and orange juice for both of us and Max took off his toque, revealing a gruesome-looking buzzcut with tufts that poked out at different lengths.

"When did you do that?" I asked him in alarm.

"Do what?" he replied nonchalantly, scratching at it.

His reflection in the sugar lid made his face distorted: skinny and concave. It reminded me of Munch's painting *The Scream*.

"You're not a girl who misses much, are you?" he said, quoting the song lyrics.

"I'm just happy to be here," I said, remembering George Harrison's television response to being asked how it felt to be a member of the greatest band of all time. But it was lost on him, and he continued to stare unsurely at nothing while putting too much sugar in the weak coffee and stirring insistently.

"Hitler was good at public speaking," Max told me without looking up.

"I always talk about Hitler over breakfast on Remembrance Day, Max," I said dryly. "Don't you think it's not the best morning to discuss this?"

"It's power. Power can make people die because of who they are."

"I don't really want to talk about death right now, Max."

"Non, c'est vrai! With his great voice he convinced countries full of soldiers to hate and kill people who were just like him! He wanted to be an artist, you know?"

"No, I didn't know that." I pretended, to appease him, and took a long drink from my coffee, averting my eyes.

"Charles Manson, too. He got young followers to kill the people he couldn't be—he wanted to be a famous musician, just like The Beatles, actually. He had a … what do you call … inferiority complex. Imagine being so upset over your own failure that you would form an army? Carve an X in your head?" Max tapped at my forehead. Maybe it was the barrier between our languages, and my lack of understanding of the deep Quebecois slang that limited our ability to find real understanding. He leaned in and kissed my chin.

"You know that I am falling in love with you?"

"You know that I am falling in love with you too?" I said it back. It was easier to say when it wasn't just those three little words and falling meant you hadn't landed yet. We ate our bacon. Max was energetic. The round metal stools at the bar shone chrome.

I listened to the clinking of glassware and running water, sizzling food and the staff hollering at each other through the open kitchen. I could see them through the pinned-up paper orders, moving quickly and organized, talking over weekend breakfast rituals, delicately placing the dry slice of orange, the fruit cup with the awful cantaloupe. I was disrupted out of my trance.

"I am going to Florida."

"What?"

"Florida."

"What's in Florida?"

"There is a skateboarding tour and they need me to be the filmer. It's for two weeks. Paid gig. Will you wait for me?" he asked while taking a huge bite out of his everything bagel.

"Will you wait for *me*?" I said, looking over his haircut. I knew what happened on those tours.

"Bien sûr, toujours! I have something for you." He took out a Polaroid picture from his camera bag. It was a picture of Cedric in his Santa costume and me hugging him tightly, trying to adjust his hat while laughing. I didn't remember the photo being taken. It caught him perfectly: his thick-set body, his brindle colours and his slouchy jowls that formed that always-sad boxer expression.

"You look so happy in the photo."

"Yeah, but it was kind of a weird night."

"You're so sensitive."

"Okay," I said.

"I leave lundi prochain," he said. "Next Monday." Ignoring my attempt to talk about Clara. He didn't seem to want to remember.

"Let's have a big dinner before I go."

"Sure, I'd love to make everyone dinner." I crossed my arms and watched Max as we poked at our breakfasts not saying much. The bacon was really fatty and not at all as crispy as we usually got it. The server was busy but I wouldn't complain about something like that anyhow. Bacon always tastes good. I pulled my arms in from my hoodie sleeves and wondered how I would fare in the Quebec winter and stared out the window. I was relieved Max said he'd wait for me. It was a line in the sand. When we left it was bright and clear. A halo of colour refracted and circled under the sun like a rainbow smile.

By the time I got on the metro there was a blistering wind outside. I listened to Sonic Youth's "Teen Age Riot" on my Discman and observed how people lined up, waited, and went through the turnstile like cattle. Rushing and slowing. At the Mont-Royal stop, which was only a few blocks away, I had an urge to ditch work and stay on the train and ride it all the way to the end. The song started and ended in my ears and I leaned my head against the window, my reflection in the blackness reminding me of the bus ride I had taken to get here. I missed home for the first time, but I knew I didn't belong there. Not yet at least. The blue and white train submerged and surfaced, platform to tunnel, stop after stop. I passed Laurier, then Rosemont, then Beaubien, all the way to Henri-Bourassa. I got out, crossed over the brick walkway and went down the stairs to catch the train going the other direction, all the way back to Mont-Royal. When I finally got to the restaurant, Thierry was nowhere to be found. The manager was angry. I hurried as much as I could, trying to prepare the courses. We were doing escargots for an appetizer. I had to go into the basement and bring up the mise en place.

I was still making the list when Thierry came in looking like he hadn't slept in a hundred years. The veins below his eyes looked black and his dirty NASCAR hat that covered his greasy blond ponytail made me realize just how ugly he was when he was on a bender. When he opened his mouth to speak everything came out dry and broken like plaster; he mustered a cough that was barren and gurgled. I went to the cellar to bring up the rest of the items for service. It was a heavy load and two trips would have been easier, but

I didn't have the time to wait. I came barrelling into the kitchen as Thierry turned around holding a pot of melting butter that he was stirring with a spatula. We ran right into each other, sending vegetables and hot butter everywhere. He was already cursing and I was already apologetic. The hot grease ran down his apron and covered every item I had been carrying, turning the prep list into a translucent shard of scrap paper. Thierry's yelling was commonplace, but today I just couldn't stand the nasty creature he could sometimes be. He clearly had been up all night, and that wasn't my fault.

"Tabarnac, Ines. You have your head in the clouds, all de time. Câlisse."

"I know, désolée."

I got to work on cleaning up the slippery mess. Guillaume came to me and put his hand out to leverage me up from the floor. I took it.

"I'd like you to come into my office."

"Okay," I said as I wiped my hand on my apron. He gestured for me to sit down. There were papers and receipts everywhere. I sat down as I was told with my hands in my lap.

"Ines, you started so strong here. You cared a lot. This restaurant has a very good reputation. I have to let you go." I was red in the face and angry. I wanted to tell him all about Thierry doing coke, but I knew that was futile. He was a trained chef. I was a visitor.

"We've offered you a lot of chances. I am sorry."

I swallowed back a sob. "I need this job."

"We needed you too."

For Max's going away dinner I picked out seven pieces of bone-in veal for our osso buco from the butcher. It sounded harder to make than it was. I seared the meat in a pan, then dusted each piece lightly with flour and placed them all in the oven for the whole day with cubes of carrot, celery, onion and garlic all covered in tomato paste and herbs. While they simmered away, I made steamed asparagus and horseradish mashed potatoes as accompaniments. I bought a few cases of beer that Lainey helped me carry over from the dép. We put them in a cooler filled with ice and they stuck out all over the place, tantalizing and cold. We put the cooler on the coffee table and wrapped it up in a tablecloth. It was exciting to have a dinner party. We put an album by a French singer on the record player and it made a little crackling sound with each turn but her voice was beautiful anyway. I even bought a poinsettia at the Jean Coutu as a centrepiece. Lainey and I danced around the living room and cracked ourselves early beers as a reward for our preparations. It had been a busy day and so we sank into the couch and waited for our guests, clinking each other's bottles on a job well done.

"Have you noticed anything strange about Max lately?" I asked.

"Besides his haircut, or how in love he is with you?" Lainey shoved me.

"I'm serious."

"I am too, it'll grow back. He's just being goofy."

"He's been buying tons of shoes."

"Retail therapy, I guess."

"Do you think he'll cheat on me in Florida?"

"Do you think you can trust him?"

"I don't know," I said, turning to her in preparation for the difficult words to come. "Lainey, I didn't take tonight off work. I got fired. I've got a bit of money saved, so I should be fine for a bit. I just wanted you to know."

Lainey hugged me. "Don't stress, Ines. We'll figure it out. The studio would have you back anytime."

"I'll think about it," I said.

When everyone arrived, Cedric wandered clumsily around the house, taking all his toys out of the box to show us. We had to keep going around after him and putting them away so it stayed tidy. Max sat at the head of the table and I sat at the other. He beamed at me, looking proud. He tried to clean up his hair, but there were still long pieces behind his ears. Lainey and Seb had been spending a lot of time together lately, and it was sweet to see how he looked at her and then looked away. Marie brought a dessert born out of the Great Depression called pouding chômeur, which in English meant "poor man's pudding" or "unemployment pudding." We didn't feel like poor men. We ate the delicious meat and sucked the marrow from the bones and licked our fingers and at dessert we dug into the warm sweet maple sugary pudding and topped it with real vanilla ice cream. The sink was filled with roasting pans and spoons and bowls, but we just left it all and moved into the living room with our bellies full and we drank more beer and clattered around, laughing. We played Blades of Steel on Nintendo and always picked the Quebec Nordiques versus the Montreal Canadiens. You could make some of the players fight if you pushed a certain set of buttons. You had to hammer on the B button until your fingers were sore and one guy fell down and they announced the winner. It was always Claude Lemieux fighting and tossing out punches. I smiled at Max, thinking about the playful face wash.

We put on Duck Hunt and took turns shooting the clays and ducks that popped out of the grass. Max kept putting the gun to his head, pulling the trigger and laughing, but I didn't think it was funny. I asked him to stop. He pulled me aside into my bedroom by my elbow. "You're embarrassing me in front of my friends, Ines."

"They're my friends too. I just don't find it funny, Max, and neither does anyone else." I was fearful to stand up to him but I didn't want him to see me as weak.

"Should I put it to your head then?" he said, putting his finger to my temple.

"Seriously, Max, that's not funny." I pushed him away.

"You're so sensitive, Ines."

He let go of my arm and went back into the room, cracking a beer and lifting his hands towards the ceiling and pretending to dance like he was at a club. Marie and I went to the kitchen to do the washing up. We had to unload the entire sink and stack everything into greasy piles beside it. I leaned on the counter and lit a smoke while Marie started the tap and added the soap. We drank from our bottles of beer and talked in hushed voices about Max getting upset with me. Marie was concerned; she had seen the way he grabbed me. I flicked my ash into the sink and she gave me a look. I told her he was just annoyed that I'd put him on the spot. I put out the smoke and used the flipper to scrape off the roasting pan, but it needed soaking. I tried the same thing with the dessert dish, but that needed soaking as well. The burnt sugar had created black bubbles around the edges, so I burst them with a knife and they broke like glass.

After we finished wiping the counters, we joined everyone in the living room. There were only a few beers left, so Max took Cedric and went to get more. We gathered around the coffee table and played a few rounds of Crazy Eights. Max still hadn't come back an hour later.

"He's just taking a walk. Lainey and I will cut through the park on our way out and see if he's there."

"Do you think he's okay?"

"I'm sure he's fine."

This had to be the end for us now. Marie sat with me while Felix played more hockey. Her presence was calming. She had this grounded way about her. Her thick, black dreads wound past her shoulders in a heavy braid. I admired her outlook, the way she worked hard, how she kept house. She never complained. She was so natural and always seemed to know what to say. We eventually took to showing each other card tricks and when we ran out of those too, I showed her 52 Pick Up, which she didn't think was funny. It was the first time I'd done the stupid trick since Clara had died and I felt sick about it. I cleaned up the cards myself and wouldn't let Marie help me.

"Ines, are you okay?" she said.

I laughed half-heartedly. "I'm not sure," I said, "I think I'm just making things up in my head."

We lounged on the sofa and I breathed heavily and pushed back tears. I leaned against Marie's shoulder. I woke up on the couch with a kink in my neck and a blanket over me, my jeans all bunched up and my shirt sliding. A memory of my sister clung to me like the fabrics and in the same uncomfortable fashion I couldn't seem to straighten it out. The living room had been cleaned up and all the bottles had been sorted and put by the door. Where had I gone in my sleep? I remembered that Max didn't come back, but Cedric was on his mat. Was it Max who'd cleaned and covered me up? I was stuck with an image of Clara and me playing together in the empty field next door to the cabin in the summer months off school. We would pick dandelions and break into song: "Mama had a baby and its head popped off!" We would flick the merry yellow weed head off into the air and rise spritely off the ground and giggle. In the fall, when they were all dried out, I would think of her too. How the weightless plumes were carried into the clouds, floating away like extinguished stars, filling the air and falling weightless like the ash from that one summer when the forest fires were bad.

The early morning's blue disguise lifted to white daylight. I made a pot of tea and ran myself a bath, hugging my knees lovingly, the water so hot that my shins stung like an eraser had been rubbed up and down them. They were the colour of ham. I put my whole face under the water and held my breath, imagining what it would be like to drown until I scared myself and could no longer resist screaming with rage. A blood vessel burst in my eye. I was confused. Max had come back to the apartment, dropped off Cedric and then left again. This must be the end. I listened to the Cranberries' album *No Need to Argue* all the way through before I got out of the tub, when the silence was all that was left. There was a song about daffodils that always reminded me of Clara. My heartbeat was echoing in my chest, hurried and heavier from the heat. I rose from the bathtub like it had been a baptism.

✤ ✤ ✤

For a Sunday it was missing that usual feeling of stillness and peace. Oversized Christmas decorations were being hung with garlands, hoisted over the traffic. On our way to Cinema du Parc, Max and I went to the art store DeSerres. Max held my hand but was quiet, with no explanation for his dinner party exit the night before.

"I didn't want to wake you," he said, avoiding the first departure all together. "You looked so peaceful." I picked out a new black Moleskine journal. Hemingway wrote in Moleskine journals and he was a stoic writer who was truthful without using too many words. It was how I found Max's movies and photos to be: he was concise, but eloquent. It looked you in the face. I had seen photos of Hemingway in his youth and thought he was handsome, but he, his father, his sister and his brother all committed suicide. I bought a black roller pen that glided across the paper without needing to be lifted. It was my favourite when I could do that and see what words took shape. I wrote on the fresh cover, in honour of Hemingway: *All my life I've looked at words as though I were seeing them for the first time.* My journals were a living progress report. I wanted more firsts and less repeats. I started writing them after Clara died. They were relics from my old life. The phone numbers now started with 514. Those journals were birthed from therapy sessions, and their spines became my bones.

Once we were in the theatre, Max took my hand and put it on his crotch. With his hand over mine, he began to knead my palm against his penis until it was hard. I tried to pull away, but he brought my hand back and kept his firmly over mine. All the shadowed faces were looking toward the screen, so I slipped my hand under the waistband of his sweatpants and gave him a matinee hand-job. I could smell the musk coming off us and wondered if anyone else could too. I was relieved he still wanted me, but then Max took my hand out and passed it back to me. He held his head and folded in a regretful bow.

"What's wrong?" I asked.

"Ines, I have to get home now."

"What? Why? The previews just ended."

"It's too noisy. I feel sick."

"What's going on?"

"I need to get out of here. Are you coming or what?" Max stood, grabbing me and pulling me up as though I didn't have a choice. I followed him outside, leaving my popcorn. Even in the cold, people huddled in the streets, all dark puffs of fur and thick breath and cigarette smoke. We hurriedly walked a few blocks but I couldn't keep up with Max. He forced his bent head towards the wind and kept charging forward. I could barely see the tower of the Big O through the thick cloud. In the summer I bought a postcard of the same view, only blue encompassed everything and gigantic flower baskets dangled from every lamppost. Back then I could never imagine the city looking sickly swollen, a patina finish that hurled wind in aggressive twists. Church bells rang, but they were muted by the wet air. Just as a ray of light was extending to warm the ground, Max and I retreated down the escalator into the darkness of the dusty metro station. We stood in the crammed train reaching for something to support us and leaning against strangers for balance. I could smell last night's liquor on our breath. I ran my tongue across my cheeks. I thought about my own drinking and the flinching of my hands after a bender, but nothing really mattered. It was only here and now. When the present got harder to live in, drinking was the gearshift out of hell.

We walked quietly to Max's and his apartment was colder inside than outside. An uncertainty bobbed in my stomach while I took in the scene of photos littering the floor and the computer screen fizzling with a black and white snowstorm. The stack of Nike shoeboxes had once been tidy, but was now overflowing with crepe paper, laces and fancy sneakers. I saw a photo on the floor of Max as a giddy child at Christmastime, playing with a train set that went all the way around the tree. His dad was helping him captain the train and his two-piece pyjamas were tight on his skinny legs. His bowl cut was precise. Even without colour in the photo you could sense the redness of it. I'd never met anyone with hair a shade of red so deep. I tried to reach for his hair, to take him into me, but he kept his back turned and stayed silent. The reach was gentle and fake, like I was a pantomime, like I didn't want him to know I was reaching. I dropped my arms to my sides.

"Are you okay, Max? What's wrong?" His eyes were vacant and perplexed, but I couldn't get behind them to why. I knew Max didn't see the world the same way as others and it exhausted him to keep stride. His creative visions were on another level. He found the ugly of the everyday grind and then he remoulded it. To me his films and photos captured the essence of life's capability, but his easygoing swagger was also apathetic. He wanted to live beyond confines, but young adulthood was pushing down on us, questioning if it could be done, if one could make a career out of art or skateboarding. If not doing either when your heart called to it meant that you'd sell out to cubicle and work for the man.

I began to strip naked and got into his bed with my journal. I traced my hand onto a fresh page and then studied the lines and pathways. I cracked a beer and took a drink and the condensation dripped onto the pages and left light splotches and made the black ink blur and run. I liked the way it looked. I coloured in my sister's ring. I worried what he thought about Clara. If he, too, blamed me for her death. He wasn't interested in knowing more about how

Clara died and that polarity to his usual caring disposition felt like a betrayal. I was ready to talk, but he was not present. Max stayed in his clothes and came and lay next to me under the covers. I took his hand and started tracing it on top of my own outline and was completely focused on my drawing until I looked and noticed his agitation. He pulled his hand away when he saw what I saw. I put the book down and he gripped me to say what words couldn't.

"They are just so different now."

"What is?" I asked him.

"My hands."

"Different than when?"

I desired to fit right beside him, to meld into the pebble bones of his spine, but through all the work it took to try and fall asleep next him in that turbulent embrace, that night I could feel him alert and restless. He turned away and got out of bed and started emptying the ashtray, a sign he would be refilling it before the night was through. I watched through half-closed eyes as he worked on videos and put photographs back into his book. I watched the shadow shapes jump around the walls and drift, a small flame of a match flare in the darkness and then an orange glow as he sucked on a joint. I questioned whether this was really love at all, or just another ill-fated experience to become jaded by. I wondered what it meant where the lines crossed in an X on my right palm, if it meant anything at all. If the lines were changing, too, like the man in the park told me. I wanted signs and symbols to tell me how to live and feel.

In the morning I followed Max down to the doorway, standing aloof on the front steps with his camera bag on one shoulder. I knew he hadn't slept at all. I was wearing one of his T-shirts and no underwear. I danced on my tippy toes from the cold cement stairs. The sidewalk had been heavily salted. He gave me his key to look after Pantouf and I held it firm under my knuckles.

"Are you sure you're okay to go on this trip?"

"Never been readier."

"Call me," I said. *Please.*

"Of course I will."

He reached his arms out and took my waist, pulling me into him and filling my body with joy. To me, a man's hands around my waist felt like the most intimate touch possible. In all my previous sexual experiences it was an area that men skipped right over. If he was touching me like this maybe everything was going to be okay. Max rested his chin on the top of my head. I breathed in his smell and exhaled my chilly breath as he held me tighter.

"Ines," he said and pulled back to look at my face. "You are everything to me."

"I love you." It was the first time I said it, the real phrase, to anyone other than my parents as a kid. By the time I left, none of us said it. If I said it now, maybe it would last.

"I love you too," he said. "I have to go, the van is waiting."

We kissed peacefully until, very slowly, he removed his lips from mine. I pulled on the hem of the T-shirt and stuck my hands in my armpits. We kissed one more time and he left, my last view his backpack and the pompom on his toque. I went back upstairs and threw on a pair of his wool socks, but still no pants. I got stoned, swept the house, did his dishes and listened to Led Zeppelin while the winds of winter whistled violently. I got to my knees and began to reorganize the shoeboxes into tidy piles for him and picked up the rest of the strewn photos and carefully placed them back in his album. If it was put together maybe we could feel that way too, but I knew in the pit of my stomach that stuffing memories into books didn't make them go away any more than locking a diary protected secrets from being released.

# Hiver

Creativity is the only thing that truly sets us apart.
It is rooted so deep and thick in us that it must burst free.
From mouth, from hand, from muse, it must show itself.
And within that,
individually,
there is darkness and there also is light.
What we choose to pursue from each is not always our choice.

❧ ❧ ❧

Without the restaurant to keep me busy I was left to my own devices and poor coping strategies. I drank every day. I checked my email constantly and hesitated to leave the house in case Max called. I knew playing it cool was the way to keep him, but I obsessed over the empty space and grew agitated at my own stupidity in believing he would wait for me. I'd log on to April's chat room on Lainey's computer when she was at school. Quickly fumbling around her Emily the Strange notebooks and pens. "Hear anything yet?" she'd say and I would type back... *Nothing. Nothing at all.* I called Marie to see if she wanted to go cruise through the underground city, but she said it was too wet and salty right now.

"Has Felix heard from the guys at all?"

"No, sorry," she said. It felt like an excuse. There was a hesitation in her voice. Something about Max and me being together bothered them, I could feel it.

After a few days I still hadn't heard from Max and it felt like a cold slap to the face. I figured he'd gotten all that he wanted from me and it was time to fold, but my stupid heart couldn't resist the idea that it had meant something. He had sent me roses, after all. I pulled the perfect thoughts of us around behind me like a pacifying baby blanket, the corners wet from sucking on the worn threads to help me sleep. I was making up all kinds of reasons in my head as to why the phone never rang or an email never appeared. In lieu of his partnership I drank more and turned the music up louder, aggressively prancing around the house like I was preparing to fight his shadow. Then, Seb called and told me he heard a rumour that

Max got fired less than halfway through the tour. I guess he had been acting strange, changed the way he talked and dressed, took all his belongings and left his camera and left the group. The skaters were worried about him, no one knew how to handle it. He just disappeared. No one knew where he went, or where he was staying. The tour forced to carry on without him.

I slept poorly, worried that it meant everything was over, that somehow I was responsible for driving him away. All the people I loved ended up gone.

The second week felt even slower. I went to the studio with April a few nights and helped with the cleaning. I'd bring beer and sweep the floor and dust and then download skate videos like Birdhouse's *The End* and éS's *Menikmati* from Kazaa, and I would eat chips and lounge in a free bedroom, all while listening to people fake masturbate while fingernails clacked away the keyboards and I'd slug back bottles of Boréale. In my boredom I thought about logging on, but the silence from Max made me feel insignificant.

The skate trip came to an end and the boys started returning to Montreal. Max didn't come home with the group and still no one heard from him. I went to Fouf's for the Wednesday night skate and the place was packed full of skateboarders and vagrants. I wasn't feeling the session on the ramp, it was too cramped to stand on the ledge and there was no time to warm up without pressure because it was too heated and loud and the skaters all dropped in one after another. It normally fed me to be wrapped up in the hurried motion of it, even if I got taken out, but I sat stationary at the bar and smoked and drank. Seb came to me in a panic.

"Max is back, Ines. He is outside."

"What the fuck? Really?"

"I don't know, Ines, he just isn't the same right now. Felix said that he was upset, or maybe he is angry. Just be careful okay? Nobody knows what to say to him."

I got up quickly from the bar stool and it rattled back and forth but caught and slowed like a metronome. I couldn't hide in the corner knowing he was outside, but I was shocked, with no plan of what to do or say. I put my skateboard behind the DJ booth and breathed hard at the bizarre moment. Black Sabbath's "Paranoid" played from the speakers and the irony slowed down the air. I walked through it and took a deep breath.

"Ines, I also have to tell you something more. There were other girls on tour, okay. C'est sûr. Felix told me. Max doesn't want you to know. Some of the guys are saying the parties just got out of hand, it's just what happens."

*Just what happens.* My heart flooded with pain at the news. We agreed to be exclusive and Max did it anyway. I swallowed it down. "Thanks, Seb, I figured as much." And I really did; this was how it always went. Boys get what they want and then they don't want it anymore. We all crave excitement, allure, new cities that make pleasure shine. To feel excited by another person. I shrugged as if to cast off the hurt and look strong, but Seb held onto my arm to tell me more.

"I'm also worried for him because he tells me things about my mother. Bad things, Ines." He looked distraught.

Now I was confused. "What do you mean?"

"He says my mother deserve to die because she was a bad person."

"Oh my god, Seb, I'm sorry."

"She had cancer, she died last year. He said she deserve to die because she cheated on my dad with her boss."

"But that doesn't make sense, he just cheated on me."

I remembered Max's comments on Halloween about my sister. I closed my eyes and listened to the chaos in the bar. Everything was about to fall apart. I went outside: the same spot where we first met and kissed amidst the drunken summer thrill-seekers. A group of skateboarders gathered around; some I recognized and others were visiting from the last leg of the tour. People dropped their cigarettes and stubbed them out on the sidewalk. Nobody was able to make eye contact with Max. I got it when I heard him talking. He was gesturing wildly and demanding everyone's attention whether they wanted it or not. His eyes were wide and black, incessant. His clothing was flashier and the red on his cap, shirt and shoes all matched. His voice carried as though he were preaching. He wore a thick gold chain. He flailed his arms with every sentence. When he saw me, he stopped and tried to contain himself. He hugged me hard and swayed me back and forth in his embrace, though his body was shaking with nervous energy. I wanted to stay nestled in that collarbone, if only to never look up and see the way his face looked. He smelled like home to me now, even felt like home to me, but to look in those eyes, it wasn't him.

Without meeting his gaze, I said into his neck, "Max, what is going on? Why didn't you tell anyone where you were? We were worried."

"Don't worry about me!" he yelled and people took notice of him again. "It's them that have to worry. They fired me."

"Seb said you left."

"Seb is a liar."

"He's your best friend—"

He cut me off. "You don't know what happened there, Ines."

"How did you get home?"

Max wasn't interested in question and answer. "Let's get out of here."

"I have to get my skateboard—"

"We get it later."

He hooked my arm through his and turned in a quick motion, forcing me to follow. We started walking up the hill towards the Plateau, past all the colourful graffiti that decorated the alley. I lit a cigarette and watched the ground, muttering under my breath, "Why didn't you call?" He talked constantly in both English and

French. It made understanding him impossible. I was nervous and sucked the smoke in through my teeth and tried to listen to see if there were any clues to what had overtaken him, but there was no discernible train of thought. He was at once elated and illogical. I started to cry and when he noticed, he got upset.

"Why are you crying, Ines? What is everyone's problem? Nothing is going on. I'm really feeling fucking amazing."

I couldn't respond. I imagined him kissing the other girls and opening their legs, wandering the streets of Miami, broadened with this new-found arrogance. Gone was the tenderness he first displayed, the way he held my bruised face in his hands and caressed my hair. I flicked my smoke butt and grabbed his hand and kept walking, trying to keep pace. I kept my head down until we got to my front door. I could tell it was hard for him not to talk rapidly. Words were welling up inside his throat and it all came out uncontrollable like vomit.

"Ines, I'm going to open a skateboard shop of my own, forget the other ones. It's going to be the best. I'm getting a new car and a new place. I'm gonna sell Nikes on eBay for triple the price. I'll be rich this way. They can't stop me. I want you to come live with me." He never cared about money before and it startled me to hear it. He paused for a second for air and then started again on the same rant. He looked skinnier and the sports jersey he wore hung off him. Over and over he told me all of these plans, at the same time bubbling over with emotion. He was fragments and mixed pieces. Max was on the verge of a dark place, and it felt like any second he could topple and be lost. I was practically holding up his physical body, like it was too exhausting for him to keep pace with himself. I was scared, already anticipating the time when I couldn't any longer and we would have to try to put the pieces back together.

I opened the door to the apartment and we packed ourselves into the foyer. We took off our shoes and I led him up the stairs and into my room. I went into the bathroom right away and watched my face for a minute in the mirror. I splashed some hot water onto it and stared again at the perplexed reflection. When I returned to him he was smoking a halfie on the balcony, stretched over the railing and looking down onto the sidewalk. He spit and raised himself up as I came outside.

"You are so beautiful, Ines, why can't you see that?" He lumbered towards me, his limbs extending like a wild cat, a larger person than he was when he left.

I swallowed hard as he pulled me into him.

"Something bad is going to happen, you know? They can't stand to see me like this."

We rocked and kissed but it was harsh. I knew I shouldn't sleep with him, I couldn't help myself. I knew he had been with other girls on tour, but at that moment I didn't care. I wasn't enough to be his only, but his hands and his fervent kisses were already covering my body, convincing me it was right. It was the only way to contain him. We stayed outside kissing until we were shaking from the cold. We made it to the futon and although I had hoped he would pay attention to my own needs before his, he was in a mood to finish only for himself. He rolled off me immediately after and went back outside and smoked again. I went under the blankets and held myself together.

"You going to sleep?" Max called from the balcony.

"Yeah, I think I will."

"Not me. Call you tomorrow." Max came in and shrugged his way back into his baggy clothes and left, no amount of dopamine allowing him to settle. I figured he would be out walking the streets, talking to strangers while smoking joints or drinking beers, unable to stop himself from frantic speech. The thought of it frightened me. I lay sleepless for hours, and in my own racing mind I felt only a slip away from the devil inside him. The darkest part of ourselves. With the dawn I fell asleep, nearly paralyzed by the mental exhaustion and confusion of what was going on in his head and how I was supposed to react.

I got up to pee and then moped back to bed. A sideways ice rain fell outside. The new kitchen window was already caked with a dirty brown spray, as if a plough had driven by and barfed up the side of our building. I wanted to be snowed in. I missed the snow back home that always seemed to stay white and held light in every flake. Sometimes what you miss is not the truth. Snow is only white while it's falling. I crawled under the covers again and I heard the phone ring and then Lainey knocked on the door.

"It's Seb. Ines, he says it's important." I got up and walked to the phone, holding its handle to my chest for a few seconds before lifting it to my ear. I put it back on the receiver with a click. Lainey poured two coffees and brought them over to the table with some cream and sugar, and in the quiet of the inside, while the angry rain pelted like a drum outside, we sat together. She didn't probe me. I stirred the beverage. Finally, I spoke.

"Max is in the hospital."

"What happened?"

"Seb called the police on him. He said they were at his apartment together after the bar last night and he got scared about the way Max was acting, says he was messed up. The cops came to the apartment and Seb let them in. Max got paranoid and mad at everyone and they ended up having to detain him and drag him out into a squad car. He's in Hôpital Saint-Luc."

"In the psych ward?"

"I don't know."

"What do we do?"

"He wants to see me."

"When can you go?"

"Tomorrow."

❦ ❦ ❦

*Love and grief must be the same. Lasting, lyrical, disappointing and distracting. They hurt in the same places, leaving holes that can't be filled. Can a person be raw and hollow forever? Only rough edges, the seasons of loss repeating themselves. I skip like a record, stuck on the bend.*

Frozen rain came down all night and showed no signs of stopping. Cedric slept with me and I took comfort in spooning his furry back and rubbing his warm tummy. He snored like a chainsaw that night and dreamt he was on the run or hunting a squirrel. When he jolted awake, I jolted awake. I listened to the stabbing rain, my mind alert. Cedric grunted and shifted and I lay still, trying to let go in my mind enough to sleep. I couldn't, so I stared at the creamy shadows on the wall and wondered if I was feeling another presence with me, or just imagining it. Sometimes Cedric would stare too, and I thought with his extrasensory abilities that he was feeling it as well, that the curtains looked amiss, but he slept again while I lay there awake, wondering about delusions and feeling at times like Clara was with me.

I thought the moon was shining into my bedroom but it was just a porch light from an adjacent apartment. It throbbed in through the glass like a halo. Icy tree branches tickled the window and occasionally spooked me, as if someone were rapping on it for me to let them in. There was no one coming for me though. Max was in there, and I was in here. That was all I knew. I wrote in my journal, I had a bath, already knowing anything I did in that moment would add to my suffering the next day. I rolled from one side of the bed to the other, trying not to think about Max in the hospital. Trying not to think about Clara's tiny body in a morgue. I pretended I was at a sleep clinic where it was so quiet you could listen to the apnea dreams of others and I waited, listening to the rain, pretending the test subjects had stopped breathing. Sometimes wishing I would stop breathing. I broke apart sticky buds and mixed them with the tip of a broken cigarette, carefully crafted a filter out of the cardboard from the rolling papers and inhaled intensely as I lit the joint with a match. My lungs filled and resisted. I breathed it all out in one giant hoot. My goal had been sleep, but my whole body buzzed. I tried to smile and think of how good it felt as blue smoke danced around my head, calming me eventually to a state of rest. It didn't feel good though, nothing could coerce me. I was kidding myself that weed would help.

I fought with vague enemies in my dreams and tossed and turned until I dreamt I was being buried standing up. My parents were shovelling dirt onto my head and Clara sat cross-legged next to the hole. Her ribbon pigtails were perfectly curled. I twitched hard like I'd fallen, shaking the cold ground from me, some landed in her lap, staining her dress and she brushed it off. In the dream I felt thankful that I was the one who had died. I couldn't tell her. I tried to say it. I tried to say I was sorry, but there was dirt in my mouth and my parents kept shovelling more on top of me. I couldn't tell her. Clara patted my head right before it was covered and said, "It's okay, let me go." And then I saw the sunflowers reaching for me and I was running to the sand.

I woke up sweaty, a terrible hurt stabbing at the back of my ears, dehydration creasing my lips closed. I craved the peace of being the first one awake again. I wanted to sip hot coffee while the pink summer mornings were born. I wanted to trace the map of Max's hip bones, to see the possibility of first light, to give it a name, but I spent so much time at night in my own head that by the morning I was exhausted and trite. The ghosts who kept me up had long since fled. My batteries remained uncharged. The day held nothing for me, though the storm had cleared and naked trees danced against the sunlight. I refrained from looking at them because it stung my tired eyes.

I thought that when I fell in love for the first time the pain would go away. I was stuck in some skewed belief that I would be saved the moment someone told me they chose me. If I was beautiful nothing would hurt; if I was chosen, my mistakes wouldn't own me. Instead, grime had only grown and nestled into my bigger, blacker pores. Water poured over me in the bath, but I never felt clean. I tasted it in my dental floss; life was shit. I stared off the balcony and smoked; there was nothing else, it had all been taken away. I watched everything like I was behind the lens of Max's camera. I saw bundled up kids on the swings in the park, urging their father to push them higher. He would push them to the moon if he could. I thought all day about what would come next. Would he be drooling out of the corners of his mouth, sedated and sick? I didn't know anything about mental illness. I loved Max, but he felt gone from me. Or did I love him just because he let me? I wanted to help him through this minefield, but I didn't know what to do and his behaviour told me he didn't want a caretaker.

I imagined him in a stuffy office lying on a chaise lounge looking up at cheap chipboard, retelling the story of how he wasn't depressed but rather amazing. I pictured doctors in white coats, their voices echoing over the buzz of the sterile room, looking at Rorschach tests, discussing algorithms, saying to each other, *He thinks this black moth is an angel, he's not of the population norm, this motherfucker is batshit crazy.* His ideas were, albeit unorganized, not entirely impossible; they seemed like attainable life goals. They were just coming out erratic. Magnified anxiety. I couldn't forget that I was a part of those plans. I wanted those things to happen to us too. I wanted to be right there with him. I jolted up and quickly got to work on caffeinating before I slept all morning and missed visiting Max. If I rushed like he had, I could accomplish anything. The phone rang and I ran to get it in time.

"Hello," I said into the void.

"Ines, it is Pierre. How are you?"

"Uh, I'm fine, why are you calling me?"

"I have a huge show booked in the new year and the girls I had lined up backed out. I am in a pinch. It pays well. April is already on board. She recommended I try you."

"At the cam studio?"

"No, it's at a swingers' club. Talk to April, she'll fill you in." He hung up.

I put the phone down and then picked it back up and called April.

"Pierre just called."

"It's a thousand bucks each for like a twenty-minute gig."

"What kind of show?"

"Basically, we open the party with a bit of a dance and then we leave with cash."

"April, I can't dance. What *kind* of show?"

"Well, that's on us, but the idea is that I fuck you with a strap-on, but with a condom on to promote safe sex, and we dance around a little and get the crowd all horny and then we leave. I know you need the money right now."

"Let me think about it. There is a lot going on right now."

"You want to talk?"

"No. I can't. I have to go. Max is in the hospital."

"Ines."

"I'm sorry. I'll explain later." I hung up.

The light in the room changed drastically from morning gold to a dark, muted grey. What did I really have to lose? There would be no one there I knew, or would ever see again.

The ice outside was treacherous, making every inch of the old sidewalk so slick it created a reflection just so you could watch yourself fall down. Carefully, I curtailed the salted cement to the front entrance of Hôpital Saint-Luc. Huge columns of steam belched their way out of the tops of the building from giant metal tubes. It looked like a power plant, all grey in the drab weather amongst the drab traffic and cold cement. I watched it for a while, attempting to comprehend the mechanics of a building huffing and puffing as hundreds of loads of laundry were done in the basement to clean bedsheets that people died on and heaters pumping through every floor to keep cold skin warm and water hot and to clean the sick from people. Tasteless meals of broth and orange Jell-O delivered on plastic trays to every floor. When I went inside Christmas trees twinkled in the switchboard room, skirted by pretend presents labelled *Patrick* and *Charles* and *Genevieve*. The Post-it-Note-yellow floor was slick with slush. The waiting room was filled with people in salt-stained boots and long puffy coats that looked like sleeping bags. I approached the counter and asked if I could see patient Maxim Labelle. The secretary had thin lips that barely parted and only moved slightly sideways. She nodded at me and pointed left to the hall.

I followed the corridor with bright and sterile lights passing overhead. I felt like I was diminishing. The end of the hall had a door heavier than a house. Its handle needed to be wound like a boat helm to be opened, and the menacing weight of it, heavy and cold, made it feel like a walk-in cooler. There was a guard and his hands were calloused. The round grey steel turned under his big fingers. There were pearls of dewy sweat on his forehead and he looked tired, like he'd been busy all night containing erratic thoughts. An orderly, witness to the fright in the eyes of the patients, watched me as he opened the door, and I reluctantly went through. The door closed with a heavy groan and then I saw him in there. His back was to me. He was in a hospital gown, the strings tied loosely in the back so that his underwear was showing. I wanted to laugh at the sight, but my throat was tight with confusion. He was yelling something to a woman behind a counter and hitting the secure plastic wall that separated them with only a circle cut out in the middle. He had a piece of chalk in his raised hand.

"Max, vous avez une visiteuse," the lady said calmly into a microphone. Another door closed behind me. He lowered his arms and when he turned to face me I was still looking around at where I was. The room had bench seats along the walls with padded plastic cushions, and in the middle, plastic chairs were pulled out from cheap wooden tables. A movable chalkboard on casters was parked in the centre of the room and adjacent to the counter were two other rooms with large, low Plexiglas windows. The walls inside were white and there were hospital beds with straps like seatbelts and overhead fluorescent lights that were wrapped in metal cages. There was no privacy. The whole place felt designed for observation. Medical personnel watched from behind the glass and I even began to feel paranoid. A young man launched himself in front of me holding an open book. He had a page marked and he was trying to show it to me, rapidly repeating himself in French and showing me the pages as he scoured over them, flipping back and forth. Stepping backwards I stumbled and slid into one of the padded seats, and he sat beside me quickly.

He pointed into my face with a look of frustration. "I have been here before, you know? Look at this!" He laughed intensely. He showed me the book. It was a French dictionary. Pointing to the words, he spoke with a heavy Quebecois accent. I could not make out what he was saying. He watched me with curiosity, his eyes fixed but stuttering. As he closed the book Max joined us on the other available seat, putting me in the middle of the two men, who suddenly looked like boys, with eyes so full of naivety I felt afraid.

"Ines, you came," Max said gently in the voice I so dearly loved. "We are both Labelles. We are brothers and we were supposed to meet now."

I exhaled and tried to get to my feet but Max took my hands in his. I grabbed his back, and they were clammy and supple. He laced his fingers through mine the same way he always did. Standing up, he pulled me with him.

"Come and see where they made me sleep."

He led me through the tables and chairs, and the young man with the dictionary followed close behind. Some eyes looked up to watch us move across the room, some made sure not to look at all. We stood outside of one of the walls with the hard plastic windows, and Max became troubled by what was inside. His movements were so restless and erratic that I flinched.

"They tied me to that bed! I couldn't even go to the bathroom. I pissed myself." He started sobbing though he looked at me sternly. There was so much fear in his red, crying eyes. He grabbed me by the shoulders, and all his weight fell onto me. "I had to sleep strapped to that bed. In my own piss."

I staggered to keep us both standing. I didn't know what to believe. Could a hospital really do that to a person?

"There is nothing wrong with me, you know that right?" Max asked me as he pulled away, suddenly sounding calm and rational. "I am not depressed, I feel great." But he looked petrified and clenched his jaw and had to concentrate to stay still. It couldn't hold, and he spun into another rapid exchange of words in French, impossible to understand they were so fast.

"Can you slow down, Max? I can't understand when you speak so quickly."

Weeping, he told me of the time he went with his mother to a Bob Dylan concert. He told me that he wanted me to go get him a newspaper so he could find a new apartment and a new car and a place to rent to start his skateboard shop.

"We can buy a Subaru Outback," he said with urgency. "I saw one for sale on a flyer on Tuesday. We can go live on the Îles-de-la-Madeleine and bring Cedric with us so he can be in the country. I can rent a space above the tattoo parlour on Saint-Dominique to make a skate shop, that space is perfect, it has big windows and ..."

And on it went, until he had tired himself and had to go drink water to keep from speaking. He seemed to be aware that he wasn't making sense but couldn't control it. I didn't even want to ask how we would live in the country and own a skate shop in the city, or take Lainey's dog, but I felt special that I was included in all these future plans. I couldn't help imagining driving in the Subaru with the dog in the back and the windows down, stopping for a dip in Lac Saint-Jean on our road trip, the sun beating down on us.

Max grabbed me by the hand and pulled me to the large chalkboard; the other Labelle followed spritely behind us with the dictionary above his head, muttering about their newfound kinship. His mania snapped me out of the vision.

"I want to show you something special," Max said, erasing the chalkboard. Coloured dust splattered the air but completely unfazed, he turned through the cloud and wrote:

*Je suis*

"I am," he said. Then he erased the letter I and moved it to its own line, which left:

*Je su s*

He looked at me with a deep look of satisfaction on his face, then turned and wrote underneath:

*I = Intelligence*

"I am Jesus," he said plainly. "And you are my queen. These people in here, they think I am depressed, but I am not. I am great like a god, like Yashua. Did you know the letter J never existed in the alphabet one hundred years ago? It is because Jesus is not a Hebrew name, it was Yashua. Yashua was Jesus."

His posturing was so magnified it pulled the room into him and took me with it. My hands shook right along with his, but out of fear rather than bravado.

"Is there someone here who I can talk to, Max?"

"You don't believe me." He said it coldly, resolutely, shrugging. "No one does."

"No, that's not it, I just don't know what to think right now. This is all really overwhelming."

Tears were welling up in his eyes again. He looked wounded, like he was a small child and I had just struck him for spilling milk.

"Can you call me from here?" I felt silly asking. He was, after all, in a psychiatric hospital, under surveillance; they probably had his shoelaces labelled and kept under lock and key. I just didn't know what else to say. I had to create a diversion, so he didn't see my own tears that threatened to fall any second. He grabbed at my cheeks and the tears started. He caught them with his thumbs. Max kissed me hard. "I love you, Ines. I am not depressed. Get me out of this place." His fingers smelled like chalk, his thumbs were calloused from carrying a skateboard. His fingernails were jagged and dirty. He smelled sour and needed a shower. He kissed me again in a series of small pecks, wiping and kissing away my tears.

"I'll come see you again when I can, okay?" I disengaged from him and stepped back. The whitewashed walls and tiny windows felt isolating. I gestured at the nurse behind the counter to open the door for me. The brightness of the room suddenly bothered my eyes. She pushed a button behind the counter and the door began to open. A red light blinked above the doorframe. Even that was kept behind bars.

The next morning I rode the metro to Place des Arts. I got a tea and let it warm my hands while I walked the streets. It was warmer out. The ice rain had ceased and thick clouds that were swollen boxed everything in, shrinking the city to a manageable size. I used to love walking around the city aimlessly. It had so much vibrancy and culture and the allure of cosmopolitan fun that sometimes soothed me but also made me feel lonely. I headed to the Old Port. I felt like I was in Europe there and despite the secret of the cam studio, the area brought a familiar comfort. A pair of Clydesdale horses pulled a carriage down a cobblestone street. Inside, a man and a woman held onto each other, draped in warm blankets. Fake flowers and garlands hung around its doors. The horses stopped and one of them took a steaming shit.

I stopped at the grocery store to get a paper for Max, but the lines were long. The woman in front of me had a twenty-two-pound turkey and three 100-dollar bills in her hand and the guy behind me was holding a microwave lasagna and a bottle of no-name cola. Would I be in the express lane my whole life? Leftover bits of mascara fell from my tired eyelashes when I wiped my hands over my face giving a whole new meaning to the term raccoon eyes. They were zombie raccoon eyes. The half-moon circles pulled everything downwards. They looked like remnants at the bottom of a coffee cup.

I headed to Saint-Luc. It was a building like any other: rectangular windows filled the front. Some lights were on, and in others the shades were drawn. I wondered where Max was. What he was doing. I wanted to sneak in and rescue him—turn this whole situation into some adventurous lark where I would run at top speed through the hallways, me pushing him in a wheelchair to freedom, the belt from his housecoat flying as we burst out the front doors, charts and gowns whipping behind us as we smiled big teeth-bearing grins of freedom. Or we'd make an escape mission down the laundry chute after a near brush with a guard whose trolley I'd push in his way. We'd land in the outside bin and a loading truck would conveniently be picking it up at the exact same time. We would take beers to a beach, feel the sun on our faces and laugh about the whole situation. I shook my head; I was delusional myself. I relied on imaginary scenes. I didn't know what was real anymore.

The streets were so empty and silent. Everything was red and green with holiday décor, and out front of Saint-Luc cops and ambulance attendants milled about. I wondered if any of the officers had escorted Max out of Seb's apartment. I felt like they were staring at me, but I was staring at them, at their badges, at their sticks and gun holsters. We put a lot of trust in people who carry guns for a living. I felt like a criminal myself and without anything left in the day to throw myself at, I just went along with visiting him in hopes that we were both going to be okay.

I went inside. I had no idea what the protocol was, what would happen in there, if anyone would notice me. I crept in, the paper tucked under my armpit, and my other hand, in my jacket pocket, fiddled with my keys. The lady behind the counter was older than the last. Her hair was piled high into a bun. It looked as though it had been styled that way for decades. A few stray hairs had made their way out and I felt certain that if she saw them that way she would tuck them right back in. She must have been on night shift. As I approached she took her glasses from a strap around her neck and placed them lightly on the tip of her nose.

I whispered to her, feeling very shy about my French.

"*Pardon?*"

"Umm, Maxim Labelle, s'il-vous-plaît. I would like to see him."

She pushed a button on the switchboard that turned red and then began blinking. The phone rang and, not breaking her concentration, she pointed to a door. She looked me up and down and I was suddenly aware of my second-hand winter garb: the too-big jacket and the SORELs with ripped laces and the tongues pulled forward.

"Third floor, down the hall." She didn't even try to speak French back to me. I slid my mitted hand up the railing. Ice fell off my boots, tracking my footprints up and up until I paused at the third floor and looked in through the window. I pulled open the heavy door and saw a small room lined with chairs. All the doors were closed except one that went to a bigger room with a lot of windows looking out onto the downtown core. A circle of chairs was placed in the centre around a folding table.

The heat was too high and sweat dripped off Max's brow, probably from the meds as well as the stagnant warmth. Icicle lights stained with yellow hung from the window. A patient got up and went to the radio, an old one, with big silver dials and brown lattice speakers. He argued with a nurse about what to listen to, and from the nurse's tone I understood that having music on was a privilege. It was his turn to pick; perhaps a reward for good behaviour. He turned the dial back and forth and everyone grunted when he stopped on a Celine Dion song. Chatter rose and he turned the volume up, laughing and singing along.

"Arrête!" Max said. "S'il-vous-plaît, mes oreilles!" It was a humorous moment, and the temporary joy felt so strange amongst the white gowns and slippers and pale faces, like someone in a concentration camp told a joke. Then the acoustics changed and the joyfulness changed too. A banjo, then Neil Young's voice rang out across the floor of the ward. "Old Man" played through fuzzy speakers and I listened to the words and revered the influence of fathers on our shaping. I didn't want to be like my old man at all.

Max's head drooped. No one spoke. I handed him the paper and he hugged me. The nurse came in and announced that it was time for breakfast, breaking up the quiet meditation the song inspired. The energy changed. Feeding time also meant pill time, which made half of the faces look pained and the other half excited. The concoction they had Max on was sitting all together in the bottom of a Dixie cup rimmed with tiny pink flamingos. He was less extravagant than the day before, but he trembled more. His eyes had gotten heavier and his mouth was dry. He tried to show me his new room, but before we could enter an orderly came and stopped us with his burly arms. We weren't allowed inside together. It was a skinny room, with an elevated single steel bed against the wall. It had one small pale pastel pillow that crinkled like hard paper. The walls were the kind that moved in on you. There was a metal table, but it too was bare since they had taken all his belongings. The room was void of anything personal.

When Max motioned for the orderly to take him to the bathroom, a man in a white coat motioned for me to follow him into an office and as he manoeuvred around the room, he settled into a plush office chair. A sign on the desk said DR. LERANDEUX. A picture of a dark-haired woman with two boys sat beside it.

"Bonjour, mademoiselle. My name is Dr. Lerandeux. I understand you do not speak French?"

"No, sorry."

"Why not?" he said, smiling, lifting his shoulders. His humour relieved me but I still looked down.

His white coat hugged his round belly and the pens in his pockets all leaned forward when he moved himself closer to me. "We have a very serious problem here, Ines." He pronounced the I in my name way too hard, it sounded like E-ness, which reminded me of when kids called me penis, which made me hate it even more. "You are the girlfriend of Monsieur Labelle, correct?"

I nodded, although I was not so sure it was true.

"We haven't been in contact with any of his family. Are you able to help us with that?"

"I don't know his mom's number, but I can try to get it for you."

"That would be very much appreciated." He sounded out his words carefully, with cheer.

I was glad he could speak English. "Can you tell me what is happening to him?"

"Ines," he said again with the long I. "I am sorry, but it isn't that straightforward. I can tell you it is going to be some time in here for him, and we will do our best to get him better quickly. I would encourage you to come and visit often. It is healthy for normalcy."

"And to improve your French," he said at last, grinning. We sat quietly for a moment and he motioned for me to go.

"Okay, thanks," I mumbled on my way out.

Max and the orderly came out of the bathroom and I watched as the attendant accompanied him to the armchairs. I went and sat in the one beside him.

"Max," I said. "They want to get a hold of your mom."

"Who is *they*?" he said, flat.

"Dr. Lerandeux. Your doctor. He needs to speak to her."

"They can't find out who she is."

"She deserves to know you are okay."

"Do I look okay to you?"

"Can you just tell me her phone number please? I could call her if you like."

"Yes, call her. Tell her I'm screwed up. Tell her she failed. It was always going to happen."

I put my hands on his knees, but he got up and went to his room, closing the door behind him. The glass window distorted the back of his head and he just stood there, neither turning around nor lying down, the only two things you could do in a room that small and undesirable. I grabbed my bag and left out the hallway. I passed rooms that looked like cells. I went out an exit door into the stairwell and descended, trying to find my way out. I went down an extra flight of stairs and into the basement. Down the corridor I passed a pharmacy lab and a janitorial room. The cement walls were wide and I was lost. I went back out the other way and tried to retrace my steps, but the doors were locked. I ended up using the service elevator. I pushed the main button, thinking I would get back to the front of the hospital, which I did, but not before stopping to let in a cleaning lady wearing a hairnet who looked me up and down like she expected me to flash her a permission slip for riding her elevator. We rode in silence. The light flicked on and off and I imagined getting stuck in the elevator with her.

When the doors finally came apart and I saw hospital staff and visitors milling about on the waxed floor. I ducked past her and out into the lobby, where sick people coughed and kids ran around and adults hid their faces behind magazines. I left through the revolving doors and found myself on René-Lévesque. There was no saving anything, and I began to cry from the fear. I prayed for him to be okay but praying made me feel disconnected from the truth. I knew there wasn't going to be an answer from God. I stopped expecting answers after Clara. So many strangers were held in that room, and for a moment Neil Young soothed their shattered dreams. I cried for the sadness of it. Their spirits were gone.

I walked to Max's apartment. Light snow dusted the ground like confectioners' sugar and the feelings of the approaching holiday made me imagine I was inside a candy house like the one our family used to make this time of year. We would cover it with white icing first. There would be a jujube chimney and a jelly bean gutter. There was always a pretzel fence. In the run up to Christmas we were allowed to take a candy off each day and eat it. Eventually the icing would hurt your teeth and the house would start to look like a foreclosure. The fence was missing pieces, liquorice laces hung off the ceiling, it would get decayed and abandoned and sit there, dilapidated and uninviting, all the best candies gone and hardened holes in their place. We never decorated the house after Clara died. Nothing this time of year had ever been the same again. I watched the light snow scatter on the sidewalk in the wind, like when I watched Mom blend the icing and the sugar would blow around the counter as she baked. I just wanted to go back to those days and have a second chance. The wind stung my eyes so that even when I stopped crying, tears still fell.

As soon as I opened his door Pantouf came out of the bedroom and glided around my ankles, mewing up at me with earnest eyes, forlorn with hunger. I went to the kitchen and poured some kibble into his dish and filled the other one up with fresh water. I cleaned the litter box and sat on the couch to look through Max's photo album. His keen eye told stories of the Montreal streets and the people who inhabited them. One time at Roy Bar, a skater bent down to pick up a dropped lighter and accidently pricked his finger with a dirty needle. Max had a photo of that moment. I kicked a shoebox of Nikes under the desk. The springs below me compressed and let out high-pitched squeals which stopped when I eventually got comfortable on the couch.

I was enjoying winter's quiet mood and felt peace with myself when there was a knock at the door. I jumped and the springs did too. There was no peephole so I lifted the latch and opened it a few inches wide. An old man with outstretched hands held a flyer foretelling the second coming of Jesus. "No," I said, feeling irked and disrupted. I waved him away, but he kept reaching his wrinkled hands out, trying to give me the flyer. I closed the door in his face. A slew of papers flew off the desk. I stood looking at the mess and felt defeated, like God was always trying to find his way into my life, like it was the only answer, to heal I must repent. I stroked Pantouf, behind his ears and cleaned up the papers, then peeked out to see if the man was still there, but there was no trace, except anyone who hadn't answered their door received a pamphlet stuck in the crack awaiting the hopeful epiphany of another life saved.

It reminded me that the pamphlets I had taken from the waiting room were scrunched up and wet in the bottom of my backpack. I laid them out on the bed and flattened them as best I could. I opened the folds and turned them to the English sides. One showed a picture of a person's face reflected in a cracked mirror. I picked them at random and started reading: *Schizophrenia. Schizoaffective disorder. Bipolar Disorder. Paranoia, mania, depression. Loving someone with mental illness.* I read through them all, trying to decipher a diagnosis. *Schizophrenia can be brought on by a genetic predisposition… New research suggests that substances, including marijuana, can bring on episodes of mania… young adults are particularly prone… frenzied spending sprees and… sexual impulses… insomnia… erratic thought and speech patterns…* Through the balcony I saw a dismal city. Under the umbrella of mood deficiency, it seemed entirely possible he had a bit of everything—hell, so did I. I wondered if Max would ever look at me with joy in his face again. I felt deeply sorry for myself, then deeply selfish. I'd lost my lover, but he'd lost himself. His passion drifted away. Our relationship felt like another life altogether. Did I ever even know him?

I stopped at the skate shop on Saint-Denis on my way home. The new Baker2G video was playing on the TV. The skating was unreal and there were so many funny and vulgar partying scenes. Skateboarding was divided into being hesh or fresh. The style was skinny jeans and studded belts or baggy cargos with a shoelace as a belt. All the videos had final tricks in slow motion. I didn't know the guy behind the counter, so I walked over to the board wall and looked at all of the graphics. They were beautiful and morbid. I watched a mom buy a complete deck for her kid for Christmas. It had a graphic of a skull with a knife through its head. I thought about how a skateboard had first found its way into my hands. How I got hooked by it—having to focus helped me stop thinking about the past. I used to hitchhike on weekends to go to the skatepark in the neighbouring town, trying to land ollies on flat ground over and over while I waited for a car to stop. There was a time that a man in a pickup stopped and he turned Lynyrd Skynyrd up really loud. He reached his hand from the drive stick and put it on my thigh, pulling on the muscle and slowly clutching into my crotch. I put my skateboard in between him and me. On and off the board, it offered a sense of protection. I couldn't wait to leave that place behind.

I wondered about the kid getting a board for Christmas, if it would last for them. If they would ever feel like it had saved their life like I did, or if they were just another kid to get excited by the fad and forget it when the next one came along. The ones it saved were different, you could tell. They came from broken homes and had secrets. Like the physical pain of learning was no match for their heartache. Without skateboarding those ones might have lost their way, but weren't we all disposable heroes anyhow? The promise of fame and sponsorship drove a lot of people to extremes, there was pressure to perform while skating and off the board the party was a necessary endeavour. You had to stand out. All it took though was one injury or a new hot shot with a gnarly front-side flip and your "career" was over before it had even started. I bought a new deck. I couldn't afford a pro model so I bought a blank, thinking it would be fun to write something on the bottom. The employee offered to grip it for me, but that was bad luck. He rolled up the tape and secured it with an elastic and I took everything home and got to work on placing the grip with precision and cutting and sanding down the sides. I took a Sharpee and started drawing black stars and hearts. I began copying Max's grip job, but instead I wrote TRUST LOVE: DON'T TRUST MEN.

✤ ✤ ✤

The outside world hadn't fallen on Max's skin since he was admitted and it was beginning to show. His freckles took on the appearance of sores and his pupils were the size of hockey pucks. His hair was messy, but not in the cute way I was used to. The back was fuzzy and his cowlicks had given birth to baby cowlicks. In fact, his head looked like it had been licked by all the farm animals. What bothered me the most was that there was no lustre to him. He was a shell of a man, wearing grey sweats and paper slippers. If he hadn't come in sick, he certainly was now.

I began missing the manic Max, at least manic Max was alive and creative. This one had stopped all talk of buying a store, renting a house, road tripping; everything about him had slowed to a half pulse. I knew those elaborate plans were never going to happen. He rarely spoke, and we never touched. I couldn't tell if he didn't want to or wasn't allowed. I asked Max if he ever saw the man with the dictionary again, but he didn't remember there being one. I wondered if I had imagined it too.

Dr. Lerandeux's office opened and a woman in a purple down jacket came out; her hair was dyed orange and gelled spiky. She wiped tears from behind her pink glasses and blew her nose into a tissue that was already used and wadded into a ball. The doctor nodded in my direction and I lifted my hand automatically to form a half wave. He looked at the lady and then at me. She came over and sat down beside me, rubbing her hands on her jeans.

"You must be Ines?" she said. "I am Deborah. Max's mother."

"Who called you?"

"Sebastien. He called me days ago, but I was out of town taking care of Max's grandmother, she is unwell. I was in Trois-Rivières. We are transferring her care to a nursing home so I couldn't leave. Now all the paperwork is done. I came here as soon as possible."

"He didn't want you to come." As soon as I said it I felt bad.

"I know this. I haven't seen him yet. I have just been talking to Dr. Lerandeux."

"Look, I'm going outside to smoke."

"May I join you?"

"Whatever," I said as I walked out of the room.

I was worried about Max seeing her, what his reaction would be, but he was her son. She followed me to the stairwell but motioned to the elevator, so I went with her and without saying anything we rode down to the main lobby, where the doors opened with a *ding* like in a hotel. We went outside and I lit a smoke. She pulled out a pack of Virginia Slims; each was as long as a piece of chalk. I lit her smoke for her. Through her first drag she clicked the snow from her boots and told me that Max was unstable and would be for a while.

"Has this ever happened before?" I asked her.

Her eyes darted back and forth through the smoke.

"Not exactly."

"It must have been hard raising him on your own." I don't know why I said it, it just came out, but I could tell by her long glance she knew I meant no harm, a softness that mothers have; they know how to take on people's words and decide if they are worth battling. Mom was similar, you could see her patience at work. I wanted that tenderness. I wondered if she had rosacea or if she was a drinker. Maybe it was just the cold. She was very colourful and small. I had a vision of Max growing up helping in her salon. Rinsing out tacky dye jobs and letting old ladies put curlers in his darling red hair while they waited for their perms to set. Deborah scooping him up off the floor and walking him around on her hip, a cigarette hanging out of the corner of her mouth as she swept up the hair with her free hand. I flicked my cigarette and the whole cherry went with it, so I chucked it and lit another one. Deborah hauled on hers and flicked it away, then lit another right after as well.

"When Max's father died," she began, "it had gotten so bad for us that it was almost no surprise when I found him."

"Found him?" I said, confused.

"Yes," she breathed. "He killed himself. I found him in the garage."

"Max told me he was hit by a car."

"Ah, well, he may have died in the car, but he was never hit by one. I'm sorry he couldn't tell you the truth. It was so hard for him. For us."

"When was this?"

"Fifteen years ago. He was sick, too. Manic depression."

Max had all those photos of him with his dad: a little boy with dilated pupils, a bowl cut and a desire to hang around his mother's knees. He was hugging them in one photo, clearly looking for attention and stalling her in her path to do the dishes or prepare supper. It was taken after his dad had died. I felt unable to speak, and we stood there, looking at each other and smoking.

"You should go see him," I managed finally, stomping out my smoke. "I'll come back later."

I saw her tears come down and I didn't know if I should take her in for a hug. Before I could decide she went on her way and I went on mine. I took one last look up at the wing where Max was kept. She turned back to me to say something, but I pretended I didn't notice and turned away, walking with my eyes cast down and my hands in my pockets. I couldn't get the image out of my head of Max's father dead in their garage. I imagined a silver Lincoln Town Car with a red interior that smelled of cigarette smoke and had an empty Pepsi can in the drink holder. His head tilted forward.

I called up April and told her everything. She invited me over. Her place was small and there were paintings and photos from concerts and magazine pictures of models covering the walls. I sat on the windowsill with a blanket, drinking wine and talking with her while she painted. Her fat cat came and kept me warm, purring by my side. We talked about our lives, how we were fearless girls who were alive and burning. She made me feel confident. I helped her clean the brushes she was done with and in the muted heat of the room I fell apart. The snow fell peacefully and through the curtains I could see it landing on the sill and collecting in a white pile. It was winter, and after the excitement and wonder of Christmas we would be left with sad, dark skies. I cried even though I didn't want to. April looked up at me from the canvas she was painting on the floor. She was using so many shades of blue and the oil paint got on her pants and her fingers. She wiped her forehead with her brush hand and got up from her work. Both her knees cracked as she straightened. She came towards me with outstretched arms and I let her hold me like she had in the abandoned silo. When she pulled away I averted my eyes and bit the corner of my lower lip, a habit I recognized as my mother's after Clara died. I pulled the skin away and bit at it and it started to feel like hamburger.

"Stay over tonight."

"Are you sure?" I asked, but April was already picking up her painting and leaning it against the wall with plastic underneath it. It was part collage and, although abstract, the faces in it were soulful and deep. She had a way of capturing distinct emotions. She was a good artist and I felt pangs of jealousy that she was so capable of so many things. I looked into the painting and then out the window, while April tried to catch my gaze. We didn't have to talk. She opened my arms and raised me up and led me to her bedroom. Her duvet was black. I stood there while April removed all the extra pillows and pulled back the covers. Her sheets were black.

"You want some pajamas?"

"No, that's okay." I took off my pants and then unhooked and threaded my bra through my shirt sleeves, crawling in under the

AMY MATTES

covers. April curled up beside me and spooned me. I always wanted
this opportunity, to be close to her like this. She brushed my hair
back with her hand and I thought about kissing her, but I knew that
if she let me, it was just an escape like all the others.

I cried that night like I never had before. I lay in bed with her
with the blanket up around my chin and her soft body comforting
me. My cheeks stung and my eyes were red and swollen, but the
tears just kept on coming, pushing themselves out and falling as
if desperate to escape while they had the chance, soaking the bedding. I didn't even try to stop them. The quiet rang in my ears. I
stared into the black silence of the night, watching the snow gather
on the telephone poles. A pair of shoes had been flung over the line
and in the slight breeze one of them went around and around in
little circles.

Before April woke up I snuck out. On the way down the outside
stairs I created a path of fresh footprints and clung cautiously to the
railing so I wouldn't fall down. They would be covered with more
snow by the time April noticed I was gone. It was still dark and I
grabbed a coffee and a stale chocolate Danish from a vendor inside
the station and waited for the train. It was always the in-between
moments where I was most comfortable with myself. I did believe
that Max's world was different than most. It came through in his
movies and glimmered in his eyes. He made beautiful connections
that not just anyone was able to see. I saw it as a gift. His photos
and films were brilliant. I listened to Linkin Park as loud as it would
go. It transported me, lost in time and space. The voice of Chester
Bennington depressing me and soothing me all at the same time. It
was an energetic anthem that disarmed me.

*❀ ❀ ❀*

Max was allowed out for Christmas, but he had to stay at his mom's, and she would have to telephone the hospital each day to let them know he hadn't wrapped the lights around his neck and jumped off the roof or got too high and drunk and passed out in a snowbank.

Deborah invited me to her high-rise apartment for Christmas Eve dinner. She wanted me to spend the night, but I told her I couldn't. I had to look after Cedric while Lainey was away. Before I left I did some MDMA off a CD case that I kept tucked away in the closet. It burned like hell, but warmed me up when it kicked in. Hoping left me strung out and strung along. I sat with the pamphlets about mental illness, about stigma and support and recognizing signs and symptoms, stories of husbands who called up stores after wives' manic spending sprees, begging to return all the merchandise. The ego taken for a lift it will never forget. Imagine having hallucinations so real they can't be dismissed. A foreign body imposing its own unquestionable version of reality. A total loss of logic.

I went to the dollar store at the last minute and got her some cinnamon scented candles and a box of chocolates. I walked down to the hospital and tried to enjoy the bustle of the evening. I headed to the hospital coffee shop to wait. The snow was being whipped around in mini cyclones. I wrapped my scarf up high around my cheeks against the spray of ice crystals. When I closed my eyes, I could almost turn the world off. The blackness and the wind; there was nothing else left. My teeth were grinding. I opened my eyes slowly, to be sure I could make it back to reality okay, then closed them again, this time for longer. I wanted to go into the blackness. I wanted to turn the world off. I wanted somebody to shake the snow globe, and for everything to tumble the way it did in my mind. A rumbling entered my consciousness, and I tried to identify it with my eyes still closed. It wasn't a skateboard, but it was similar. My eyes opened, and a homeless man pushed his shopping cart full of cans ever onward. The wheels were squeaky and the cans shook and rattled against each other.

In the coffee shop I sat on the edge of this demented planet, the hum and buzzing of coffee stirring, emotions brewing. The smell of disinfectant and rubber pervaded, assuring everyone that they were in fact still in a hospital. The place was a study in the holiday blues: big noses stayed stuck in newspapers; far-flinging gazes got lost out the window; low-slung faces inspected their lonely drinks; all these people looked like they were waiting for something that never came.

I tried to focus on my love for Max, who could eventually live his life again, if by very different rules, but my hopefulness was extinguished. I was in the company of a disorder that reshapes reality and spits you out amnesiac. I remembered his clear eyes and wide open smile, his unassuming nature, and to know it was gone made the whole world feel exclusionary. He didn't really want a future with me.

"You're sitting in my office."

Max was looming above me, his expression untidy. A grey wool toque was tucked over one ear and the other was exposed. It was the first time I had seen him in his own clothes since he was hospitalized; they were the same ones from the night he was arrested. His jeans were crinkled and his shirt, which was flashy and logoed, was really dirty. I could tell he felt unkempt, and he pulled at his clothes, trying to make them feel like his own again.

"You're sitting in my office."

"I'm what?"

"Sitting in my office. This is the exact table where I come to sit."

"Oh," I said.

"Are we going to my mother's?"

"Yeah, is that okay?"

"I think so."

He reached for my hand and pulled me up from the table, which I bonked with my knee so that it teetered and spilled my coffee. I smiled a thin line of disapproval at myself and let out a sigh. He led me into the hospital foyer where I had to sign him out, giving them my promise that he would return on December 26 by four o'clock. They called a taxi for us, and we waited outside under the big pillars, surrounded by cement, the snow whirling and cars driving by, their headlights bright even though it wasn't dark yet. It was hard to see through the weather. In the taxi we were silent and through the foggy windows we both stared out at the city. Max drew a heart in the condensation.

Max sat down on the edge of the sidewalk outside the door of Deborah's building. The snow turned into sloppy rain. The drops were so heavy they bounced back out of the ground. The recycle bin that was left out collected the rain and turned the frozen papers to mush. He sat beside it in silence on the cold cement, rolling a halfie. I watched him lick the glue strip, his head bending to it, which made me imagine all his tormented thoughts forming into keyhole shapes, and I understood then that he was and always had been using substances to self-medicate. A trait I recognized in myself. Searching his pockets for the lighter was like looking for a missing key, one that just wouldn't fit the lock. We were both searching for something we couldn't find or feel. When he finally found it and lit the joint I watched his face glow orange and then turn black against the flare of the ember.

Deborah buzzed us up. She had a balcony that had been converted into a sunroom. There was a plastic table with a floral plastic tablecloth attached to it with metal clips as if it could have blown away. The apartment was clean. She played the radio low. An opera-style carol that sounded like "Joy to the World" had trumpets that made me jolt out of my seat every time they blared. I was nervous. I was high on the MDMA, but I had to carry the conversation, since Max was comatose from his medication and the weed. I had to excuse myself and go throw up bile in the toilet. The bathroom had a matching purple bathmat and toilet seat cover, which I rested my face on once I'd puked, wiping the yellow from my mouth and feeling my stomach burn empty and my face swell hot and pink. Looking in the mirror, I saw waves undulate under my skin.

Deborah poured us each a rum and eggnog. I whirled the ice cubes around, trying to think of what to say. Max sat in the armchair with his hands folded in his lap, as if he were posing for a painting; he was certainly still enough. The eggnog was cheap and thin and the rum scorched my already burning throat. He hung his head lower. I inspected the bruises on my elbow. I played with the Velcro on the couch that held pieces of fabric over the armrests, lifting it up and sticking it back down. I was crashing, Max was vacant and Deborah was doing her best to keep the evening flowing. We ate dinner on the enclosed deck. She lit some tall red candles and they burned poorly because the wicks were too high. It was a fire hazard, but I didn't want to say anything that might spoil our attempted mood. She asked Max something in French and then took both our hands in hers. I assumed we were going to say grace. Max's fingertips were cold, but I held his hand tightly and he lifted his head and said, "Hail Mary, full of grace, pull down your pants and sit on my face." A burst of laughter escaped me. Deborah gave me a look of scorn but allowed a thin smile after which her eyes softened and we all burst into laughter. In another moment Deborah was crying; her blue mascara puddled in the corners of her eyes and she wiped it away and said, "Merry fucking Christmas." She and I raised our glasses and Max his can of Pepsi and we cheersed. She'd made a pre-stuffed turkey that was small and dry. I chewed and chewed. I was dry too and couldn't get much down. Max's appetite had changed as well, and he slowly cut his food into pieces and then rolled them back and forth with his fork. Even the peas were sullen. The spectres of special holiday feelings we knew we were without hung above our heads like sad balloons. We didn't even try to grab at them. After dinner I lit a cigarette and blew my smoke towards them and fiddled with the paper napkin and the plastic table cover. Max seemed to have entered into a daze and even Deborah finally gave in and poured the drinks stronger.

She had a fake Christmas tree with some presents under it. We sat in the living room after dinner to open them and Deborah handed me a gift with a card with Rudolph on it, his nose a felted red ball. It was a French day planner that came with a matching pen. It was thoughtful. She opened my gift and smelled the candles, genuinely enjoying them. I felt silly that they were so cheap, but I could tell she appreciated it. Her candles were cheap too. We opened the chocolates and passed them around until the box was gone. She liked all the fruit-filled ones and I liked all the ones filled with caramel and nuts, and our moods lifted at this exchange. I felt pleasure quicken my heart. Sharing this normal family holiday experience was something I had missed.

She'd bought Max a pair of slippers so he wouldn't have to wear the disposable hospital ones anymore. It was a thoughtful gift too, but a sorry replacement for Max's obsession with Nikes. I'd bought a small frame and cut out a quote that really spoke to me from a skateboarding magazine. It was a journal entry of a pro skater. He said your soul can you keep you company. That a man must know himself. I'd hoped it would touch Max the way it touched me. That it is possible to be unconcerned with greatness, if you know who you are. Whatever I could do to keep reaching out, to show him that he could get better. He glanced at it but didn't read the whole thing. He blinked very slowly, said he was tired and excused himself to lie down in the room that belonged to him as a child.

There were family photos on the walls like the ones you would get done at Sears: the three of them in front of a fake backdrop—a nature scene, a marbled wall—the carpeted levels invisible below their feet. One photo showed Max as a baby, propped up on one elbow, smiling brightly. His eyes were like huge precious stones, dark green like seaweed and brown too, like sand. I helped Deborah with the dishes, which was awkward because you could only fit two people in the kitchen and when the dishwasher door was open we were both trapped in the small space together. We did find a rhythm, in which I scraped and tidied up and she rinsed and loaded the dishwasher, which was a yucky yellow colour and had to be plugged in from the sink taps.

"Ines, can you love him like this?"

"I think so."

"You say that now."

I told her that I was reading pamphlets about mental illness to learn everything I could to support him, when Max interrupted us from the room, yelling out, "There is nothing wrong with me."

I went to him and asked in a low whisper from the doorway, "What did you say?"

I peered back at Deborah, who was busying herself stacking dirty pots and pans on the counter. She looked up at me and shrugged, while she moved to playing with the potholders.

"It doesn't matter, Ines."

"Of course, it does."

"I don't need to take pills. I was fine. I was not depressed and now look at me, I am a waste of skin. I want it back. I want me back." I came into the room fully and noticed that he had bunk beds. They were wooden and had been painted navy blue. He lay under a camouflage bedspread, which was pulled right over his head.

"Mind if I take top bunk?" I asked him.

"Ines, I am not sick."

I started climbing up the ladder, which creaked as I put pressure on it. I felt like it would break; it was a youth-sized bed. I didn't know how to reply, since I disagreed.

"I want to be here for you, Max."

He didn't reply for a long time. Then he said again, "I am not sick."

Glow-in-the-dark stars dotted the ceiling, and in the low green light they cast, I could see an old Bones Brigade poster on the wall. There were canker sores forming on my tongue and I couldn't help but bite at them. I swallowed so hard and dry I felt his mom would hear it in the other room. I was so fucking tired. I stared at the roof and Max stared at the bottom of my bed. He knocked on the frame. "Are you there?"

"I'm here."

"I'm not taking those pills no more."

"Are you sure that's a good idea?"

"You don't know what this feels like."

We lay there for some time. I fell asleep chewing the skin of my lips. When I woke up it was darker; the stars had worn out, and all the lights had been extinguished in the living room, except for a flicker coming from the TV. I swung my head down to look at Max in the bottom bunk and my hair dangled in my face. I thought of waking him up but decided not to. I got out of the bunk carefully but it was so noisy I winced every time I moved. When I came out into the living room, I found Deborah sleeping on the couch as an infomercial for a rotisserie oven flashed on the screen. "Set it and forget it," the man kept saying. A burned down cigarette filter rested between Deborah's index and middle fingers. She still wore her wedding ring. I took the filter and put it in the ashtray and wiped the ash off the couch.

With the flashes of light off the TV I grabbed my boots from the plastic mat. They were covered in gravel and ruined from the salt. The clock on the oven said 3:33. I thought of Clara and myself waking up first thing on Christmas Day and being allowed to go peek in our stockings. They always had a lump of coal in them as a joke. I pulled my zipper up to the top and went out into the hallway, taking one last look at the pictures on the wall. I noticed Max's backpack on the floor and I opened it. There was a pill bottle addressed to Maximilian André Labelle for lithium. I hadn't even known his middle name. I put it back in the bag and walked out the door. There was a courtesy phone for taxis in the lobby; walking from Verdun would be ridiculous. I made the call, then ran my fingers along the mirrors on the wall. I sat on the curb and smoked. My sour, empty stomach wailed. In the cab the driver tilted his mirror and gave me a strange look. I chewed my nails and thought about telling him, "Yes, monsieur, I understand I look weird. I have no family here and my boy-friend is crazy, and my sister is dead." But I refrained. I wanted to be defined by better memories. He probably wanted nothing more than to be in his own bed or putting presents under his tree for his children, waking up to a hot coffee and excitement. We didn't speak. John Lennon played on the radio. The city was more still than I'd ever seen it before. It was magic at this moment, all the lights and decorations. This time tomorrow they would mean nothing at all.

When I got to my apartment I searched my pockets, my purse, my jeans for my keys, but I couldn't find them. I grabbed at the handle with both hands and body checked the door, which burst open and launched me into the landing. I loped up the stairs in my heavy boots to the sound of Cedric pawing around near the door. I let him out to pee and made sure to slam the door shut hard. Lainey had decorated the ficus with twinkly lights and underneath it she'd put a package that had arrived from my parents. On the table there were still scraps of paper from where I'd cut out the quote from the skateboarding magazine. I realized I'd left not only my keys but my present from Deborah at her apartment, which made me feel terrible. I unplugged the phone, pulled all the curtains and searched my pockets for the half tab of ecstasy that I had left over. I unwrapped it from the lottery ticket it was folded in, crushed it up on top of the CD case and snorted it through a five-dollar bill. I took a shower and then wrote in my journal. I started writing a letter to myself, my dead self.

*It's not your fault.*

In the morning I made coffee and took it with me into Carré Saint-Louis with Cedric. I sat on the top of a bench since there was so much snow it covered the seat. I curled my fingers around the cup, taking satisfaction in the billowing steam and the freezing cold day. We walked up Saint-Denis. Cars drove past us on their way to brunches and hugs with loved ones who were hustling away in kitchens all morning, basting birds and putting out trays of cold cuts and cheeses and pickles. I thought about the wish I had written and set free, how it had come back to me tenfold, warped and seemingly cruel. Cedric stopped on the sidewalk and hunched into position. I wrapped the bag around the turd and chucked it in the trash. *So, this is Christmas,* I hummed. My first one alone, even though they all felt lonely after Clara died.

I took Cedric home and left again cutting up rue Rachel towards the Mountain and along avenue du Parc until I got to Dusty's. I ordered fresh orange juice and a classic eggs benny and a specialty coffee with Frangelico and an extra side of bacon, which made me think of Max's breakfast bacon program. I didn't eat much of it, but the attempt to create a moment, evoke an atmosphere was there. Oldies played like usual and there were others who were by themselves, so we dined alone together. It was the environment that nourished me. When I got back to my apartment Max was sitting on the stoop and shaking with his arms crossed. I brought him upstairs and we lay together on the couch, wrapped in blankets.

Conversation didn't come easy and I could sense that we were both high in different ways. While Max slack-eye stared, my jaw clenched and surges moved through my insides. I took my hand in his, but he pulled it away.

"It's another reason I don't take the pills no more."

"What's that?"

"My sex. I feel nothing there too. I'm worried."

"It's okay, Max," I told him. "We don't have to do anything. I just want to be here with you, that's all."

"You don't understand. Before this I was engaging, people were interested in me, and now I offer nothing."

"I know about the other girls." I blurted it out. The ecstasy made me honest. I wasn't even sure if I had anything else to say about it, but I wanted him to know that I knew. His expression stayed vacant. He wiped the dryness in the corners of his mouth with his fingers and wrinkled up his forehead in thought.

"Who told you? I can't explain it, okay. There was a lot of parties and girls and the girls were just there, they wanted me to take them. I couldn't refuse."

"I'm just trying to make sense of it all. I thought we made a promise to each other?"

"Well, you can't understand." There was a long pause and then Max grew excited. "I know, let's go for dinner at the bistro."

"It's Christmas, Max, they're closed today."

"Well tomorrow then. I haven't even been before. I can get one of those steaks you're always talking about."

"I don't work there anymore, Max. I got fired."

"What?" Max leaped from the couch and slammed his fist onto the coffee table. "Why didn't you tell me?"

"I don't know. It just wasn't a big deal to me I guess." There was another long pause and Max sat down again beside me.

"I don't think you should stop taking your pills, Max." I shook my head, my eyes fluttered. Pills, no different than the ones I was on.

"Stay out of my fucking business, Ines." Max got up and tossed the blankets towards me. He went downstairs to the door and I could hear him putting on his shoes and coat.

"Here are your keys." He tossed them up the stairs and they landed on the floor at my feet. "And the present from my mom." The book skidded across the floor. The door closed and I stuck my face into the wad of blankets. I closed my eyes against the possibilities. My heart felt so cold it could have put out an apartment fire. I imagined him walking around the Plateau again, smoking weed and telling strangers stories. He wasn't even sorry about the other girls. Why did I let him treat me that way? I couldn't help thinking that they were the perfect excuse: the easiest way out of this situation. And why the fuck not? I hated to think of his hands on someone else's body, un-hooking their bras the way he had mine, his skin on theirs—but I knew that wasn't him. He wasn't trying to hurt me. The thought that he would kill himself like his father crossed my mind and made me shudder. Then I'd be responsible for two deaths. Lost in the crazy business plans, the car, the house in the country, I was in those beautiful ideas. I loved him for his wide open heart and his dirt-encrusted fingers that had gripped my own and held me close and made me believe that love was possible, even in wreckage. I loved his smell, the grunge of sweat that emanated from his T-shirts when we skated in the heat of summer and the city was bustling, green and fertile. The feeling of holding him close and resting my head against his damp neck, against the narrow strength of his shoulders, his freckled, smooth skin. A sob broke from me and filled the empty apartment. He was gone, and I would not be the person to bring him back. He had practically told me so with his leaving. We were done, and I mourned the death of us. The grief stole my breath and made my ribs ache and I couldn't breathe.

The phone rang and startled me. It was a tradition in my family to say "Merry Christmas" but I couldn't be bothered. In my head

I heard my dad's voice saying it before I even answered. I did love my father and speaking with him reminded me of good things, how he always sounded like he was about to cry when he said goodbye. I thought it was his way of saying *I love you* because Clara's death made every goodbye feel like it could be the last, but my parents were disappointed by me, I knew that. I picked up the phone and held it midair for a brief second, then I put it back down without saying hello and unplugged it from the wall. I wondered if they ever wished it was me who'd died instead. I lay back on the couch and closed my eyes as if I could shut out the world. I held my breath for long moments and then exhaled as hard as I could, giving me a head rush that made me dizzy.

I fell asleep with my arms on my chest like I was in a coffin. I had a bizarre dream that I wanted to write down before I forgot, but then I did. Mom bought me a dream decoding book for my birthday when I was sixteen. They didn't really know what I was into by then, but I slept a lot, so I guess she figured I probably liked to dream. It didn't seem to be reliable; it said things like if you dreamt that your teeth were falling out it meant you were going to get pregnant. I had never been pregnant, but I had friends who'd had abortions. Max and I used condoms, most of the time. But I would try to hold him inside me in the final thrusts because it felt so good I didn't want to ever let him go. He would exhaust himself trying to control it and at the last second he would remove himself, spilling onto my stomach, and then collapse on top of me and we'd pant for minutes at a time until we shifted and got a towel and pulled ourselves apart. It was those times when my senses were overcome that I felt cherished by him, like my body was loveable. I got up and put on the radio, desperate to pull away from the memories of our relationship. I was confused by lust and I didn't want the film of it on me anymore. Pink Floyd's "Mother" played from the speakers. I turned it up as loud as it would go and twirled around, shaking it off. *Mother* was another loaded word. I tumbled, diminished,

when the final notes played lower, I stopped my wayward dance
and crumpled on the floor like a discarded doll.

On Boxing Day morning the house was so quiet I didn't know if I could speak, but I finally called my parents. I didn't want to tell them that my boyfriend was on a holiday pass out of lock-up from a psychiatric hospital but I knew they were expecting to hear from me. I opened a beer and took a breath in preparation to hide behind the line in any way I could.

"Hi."

"Ines, we've been worried about you."

"Don't worry about me, Mom, I'm fine. I was just out all day."

"Did you have someone to spend Christmas with?"

"Yeah Mom, I did. I had dinner at a friend's. It's um … cold here right now."

"Did you open your gift yet?"

"Oh no, sorry, I haven't."

"What's wrong, Ines?"

"Nothing, Mom."

"I wish you would tell me. We never hear from you."

I broke down and told her all about Max. How I loved a man who had changed from someone tender to fierce. I held onto the fear that this was happening because I was unlovable, that it stemmed from Clara dying, following me into adulthood, like a gallows lasso, ready to pull me back in. Max and April had showed me that I wasn't broken. I wanted her to know that. I just wanted to hear her say that she didn't blame me for Clara's death, that she was sorry for the silence. I knew it broke us all, but I was a child. Only a child. An only child, a lonely child.

"Oh Ines, we wish we could be there to hug you."

"I know, Mom," I whispered, defeated. I wasn't sure I could bear the conversation any longer.

"I think I'm just going to go," I managed, feeling like a child all over again. "I will call you more often, okay. I'm sorry."

"Don't be sorry, sweetheart," she said. "Do you want to talk to your father?"

"I don't think I can right now."

"Okay," she said. "Take care."

I had no will to try to explain to him that I was in love with an unwell man who cheated on me, nor betray in my speech that I had my own residual drug problem. He was a *marijuana is a gateway drug* type of guy, and he had little time for talking about messy feelings. He expected his daughter to be treated like gold. Problem was, no one had taught her the value of it.

I went to Max's and an overdue gas bill hung on the door of his apartment. When you cash out on life for a bit, it's always determined to catch up, even during the holidays. No one likes forms, no one wants to be a number. Max had no choice now but to be defined by other people's rules and judgements. We were faceless in the grand scheme of things, and true to the times, no one fucking cared. It was musty and seemed abandoned after all his computers and cameras had been packed up. Seb was storing them and taking Pantouf to his place since we didn't know how long Max would be committed for. I helped Seb put the last few boxes into the trunk of his car. Back inside I looked out behind the dark pulled curtains at the sun warming the roofs. It made the frost melt and a slow steam appear in its place. I couldn't remember the last time I had woken up with the sun, in the morning; I couldn't remember being awake and it not being dark. I stood watching the day like an empty shell, not feeling.

"You look tired, Ines," Seb told me. He put his hand on my shoulder and I cowered at the unexpectedness of touch.

"I am tired," I said, pulling the curtains back together. "But you shouldn't tell people that."

"You have to take care of yourself, if you're going to take care of him."

I said nothing, but he was right. Seb had so much integrity; Max was lucky to have him. He was loyal and he had done what he thought was right. Had he not, I might have had to call the cops on Max myself. Max could have gotten himself into a lot of trouble.

"Max told me he was stopping his meds," I said.

"Do you think he made it back to the hospital okay?"

I imagined him at his mom's, still sleeping, or standing leaden in the shower. I wondered if he would truly go through with it, or whether he would think better of it and stay on them enough to stabilize. I cleaned the cat box and brought it to the car. I held Pantouf on my lap and Seb drove me back to my house. Pantouf brought his pink nose up to my chin and ran it along, curling his head back and forth and letting out a tender meow, grateful for the change of scenery and the company.

"I told Max that I knew about the girls on tour."

"That's okay. Everything is fair game right now, Ines. It's not your fault."

Seb pulled up to our place and as I got out I could hear the phone ringing upstairs. I ran to get it.

"Hello," I said, out of breath.

"Ines, it's Deb. I took Max back to the hospital. He needs help. I don't know what he was talking about half the time. I wanted you to know." I could tell she was taking a long drag off her cigarette by the pause she took at the end.

"Okay. Merci. Did he say anything about me?" I wanted her to sense my concern, to tell me everything was going to be okay, but she didn't.

"No, nothing. Désolée." She hung up.

I wondered if he had gone willingly. I ran back down the stairs in hopes that Seb hadn't left yet, but his car was gone and the puffs of exhaust were all I could smell in the cold air.

I came back to the apartment but the silence was damning. I cabbed to the hospital and when I saw Max the constant prodding had made him gaunt and aloof. He received no human touch outside of his medical care. He slipped back into psychosis and began new therapies. It seemed a fine line between treatment and torture. Nurses drew blood from him to see where his levels were sitting. He looked relieved to see me and he caved into my collarbone when I went to him. There were tears welling up again in his eyes.

"Max, what's wrong?" I asked at the sight of him.

"I am not sure. I am just happy you are here again."

I grabbed him another newspaper with the hope that we could scour it together with plans for when he was released, but he was numb to the idea, and unable to focus. He didn't seem to recall his erratic plans to open a store and take me to the country, which I secretly longed for. His rational mind had begun to return, and the seductions of his insanity were replaced by sedated sense. He had come back from the boundary. I told myself that if we could just get through this winter, get through our tears, everything would turn out okay.

"What is the point of looking, Ines, if I don't know how long I'll be here?"

"I don't know. I guess I just thought it would be good to look and get an idea of what's out there."

"I live here now."

"C'mon, Max, don't say that. You'll be out sometime soon, I know it."

"I am a ghost to the outside world."

In some ways he was right. His energy levels were low and his memories were sparse. He couldn't piece together why he'd ended up there. He was too defeated to try to come to terms with it. The frenetic restlessness had died. Deborah didn't make much of an effort to visit and the residue of the holidays still had our friends pulled in many directions to be with family and have dinners in warm and cozy homes, celebrating. Meanwhile Max was grey-blue as the frozen sky, frigid like the empty air in the ward. And I was either alone with him, or alone in the city, both of us medicated. The sun tried its best to shine that day, yet everything was so frozen it looked ready to snap and break into a million tiny pieces. Crystals sparkled everywhere and rainbows of frost dazzled as it flew from buildings. The brightness was impossible but I thought to myself if the rest of winter could stay like this, it wouldn't be so bad. I would get through it. The sunshine didn't last, though, and the week between Christmas and New Year's beat us hard with icy rain and angry winds.

♣ ♣ ♣

Change can be slow. You don't notice it creeping in, even if others do. It can be fast; overnight you and everyone you know are different. That's how it was after Clara died. Immediately and irreparably different: now marked by death. Mom and Dad, ever after those poor people whose daughter drowned. Our family was forced to move forward without its central piece, becoming the subject of much discussion and suspicion. For years, I believed that everyone in my town blamed me, and I didn't want to feel worthless anymore.

When Lainey returned from her parents', she walked up the stairs. I was playing on the floor with Cedric, trailing a ball around and watching him swat at it. There was dust all over the back of my black sweater from the floor. As soon as the key turned in the lock Cedric was gone, running down the stairs as fast as he could like he knew it was her before I did. She called hello from the boot room and I thought she sounded like a widowed woman by the way she didn't seem to expect an answer. "I'm up here!" I yelled while she ruffled with bags and shoes in preparation to hike the stairs.

"Oh, Ines! I am so happy you're home, my family was driving me crazy."

Lainey hoofed her way up the stairs and the bags rustled and made scratching sounds against the walls. She struggled through the doorway with a wide smile on her face, then stopped as our eyes met.

"You look like hell, Ines. What is going on here?"

I tried to explain that I had been busy, and stressed, but she interrupted me.

"There is VCR under your nose, what the fuck?"

"VCR?" I said, scratching at my inner nostril.

"Visible coke residue."

"Oh, it's not coke," I told her, feeling panicked by the look on her face. "It's MDMA."

She rolled her eyes in disapproval. "You don't snort MDMA, dummy, you just eat it. Your nose must be on fire." She berated me, but I could tell from a guilty glance or two that she felt bad for April having introduced me to it in the first place.

"It's not like I'm addicted," I told her.

"How can you say that? Look at this house! You certainly haven't been taking care of things. Look at all those bottles!"

"This stuff with Max just has me freaked out." I gathered a large dust bunny from the legs of the couch and began getting up off the floor.

"Okay, for real? Max is in the hospital and it's not his fault. If you don't get your shit together, you'll be there too."

This hurt. Of course Max didn't have a choice in losing his sanity, but to relate it to my stupid circumstance was a little too close to the bone. Lainey was so good at juggling every facet of her life. I felt stifled by her achievements and knew she was right on some level.

"Where are you even getting this stuff from?"

"Down on Sainte-Catherine by MusiquePlus."

"You're just buying this on the street? Do you even know what's in this? It could be meth."

"What difference does it make?"

The anger I had been worried about suddenly flared in Lainey's face. She swallowed and when she spoke her voice was low and forceful. "You need to pull yourself together, Ines." She picked up her stuff and went into her room, closing the door behind her and Cedric, leaving me at my pity party. I sat on the floor again and opened the gift from my parents. The card was written in my mother's beautiful cursive and Dad wrote in the card that he was proud of me for living life on my own terms. I was sure that meant that he didn't understand why I did what I did. To be fair, I barely understood it myself. It was a new winter jacket. A puffy one like all the locals wore, filled with goose down and with a fur-lined hood. Utilitarian and useful. *Stay Warm, Merry Christmas.* I rolled the tag into a ball and threw it on the floor with the dust bunnies and went to get the broom.

My eyes fluttered in a rush from the drugs. Time contracted and expanded. I felt like an outpatient with just a touch more capability than the patients in the ward. I was going to break up with Max. I tried to ignore the voice that said so, because it was giving up and I was tired of doing that and Max needed me now, more than I needed the truth.

New Year's Eve when I was growing up was a letdown. There was so much hype for a party and pressure to assume a new identity the next day, be brand new for no reason, other than to pretend it would improve things. In my experience, it was a few weeks of running strong and when the shine wore off it was back to the usual habits. I found ways to justify having another cigarette or drinking as much as I could to numb out. There was always a reason to keep doing something and not enough of one to stop. Wrinkles and poor metabolism weren't part of my problems.

Seb made a reservation for him and Lainey at a fancy Quebecois French restaurant. April took on a private date through the studio. She would get the sugar daddy treatment for twenty-four hours and an unfathomable amount of money to spend the night with some lonely chap. Pierre would monitor her safety. It was a business transaction. She thought New Year's was bogus too, so she saw it as a chance to make bank. I wondered about going to visit Max for the evening, but it was a dour thought to imagine myself placed among the sedated wearing paper hats, eating cake that crumbled in our dry mouths, our movements observed and recorded while *A Christmas Story* played on the rollout TV.

I decided to call Marie. I was surprised when she invited me
over for dinner and drinks with her and Felix.

"All right," I said on the phone, "what can I bring?"

"Nothing," she said. "We just want to see you."

I went to the dép and picked out two bottles of red and cabbed
over. I sniffed at my underarms, nervous what they thought they
knew about Max and me. Marie had a small, fake Christmas tree
neatly arranged on a table. There were tapered candles on the
windowsills and white lights hung in droopy unison around the
living room.

She had made a shepherd's pie but called it pâté chinois. While
it baked the house filled with the aroma of thyme, we drank the
heavy reds in gulps and I twirled my glass around and sniffed at it
as though I knew anything about the complexity of wine.

"So how is Max?" Felix asked while Marie put her oven mitts
down and rustled in the kitchen. She puffed on a joint and passed it
to Felix who took a haul and passed it to me.

"I don't know. Not good. He was talking about being Jesus. It's
not him. I know that much."

Felix sniffed at his glass and stifled a laugh that was also mixed
with concern. If it was for me or Max I couldn't tell.

"Is he going to be home soon?" Marie asked.

"I am not sure. He was allowed to go to his mom's for Christmas
but it didn't go well."

Marie reached into the cupboard above her and came over to
the table with a gift resting in her arms. She placed in front of me
and sat and poured herself some more wine. I stared down at the
reindeer wrapping paper, elated by the gesture, unsure where to
begin.

"We've been meaning to give this to you for a while, but we
haven't seen you."

"I know. There's been a lot going on."

"I get it," Marie said. "We've been busy too."

"You guys have always taken such good care of me," I said, scooping a creamy, gooey piece of brie with a cracker. I crunched it and started to peel back the tape and lift the flaps of the package. I started to see a long, black box and as I peeled the paper away the words Victorinox appeared on the front. I opened the case and nestled in velvet was a stunning chef's knife reflecting my wide eyes.

"Wow," I said.

"I get a deal through work," Marie shrugged.

"I can't accept this, you guys," I said.

"Of course you can. It's nothing," Marie said.

"I don't work at the restaurant anymore. I got fired." I hung my head.

"You will still need to eat." Felix laughed. I got up and hugged each of them. I held tight and took in their bodies.

"I could see if we need anyone on set?" Marie offered.

We sat down to eat together and we raised our glasses.

"What's your New Year's resolution?"

"To be happy," I said. "Do you guys have one?"

"No," Felix said, "don't need a special day to plan my life."

"I want to quit smoking," Marie said as she grabbed another one. "After this pack."

We sat and chatted. Marie had some sparklers and horns for the countdown, but I was faded. I felt like a third wheel when they conversed in French. Close to eleven I decided to pack it in. I promised I would be okay to walk. They kissed me on both cheeks and closed the door behind me. "Bonne année," I said and held the wall as I left the brick stairs out into the night streets. A halo of light from the lamppost told me it was snowing. The cold air hit my nostrils and my feet slid. I acquainted myself in the direction of home and began trudging with the knife box under my arm. I dropped into a drunken shiver. My thoughts ran and I tried to keep up with them. I was stumbling on the icy sidewalks. Swaying side to side. I stopped and took the knife out of the box and looked at it. I held it in my hands admiring its beauty, but I was too drunk to stand and I dropped it in the snow. I picked it up again and tried to wrestle it into the box but it was slippery, the wet handle slipped again and I couldn't coordinate myself to put it safely away. I leaned into the knife while trying. It was sharp and I felt the tip penetrate the fabric of my down jacket and prick into my abdomen. I dropped the knife again and I held myself. I bent to pick it up and fell onto the ice face first. I steadied and came to. I lifted my jacket and saw that my stomach was bleeding. The incision was not deep, but it bled. I got the knife back into the box and zipped it into my jacket and continued to walk and stride drunk to my front door. When I reached the steps, I grabbed for walls and barfed the entire dinner and red wine all over the entrance to our home. My stomach bleeding from a self-inflicted laceration. I was well on my way to doing the opposite of being happy. I vowed to never drink red wine again. My Discman had slipped from my coat and broke in the mess of regurgitated food. I grabbed the CD out and threw it against the wall and it broke too. I fell to my knees. The final moments of the year an absolute reckoning.

✿ ✿ ✿

The day of the show was cold, windless and vapid. I slept until the afternoon and when I finally got up I paced around. I rearranged the furniture in my room, but after I moved the bed I couldn't plug in the lamp and in the only other place the bed would fit, the balcony door wouldn't open. I moved it all back and sat down on the edge of the futon. Lainey hadn't come home on New Year's Day, so I took Cedric for a walk.

April came over. Under her long coat she was dressed in a white lacy two-piece, and her backpack was full of lingerie for me to try on. She pulled out a black two-piece set and offered it to me.

"Try this. You in black and I'll wear the white. Then we're kinda like bad girl, good girl."

I didn't mention that I thought she should be the bad girl in black. She was so much more provocative than me and in control—not to mention she would be doing the fucking. I put it on, and the chest was loose and flappy on me. I was scared. I wasn't innocent, but this was a first. She had on white, over-the-knee pleather heeled boots, like Julia Roberts wore in *Pretty Woman*, and she had a black pair for me. They were fuck-me boots if I'd ever seen any. My kneecaps fit perfectly into the tops and they stayed up without issue. The plastic was shiny and reminded me of Catwoman.

I looked at myself in the mirror and didn't recognize the person standing there. April stood behind me. She put one hand on my stomach and the other on my back and pulled me up straight.

"Rise up, Ines," she said. "Be demanding."

My skin was so pale against the black lace and pleather.

"What happened to you?" she said.

"It was an accident," I said.

April curled my hair and brushed it out so it was big, and I flipped it back and laughed while she covered my eyes with one hand and doused me in extra-firm-hold hairspray. She put thick black eyeliner on me and curled my eyelashes.

"I don't know what I'm doing, April."

"That's okay, just follow my lead. We'll practise here first. I brought some wine."

She lengthened the word bro—ught as she said it and it reminded me of when we first met. In my fondness for her I persisted, feeling undone and turned off by the thought of wine.

"I'm a disaster."

"You are a beautiful disaster," she said gently, then kissed me on the forehead and went to the kitchen to get some glasses.

I looked in the mirror, tilted my hip and placed my hands on my stomach. I was afraid of myself in that moment. The power of my body, the idea that people were going to pay money to see it. April came back with two mismatched coffee mugs brimming with cheap red. We clinked glasses and said "Santé" and I took a huge gulp, which burned my throat and dribbled down my chin. She took a CD out of her bag and put it on the player: "Teardrop" by Massive Attack.

"The dance will just be the length of this song," she called over its pulsing.

April turned around and sashayed towards me. "Just feel the music, Ines."

I closed my eyes and tried to relax and enjoy myself. I felt so nervous I wanted to cry or burst out laughing or both.

"This is serious," she said. I stood there and closed my eyes, trying to feel calm and sexy and confident. When I opened my eyes, April was taking the strap-on out of her bag. It was the first time I had seen one. The strap was all black and a hard purple dick thrust from it. The back laced up like a corset.

April noticed the look on my face. "Don't worry, it's clean."

"I've never…"

April paused the song.

"Are you sure you're okay with this?"

"Yeah, I am." I downed the rest of my wine and poured another glass and hit play.

We practised the dance a few more times and finished the wine. April called a taxi and I went to the bathroom. I stared into the mirror and told myself I could do this, all the while wishing I had about a thousand Xanax to pop and more MDMA.

"Okay, babe, the cab is outside. We've got to go."

The club was at the top of rue Saint-Laurent. I had walked by it a hundred times before but never noticed what it was. There was no sign and as far as I could tell it didn't even have a name. The windows were boarded up and painted over and the front entrance made it look like the doors were permanently closed. We arrived just after 11 p.m. and it was just beginning to fill up with people. April gave the CD to the DJ who was behind a black caged wall, elevated above the dance floor which looked like a wrestling ring because of the way the cage continued to wrap around it. The manager approached and asked us if we were Scarlett and Madison, then led us downstairs to the office where we locked up our purses and coats. As we walked through the basement to get to the tiny office, which was basically just a computer desk and a safe in a windowless closet, we passed several rooms, large and small, with beds everywhere and even a shower. The beds were all made and peppered with decorative pillows. I wondered who cleaned and made them.

Back upstairs, we hung around the bar drinking double gin and tonics until the show was supposed to start.

"You're going to be great, Ines, I know it," April said. The drinks were beginning to take effect and I began to believe it too. I looked around the crowd of mostly middle-aged couples. The women were trying hard to be sexy and the men played at being aloof though it didn't take much to imagine they were thrilled to be there, with or without their consenting partners. The room vibrated with anticipation and I realized what happened in those beds long after we left was the real show. These people would no longer be thinking of us, and they wouldn't remember our faces. We were just appetizers. With this understanding in mind I turned to clink glasses with April, feeling lighter and readier. I decided the best course of action was to own it completely—and not make eye contact with anyone.

The DJ announced us in French and then English and we stood on the sidelines of the caged booth until we heard our names. The song began to play and we moved out onto the stage. The crowd of people gathered closer around us. We danced together and stroked each other's breasts. We went to kiss but April tossed her head away from mine at the last second, teasing. As we had practised, I began by dominating April first. I danced her against the black cage and she grasped onto it with her hands while I lowered myself to a squat and ground up against her. I could feel her long black hair on my shoulders and smelled the sweat from both of us as the room heated up. The nervousness left me when I had my back to the audience. I had never seen April wear white before. The lace bra held her large breasts beautifully. Her nipples grew more visible against the white as they hardened and darkened. Just as I went to pull the lace down and expose them, she fake kicked me and I tossed myself forward to the ground and crawled along the floor with my ass in the air to the centre of the stage. It hurt my knees, but I didn't care. April followed. She circled around me, then spanked me a couple of times. I looked up at the faces and caught the eyes of a couple watching intently while sipping their cocktails. I looked down again, feeling embarrassed.

When I returned to the present moment I realized that April was no longer behind me; she had gone into the wing for the strap-on. I stayed on all fours, crawling like a wild cat to the slow melodic music while she attached the strap-on to her body and then opened a condom wrapper with her mouth. She spit out the torn-off piece and rolled the condom over the dildo. I looked up and found myself at eye level with several hands stroking legs and crotches. I looked down. April ran her hands up and down my back while I flipped my hair back like I couldn't get enough. When she entered me from behind she held my hips and pulled me back towards her. To the beat of the song she pushed into me, no more than four or five times, and my hips and ass jiggled against her. The music ended and the lights went off. I stared at the floor, still on my hands and knees. April pulled out and grabbed me by the elbow to help me up. We scurried back into the wings, the heels clopping on the hardwood, while people applauded and we headed back downstairs into the office.

"Great job, ladies, well done. That was awesome," the manager greeted us, counting out twenties from the safe. "Have a few drinks upstairs if you want, on the house. Thanks so much." He arranged the cash into two piles and then handed one to each of us. April and I looked at each other with our eyes wide. We put on our coats and went upstairs, past all the empty beds waiting for sex and debauchery. The dance floor was full and the room was still dark save for some strobes and a few spotlights on the DJ booth.

"Do you want to stay for a drink, April?"

"I can't. I told Pierre I'd cover a shift, he's short-staffed."

"Okay, gotcha."

April had her backpack on and we stood there for an awkward moment. "Thanks so much for doing this, Ines. You did great." She kissed my cheek. "I have to go."

She left and I sat at one of the bar stools and ordered another double gin and tonic. A woman in her forties approached me and asked if I wanted to join her and her boyfriend downstairs. She pointed him out a few feet away and he lifted his drink in my direction. He was backlit by the pulsing strobe lights so I couldn't see his features, but when she pulled her hair behind her ears and placed a warm hand coyly on my shoulder, for a second I thought it was Multiple Scorgasm. But if she was really too shy to have a three-some, it couldn't have been her.

"I'm sorry, I can't. No fraternizing with the patrons. House rules." I pulled the cold gin through the straw till it was gone in a few gulps and it fizzed in my stomach. I started to reconsider their offer, but she disappeared into the flickering glow and they were taken together by the bass into a sea of options. I zipped up my new winter coat and walked out into the street, suddenly very aware of the outfit I had on underneath, and the fact that my boots said *Fuck me*. It was freezing and the mucus in my nose turned to ice. I tried to flag down a cab, but it had people in it. I felt like they were staring at me. I felt ashamed of myself. I walked a little down the sidewalk and imagined I was a sex worker in the wrong neighbourhood. I felt for the money in my pocket to be sure it was still there. A cab finally stopped and I jumped in the backseat. My apartment wasn't that far away and it only cost seven dollars to get there. I gave the driver a twenty and didn't ask for change.

＊ ＊ ＊

When I got out of the cab I flipped up the fur hood, keenly aware that the driver was watching me. I began walking towards the apartment, I noticed there was a man sitting on our front steps. Before I had a chance to grow nervous I realized it was Max. He was wearing a brand new pair of Nikes and had his head in his hands on his lap. I trod carefully on the icy cement in April's boots, and the sound of the heels gouging in the slated sidewalk roused his attention. "Ines, what are you wearing? What are you doing?"

I had questions of my own.

"What are you doing here? When did you get out of the hospital?"

We were talking over each other and both stopped. He stood and I hugged him hard. In April's boots I was nearly as tall as he was. He rested his chin on the top of my head and we embraced until it was too much for me.

"Come inside, it's freezing."

"What are you wearing?" he asked me again.

"What are you wearing?" I said.

I didn't stop to take the boots off in the foyer and we both clambered upstairs. Lainey was working at the cam studio and Cedric greeted us with excitement. Max sat on the couch and looked around the room like it was his first time there. A thick gold chain peeked out from beneath the collar of his coat. I had never seen it on him before. I motioned for him to come into my room and closed the door behind us. It felt like we needed to be private, even within the walls of the inanimate, empty house.

"Why are you dressed like this?"

"I was at a club."

"Like that? What club?"

I didn't know what to say and like most situations in which I was at a loss for words or too moved or surprised to come up with any, I began to cry. I folded into Max's lap, grateful for his lucidity, and even though I hadn't planned on it, the release of tears came easy. Max patted my hair, which felt crunchy from the product.

Eventually I managed a reply. "Can we talk in the morning? I just want to go to bed."

Max's eyes were wider than I'd seen them since he went in. His pupils were fixed on me, intent on finding what they were looking for. But he slipped off his Nikes—brand-spanking-new and all white save for the blue swoosh. He had brand new Nike socks on underneath. He moved them neatly into the corner and sat beside me again, resting his hand on my lap. I looked down at myself, wondering how I had just done what I did. I knew what it looked like to Max. It looked like I was working the corner. I felt for the money again in my pocket and decided to leave it there. I zipped up the pocket and began to undress. I took off the outfit and pulled on some sweatpants and a tank. I put on a pair of wool socks and crawled under the covers. Max continued to sit, puzzled by my extreme look. Still sick and medicated, he moved slow. He began taking his jacket off. He folded it and laid it down on the floor beside him. I heard a container of pills jingle in one of the pockets; he gave me an odd glance and I paid no mind. Neither of us was in the mood for talking.

We lay down on the futon and I nestled into the indent of his shoulder, smelling his scent while his chest rose and fell and I listened to his heartbeat, striding in slow motion. His heart was a seashell and I listened for the sounds of the ocean. His breathing was calm and sleepy, and it lulled me into memories of the summer when we lay tangled in his bed in the wet humidity. I rode the wave of that moment, forgetting all the demons in the undertow.

There was no place I'd rather have been. My throat closed up at the thought and I stifled more tears, but it was no use. They fell anyway and wetted his white shirt. He stroked my hair and pulled it back from my stinging eyes, combing it gently with his fingertips. A grateful and tired sleep fell over me and I surrendered to how lost I was in the world. I wasn't tough at all. In the buzz of the intoxication I wanted to end everything.

I dreamt of water, only this time I was drowning in it. My legs were treading so hard they churned and created a rumble like a heavy spin cycle. In my hands, held high above my head, was Clara's teddy bear. I was trying to keep him from getting wet. The bear had a red ribbon tied around his neck. I pushed him to the sky as the abyss tried to pull me below. I stretched so hard for so long, I thought I was going to snap in half. My screams for help made so much racket the birds flew from the trees.

One winter, a deer had fallen in the lake as the water was freezing over. She was stuck there, and there was nothing anyone could do to free her without risking death. She was forced to surrender, caught between the water and the air, until she died. She remained there until the melt, when the ice released her bones and wisdom back into the lake. She sank and became nothing, as cutthroat trout feasted on her innards. In my dream I became that deer, frozen in time. Unable to keep hold of the teddy bear. It drifted weightlessly into the dark, unravelling. In my fingertips, only the dangling red ribbon.

"Clara Bella!" I heard them calling. They call grew more frantic and it became a yell.

"Clara Bella!"

When I woke up it was the afternoon. Max was still beside me. I had grown so used to his abandonment during the chaos that it felt like a cosmic gift. I smiled to myself, remembering how he had comforted me and held me through the night. I pulled his arms around me under the blankets and he stirred. He rubbed my legs and I wiggled my hips into him, and we rocked that way until he was ready to enter me and as he finished, for the first time inside me, I ached for all that we once were and would never be again.

I got up and went to the bathroom. It stung to urinate. I reached down to pat my swollen vulva dry and noticed something on the paper: a broken piece of the condom from the show. I remembered April saying something in the wings about forgetting to bring lube. Since I'd never been fucked with a fake dick before I had no idea that you needed it. I threw it in the overflowing garbage bin and felt ugly and ashamed of myself, disgusted by my body. Max was asleep again. He looked so innocent with his hair all ruffled. Until last night I hadn't seen or felt him move so purposefully since the episode. I left him there to rest. I wasn't ready to talk yet. I got dressed and went out for a walk, I went to the restaurant, in hopes of getting my last paycheque and tips. The walk up was strange and desolate. It was so quiet outside it felt like science fiction. Icicles hung menacingly from the power lines, looking like they could crack and fall and split a person in half. There were no doors or windows open, and for a metropolitan city, the Plateau in January was sparse. Thierry was the only one at the restaurant. I peeked through the glass and knocked. My breath heaving into my hands to warm them. He came and unlocked the door for me and invited me in. I was nervous to see him because of what I had done, but Thierry was in a surprisingly pleasant mood.

"Ines, my girl, comment ça va? Come in, it's freezing."

"Hi, Thierry." I stood with my hands back in my pockets, waiting again to be motioned inside. It didn't feel like a space I could take that kind of permission over any longer. The wooden door in the floor was open and I could tell Thierry had been pulling out bags of sugar and flour; the heavy sacks lay around in odd places, slumped over like tired, dried-out drunks. I thought about asking him for some of his coke.

"I just made fresh crème brûlées, you should have one."

"I don't know, Thierry, I should probably just get going."

"*Non non non* ... I refuse. It is cold and here it is warm. Stay for some last time."

Thierry was wearing his NASCAR hat that had food bits stuck to it and his apron was stained with sauces and oils. His ginger beard was sparse.

"Okay, if you insist." I pulled myself up onto a stool at the bar while Thierry began making us coffees. The machine hissed and purred as he steamed the milk in a metal cup and the espresso poured out black and thick, the crema even. He poured the milk carefully, handed me one and went to the kitchen with his own. I could hear him whistling and then heard the ignition of the torch. He came back with two crème brûlées and two spoons, and he pulled up to the bar beside me.

"You know, Guillaume is a very understanding fellow. Why do you think I still have my job here?" He laughed hard and adjusted his hat. From his black chef pants pocket, he pulled out a cheque folded in half and a small brown envelope with my kitchen tips. "Guillaume is a good man, Ines," he persisted, holding up the papers so that I would meet his gaze. I took the cheque and opened it. It had a four-hundred-dollar severance on it. In the memo was written *Thank you for all your hard work, take care of yourself.* I cracked the burnt sugar carefully and it spidered out like a broken window or the puddles of ice everywhere outside. I put the cheque and the tips in my pocket. My money from the show was still there.

"Why did you come to Canada, Thierry?"

"Paris, my friend, is a cruel mistress. Don't give yourself away to her, Ines."

"But I want to see the Eiffel Tower and drink coffee and eat expensive cheese."

"Paris," he sighed, pronouncing it in French without the S. "The city of lights, the city of romance..." And then he stopped and shrugged.

I gave Thierry a hug. He smelled oily, but I held him tight. He was such a small man, in big clothes, but when his callousness softened, I knew he had the best intentions. He taught me a lot about food and cooking. Once he had confidence in me, I was an opportunity for him to do less, but today I felt like he cared. I finished my dessert quickly and looked around the tiny restaurant one last time: the low wooden roof and the small intimate tables, perfectly set with crisp white linens. Their symmetry and extravagance were comforting. I left and the sky outside was turquoise blue, boastful that it could not be replicated. Like a mood ring, it changed suddenly, and indigo fell over the city like a blanket. I looked at Clara's ring on my necklace wishing it would change too.

I stopped at a café on the way back through the Plateau and ordered another espresso and a croissant with marzipan on the inside and toasted almonds and sprinkled icing sugar on top. I lived on coffee and bread and pastries. I thumbed through my journal and thought on how I had made it to this dazzling brick city of sunshine, which had turned so cold and barren when love soured. Why had I thought love would be flawless? I didn't know what it required. I was still learning to love myself. I felt outside of my body all the more after last night's performance. I had pounded it with drugs and alcohol for weeks, months, years. I wished I didn't do half of what I did, and I vowed to make better choices. What happened to my mother that made her unable to give me any self-esteem at all? Of course, I knew the answer: the nightmare of losing a child ruined her ability to have any herself. And I knew the more important answer too: that I had no right to blame others for my own failures. Clara's death wasn't my fault, it was a tragedy. No more than Max was a criminal for his own mental health. I had watched him sleeping in peace, and he was still a good person.

When I got back to the apartment Max was sitting on the couch watching TV with Cedric curled in his lap. As I got closer to him, I realized he had all the pamphlets I had collected from the hospital in his hand. I sat beside him and he paused the movie and put the remote down on the table next to the couch.

"Why do you have all this, Ines?"

It wasn't what I had expected him to say.

"I want to try and understand what's going on. I want to help. I want to be here for you."

He smiled and looked at me like he loved me again, but then his smile cracked.

"Well, you're wasting your time. I'm not your project fix it."

The aftermath of Max's treatment was that he was swollen in places I wasn't used to seeing. His cheeks puffed and his legs ambled with less grace. He told me he was taking his lithium daily.

"You know the doctors don't even know why this stuff works," he told me as he took one pill and drank a large glass of water. I held his gaze while he held the pill in his mouth. Cedric jumped up, nudging beside him, rubbing himself against his arms as if to say he missed him. When I looked up I saw Max remove the pill from his mouth. His hand trembled slightly as he put down the glass and ran his hand down the animal's spine. I watched some of the water dribble down his chin. He hadn't left my apartment since I found him standing outside. His Nikes were still neatly tucked in the corner. When he tilted his hand to his mouth I noticed that he was still wearing his hospital ID bracelet. It peeked out from his brand new crew neck sweatshirt.

"Why are you still wearing that?"

"This? This is my new ID." He pulled at the plastic strap. His arrogant defiance hadn't softened with the other symptoms and there was no arguing its purpose. This was his measly badge of honour, proof of his now forever label.

"Where did you get that chain?"

"I bought it in Florida."

"Were you released or did you just leave?"

"Ines, don't," he said and then after a moment he flinched into a softer version.

"I feel like my pursuits have burnt out. I'm extinguished."

I couldn't tell if it was a bad French to English translation, but I thought what he was saying was beautiful. We still hadn't talked about where I had been on the weekend and I could tell Max was growing tired of answering questions about his illness—though he didn't call it that, I did.

When he asked me again what I'd been doing the night he showed up I tried to explain the events leading up to the show: that I hadn't been sleeping well and had no money left, I got fired, but he wanted me to cut to the chase. The underlying circumstances were meaningless to him. So I explained that April needed some help for a performance at a club. I told him it was just a dance. I wanted to help out my friend, as she had helped me.

"How much, Ines?"

"A couple hundred."

"Did you take your clothes off?"

"No."

"I don't believe you."

I wondered if the audience saw the condom break, if they thought about what my parents would say, if they felt sorry for me or disgusted by me. Did they know it was broken and aging inside me? It seemed easy for April; we were paid to be sexy and it was as simple as that. I was a broken receiving line, too scared to yell. I stood up and walked out from my bedroom to the balcony to smoke. I threw on my jacket and hung my head, feeling like a coward for lying to Max and to myself. I spared him the full extent of the truth, and he spared me his too; he wasn't taking his pills and I knew it. I found one in the couch cushion and there was never any less in the bottle.

I hauled on the cigarette and let it fill my lungs and thoughts. I felt the money in my pocket. I smoked right down to the filter and when Max came out to smoke a joint I lit another. Maybe after this pack I'd quit.

"Prescription?" I said jokingly, nodded to his joint.

"Je suis en liberté conditionnelle."

"I don't understand."

"I am released conditionally. I am in prison. I am out, but I am in prison." He took a toke on the joint and the end glowed bright crackling orange. "You know I am going to sell those Nikes on eBay and get rich."

I swallowed. "Will you still make movies?"

"Skateboarding is for kids. I want to make money."

"But I love your movies." I smoked and hoped doing so would keep my tears at bay. I was so weak.

I saw Lainey round the corner down below. She'd gone to the university to return some books and pick up some new ones from the library. She held her clothes tight like it would make her warmer. She had opaque black tights on and a mid-length corduroy skirt under her big coat. Her boots were leather and good quality. Her blonde bob was neatly arched under her toque that matched the colour of her boots. She pulled her toque down further against the cold. She looked like a student, like a good student.

"Motherfucker it is cold out there!" she sang as the door slammed behind her. "Ines?"

I came in from the patio and left Max outside to smoke his joint. "I'm up here." As I said it I was already coming to the top of the stairs to meet her. "Max is here," I whispered in a slight panic.

"Jesus, really? How is he?"

"I'm still trying to figure that out."

Seb came over shortly after and I saw him round the corner to our apartment in the same hurried state that Lainey had been in. I stood smoking yet another cigarette. He held a scarf over his mouth, as though breathing the air would kill him. Lainey and Seb kissed each other on each cheek, but I watched them linger and felt excited for them and the interest their kisses expressed. It was the first time they were seeing each other in the New Year. Seb suggested in his usual joyful tone going for drinks across the street at Brasserie Cherrier. It was an old person's hangout and there was a jukebox and the CDs spun around and around and flashed silver.

Lainey and I split a half litre of cheap red wine which I didn't really want because it made me sad and sick. The troubling thoughts would get stuck in my head and it would hurt in the morning. I preferred the blast of whiskey or the slow carelessness of beer. The satisfaction from finishing a bottle and putting it down, like a job well done or a cheers to the day's end. I never stabbed myself from beer. Max went up to the bar and chatted to the strangers beside him. Eventually he came back with four shots of tequila. We were all concerned for him and walking on eggshells, but he was a bull and if his mind was made up, there was no room for negotiation. We drank the shots and sucked on the old browning limes and made faces at each other, pretending to have enjoyed the gasoline burn of the liquor. When Max got up and went back to the bar for more, Seb sighed in obvious fret. Bull enters a china shop.

"Tabarnac. You guys, what is going on? He is so bizarre right now."

I stared at him. Seb was usually the optimistic one.

"I think he is just trying to pretend everything is normal right now," I replied, not wanting to address my own concerns.

"He shouldn't be drinking."

"We know," Lainey said.

Max took the lumberjack hat off the head of the man sitting at the bar and put it on his own. It had fuzzy grey earflaps and was red and black plaid. He came back over to the table and tried to get me to dance with him, but I didn't want to get out of my seat.

The bar was practically empty, but the eyes that were there were on us. Maybe just for entertainment value, but I knew that the more Max drank the more he was struggling to hold everything steady inside him. The song changed. The CD lifted and shifted, and Neil Young's "Old Man" came on and the psych ward came reeling back to me. The energy in the whole bar went down a notch as if every one of the bar's patrons began drowning their olives and thinking to extremes.

Max finally sat down; he took off the man's hat and placed it on the table in front of him. He lit a cigarette and pulled on it slowly. I stared out the window and watched a couple of squeegee punks huddle together and light smokes for one another. One of them had a massive red and black mohawk. I wondered how he kept it so stiff in the snow. His patchy leather jacket wasn't even done up. I wondered what it would be like to have sex with them and what they smelled like. If they were truly as tough as their exteriors exuded. Montreal appeared to have a way of accommodating all people, but under the surface there was poverty and nationalist factions. Most everyone was just trying to get along. It was a melting pot, but everyone had their quadrants and spaces. The squeegee punks took over the streets. This was their territory, especially at the bottom of Saint-Denis.

Lainey broke the silence with a lighthearted invitation. "We should go to the cabane à sucre one of these days." It was her totally earnest way of making others feel at ease.

"That sounds like a great idea to me." A positive acceptance from Seb, delivered in his totally earnest way of making others feel heard. But Max was not in tune with the rest of us. He crossed his legs and sat back deep in his chair. He smoked the cigarette and methodically blew the smoke back to us at the table. Lainey fanned it out of her way while Seb and I tried to piece together what his next move was going to be.

✼  ✼  ✼

Max came over with tickets for a hockey game. I felt petrified. I wondered where he got the money for them, but I didn't bother asking. He never gave me a straight answer. I wanted to stay in and watch a movie and wear slippers and cuddle on the couch with a blanket, but Max was determined, and when he had that look on his face it was either go and be there in case anything happened or don't go and worry what would.

He snuck a mickey of rye into the arena in his underwear and I tried again to remind him that he shouldn't drink while taking his medication, but he wouldn't hear it. He heard nothing. It was like he was a puppet being orchestrated by a presence bigger than us both, like he was never quite fully in control of himself. He was his own weather system.

"Ines, I am fine," he rebutted. "I feel good, I'm on top of the world."

We arrived after the puck dropped and everyone was already engaged in the action. Even from up high you could hear the blades of the players' skates cut the ice and the boom of the boards as the men slammed each other against them. They looked so small from where we were, but they moved so fast. The arena had a stale athletic smell to it, like it had wafted all the way from the change rooms into the rink, over the boards, and up into the stands. Jerseys hung from the rafters and the fans were so excited and happy. Max and I found our seats and shuffled our way past people's knees down the rows. People's heads peered around us as we blocked their view. Max moved like he was in a hurry to get to our seats, but when we got there, he couldn't sit still. He would stand up and yell or sit and squirm and check his pockets and drink his soda, which he'd poured rye into, then elbow the guy next to him, who kept looking over at us queerly. We were only there for a few minutes before Max announced that he was going to get a beer. I didn't say anything this time and let him march his way back through the annoyed people. He seemed to take up so much space. I rested my elbows on my knees and my chin in my palms. I half watched the game and half watched for Max, expecting him to come up to the opening and barrel once more into the aisles. The Canadiens scored and everyone launched out of their seats, yelling and whooping. A song came on the loudspeaker and all the fans clapped along and sang "Olé, olé, olé," which I thought was only a European soccer chant, but it was alive and well in the stadium. When Max still hadn't come back after the goal I began to get worried. I made my way into the ring and searched the food and drink stands for him, but I couldn't see him.

I walked the round halls, which were empty except for the merchants waiting to sell overpriced drinks and pretzels and hot dogs at the first intermission. I saw Max. He was yelling at a bartender at a beer kiosk, his arms flailing around exuberantly. I walked faster and called out his name, trying to get to him in time.

"Max," I said. "Max!" He couldn't hear me. The man behind the counter wouldn't sell him a beer because he didn't have any photo ID. Max held up his arm, aggressively showing the man his hospital bracelet and yelling, "This is my ID!" I tried to calm him and tell him that he needed his licence, but it wasn't working.

"You see this? This is my fucking ID."

"Max, please stop."

"Câlisse, Ines, enough!"

It happened fast. There was a ringing in my ears. I watched him from my position on the ground. The security guards were grabbing him and pinning his arms back. They pushed his head down and led him out of the exit doors. I wasn't sure how I got on the ground. People were speaking French to me and trying to help me up. Max was saying sorry over and over again.

"Désolé, désolé, désolé." A beautiful French word that reminded me of sunshine. It was an accident. Max would never hit me; that was not his nature. There was buildup and confusion, frustration. He wouldn't take that stupid bracelet off. He doesn't remember who he is without it. I tripped over my own stupid feet. The floor was slippery from all the winter boots. Caution signs dotted the halls and the ends of every sopping dirty rug. As they threw him out of the game, the Canadiens scored again. The building exploded with cheer. I found my feet with a stranger's help and was asked a dozen times if I was okay. I persistently answered yes. People watched me with eyes that said otherwise. I walked outside after Max. The city was fine. It didn't budge. I half expected it might have halted when I walked out of the arena, for all the passersby to turn and stare. Everything would go silent and the lights would go out in decrescendo, like at the end of a play. The snow globe, shaken up, would start to settle. I felt small. I was a country mouse in a rat race and no heads turned to see my heart spilling out all over the sidewalk. I thought about walking the streets to look for Max, but it was futile and I was afraid. I knew he was afraid too. Both afraid of who we really were. I looked in all directions but I wasn't sure which was which. I tried to get my bearings, but I throbbed at the lights in the financial district and didn't know my way out of the area. I couldn't see the cross on the top of Mont-Royal, nor the St. Lawrence River. I got in the first cab I could hail down, while the lights of all the offices glared at me.

Lainey was working at the studio and the house felt emptier than ever. I closed my bedroom door and stared at myself in the mirror. I noticed a red dent where Max's hand had caught the edge of my eye. I stood there, suspended between adolescence and adulthood, clinging to the promise of a future I didn't want any-more. I burned with rage at the sight of myself; an angry, lost girl. I smashed the cheap mirror with my fist and it cut my knuckles like a bar fight. I sat on the floor and sobbed amongst the broken glass. Dad taught us never to stay with a man who laid his hands on us. His own father was abusive; there was a violent streak in my bloodline that wouldn't be passed down. I made up my mind, walking away was not a weakness. I swept up the glass and dumped it. I cleaned my hand and put on Band-Aids.

I went to the Jean Coutu right when I woke up to get the photo taken. I filled out the application on the bench while I waited for it to be processed. One day of my life, captured in time, where nothing of any material significance happened, except that I made a decision to change. Trapped in the flash. The dead reckoning was over. My hood and headphones showing, my eyebrows thin, my skin pale. A vacant sadness. I put my headphones back on as I left and walked down the sidewalks of rue Drolet. Always with a soundtrack to the pain, I listened to the Cure's "Pictures of You" on repeat. The homes within the brick walls and painted doors looked so cozy and I peered into the windows for a glimpse inside the life of someone else. In Carré Saint-Louis the park looked like *The Secret Garden*. The fountain's dribble was frozen in time. I missed the leaves on the trees. I studied the one I had tied my wish to. The branches were exposed and no longer reached for the sky but drooped towards the ground. They weren't strong enough to hold themselves up against the ice and snow. When I got home I called my mom.

"Ines, it's so good to hear from you. How are you?"

"I'm okay."

"What's wrong?"

"I'm fine. I just want to tell you that I'm going to be leaving Montreal."

"Are you coming home?"

"No. Not yet. I saved enough money from cooking. I'm going to Paris."

The other end was silent. I fiddled with the passport picture: the saddest photo I had ever seen of myself. Black and empty eyes, a pretty, youthful face, that person trapped in the flash was angry and sullen and free; a dangerous combination.

"Have you talked to your aunt? You know, you could maybe stay with her in England first?" It was the most encouraging statement from her yet.

"I'll email her right now. I love you guys. I'm doing really well." Lies get easy when you tell them all the time. It rolled off my tongue. "Goodbye, Mom."

"Wait, Ines. Please don't keep running away. You know, we love you, don't you?"

"I'm working that one out right now, Mom. I gotta go."

I emailed my Aunt Karen right away. She'd lived in England since Clara and I were kids. *Karen spends more money on her shoes than she does on her rent,* my mom would always say. She had no kids and no partner, so it seemed like that was her prerogative. *If you look good, you feel good* was something she said often. I wondered if she ever got lonely. I didn't think so. I hoped she'd be excited to hear from me regardless.

☙ ☙ ☙

I had to bring Madison Bancroft back. I worked at the cam studio until my passport arrived. I was in control this time, hungry for the money that I could spend travelling. I was better with the equipment and better equipped at acting nonchalant. It didn't matter who saw me. I wasn't trying to impress anyone anymore. I was a real-life fantasy: the girl who ran away to the big city to find love and adventure and found herself in a fake bedroom talking dirty through a microphone. Her knuckles cut, her stomach opened, her arm weak. The clients either liked my vulnerability or it made them angry. In the forum they wrote *You're ugly* and *Let me see your pussy* and *Your tits are flat.* Others would stick up for me and write back *Get lost, Madison is amazing* and *Don't listen to them, you're gorgeous* and I wondered if they were kind in hopes of being offered a free taste or if they truly thought I was enjoyable, but it didn't matter what they thought. I kept rehearsing in my mind that I would tell anyone who said they knew me: that *they didn't know me anymore.* I kicked the bad guys out and let the others stroke my ego. I even bought a couple new matching bra and underwear sets that were expensive and tasteful. They were still all black. I felt for the first time womanly and secure. April did my makeup one night and I felt like I was hiding in plain sight. The curved black liner flicked towards my temples and my red lips curved larger than my true mouth. I was a caricature of myself. April blotted my lipstick and I smacked the Kleenex with excitement.

"Look at you."

The makeup was fun, but by the end of the night it irritated my face. During a shift I was about to smoke a cigarette for the foot fetish guy when Lainey logged on to my chat room from her home computer. I thought maybe she just wanted to say hey and check in, but she typed frantically and in caps.

AGATHA THRASH: *YOU NEED TO CALL HOME.*

Where was home? My parents? Our place? As I prepared to abandon the city it seemed more and more like I had no home, that nothing was mine. I only owned a futon. I had milk crates for bedside tables. I didn't even buy groceries.

AGATHA THRASH: *CALL ME.*

I finished the private show. Foot fetish guys were the best, an easy score; I didn't have to *ooh* and *ahh* or fake jack off. They didn't want to see my face. Customers who wanted a close-up of my face unnerved me. I never got over the fear that I would be recognized. *Have you heard that that poor Ines Moreland girl is doing porn? I heard she was in an orgy where she got spit roasted by two men. Must be because her sister died.* Small-town minds don't see the difference between getting paid to masturbate and getting cum in every orifice. Maybe there wasn't any, but that wasn't about to define me. I turned off the camera after the show, stripped the bed, peeled the Saran Wrap off the keyboard and wiped everything down with a Lysol wipe. I went to the bathroom and flushed my cigarette butt down the toilet and rinsed out the ashtray in the sink. Pierre didn't mind us smoking inside, so I lit another while I went to his office to call Lainey. I put my feet up on the desk and folded my arms. Pierre looked indulgently my way as I picked up the phone and nestled it in the crook between my collarbone and my ear.

"Getting pretty comfortable here, I'd say."

I winked at him. Lainey picked up.

"Hey, what's going on?"

"Fuck Ines, I have been waiting by this phone for like twenty minutes."

"Calm down. I had a good client."

"Well, this is urgent."

"What's going on?"

"Max was arrested. He's in jail."

"He's in jail?"

"Seb said he's going to pick him up and he wants you to go with him."

"Why me?"

I was apprehensive to see the brash version of him. I felt done with the uncontainable. I let go of any hope for a future with Max and instead envisioned a future of my own. I changed into my jeans and a hoodie and walked to Seb's apartment. We drove to the cop shop to see Max, and he was forlorn. He'd spent the night on a hard cot, his arms bound behind him, with no blankets, in a cold, empty cell room. He hadn't slept and his eyes were caverns of sorry. The police had brought him a McDonald's breakfast, but it sat untouched on the floor, the shiny oil from the hashbrown stained the box and caused it to sag. Max, Seb and the officer who opened the cell spoke in French for a while and then a policeman, who was wearing a bulletproof vest, escorted Max out and unlocked his handcuffs. I didn't want to ask how he'd ended up there. It was intimidating to watch the uniformed men and women walking around, looking like they had important things to do. There was no bail and from the tone of the officer I inferred that far from being angry, or considering this a legal matter, they pitied Max and decided he just needed to cool off for a night. Likely they saw he was outside of himself, a mental health issue, not a criminal one.

The evening streetlights had halos that shone on the sidewalks of the Plateau. Everything had shrunk in on itself: cars were buried by snow so only the tops could be seen. Shovelling seemed to have been abandoned mid-go, as though halfway through people hit a foot of impenetrable ice. The snow fell again and again, creating a fortress over bikes and cars and benches and balconies. The salt did very little to manage it, but crunched under our feet and ate at the fabric of our boots as we walked. Fat snowflakes began to fall, and one landed on the tip of my eyelashes. I felt it melt as I blinked. A snow tear. My pulse hurried. I breathed deep and welcomed the cold pain of it.

"Did I hurt you?" Max said quietly.

"No, you didn't hurt me, Max," I lied.

We walked. He either wouldn't or couldn't tell me what had happened since I last saw him. All he would say was that he went to a bar and was arrested. He called the cops pigs and spat on the sidewalk when he mentioned them. I didn't bother mentioning how kind they'd been to him, how they could have taken him right back to the hospital.

"I'm still taking the pills," he volunteered, as if this would please me and put everything back in order. "Come to New York with me! That's where I'm going."

"I can't, Max. Don't be ridiculous."

"It's just a bus ride away. We can go to Times Square and stay in a hotel."

As Max gushed about the next fantastical adventure he wanted to go on, I thought about telling him of the one I was planning, but I couldn't make myself do it. Seb glanced back and forth at us and then walked a few paces behind. I kept my hands in my pockets firmly though Max tried to take them out and cup my palms in his. I didn't want him to see the cuts. When he leaned in to kiss me, I knew it was time to speak.

"I'm leaving Montreal, Max. I'm going to Paris."

"Yes, let's go to Paris! We can drink wine and eat cheese and bread. Like when we went to Quebec City." His gestures were full again, the grandeur of his vision, our plans.

"I can't, Max. I have to go alone."

He dropped his hands. "You're breaking up with me?"

The words hurt to hear. I looked him in the eye, hoping for a moment of lucidity. "I don't think we're really together."

"Ines."

"I'm sorry, Max. I thought I could do this. I wanted to help you, but you aren't ready to help yourself."

It was not that I thought so highly of myself that I believed losing me spelled the end for him, but I could feel it. His dejection was palpable. When we said goodnight, he assured me again that he was taking his pills. I never heard them jingle in his pocket like that first night, and they weren't in the plastic bag the police gave back to him with all his personals.

*※ ※ ※*

*Nothing feels as it should as I prepare to leave the city. It's a different place to me now, beleaguered, so I move on. I'm back in liminal space. The first taste of anonymity to the decay of Fall, his fall, my fall, frozen in blue, waiting for the thaw.*

Our mother once said that Clara and I had been named for the wrong grandmothers. I was more like Grandma Clara, and Clara was more like Grandma Ines. It made sense to me now. Clara, my dad's mom, was bitter and cold and drank orange juice with vodka at breakfast. Grandma Ines taught us how to paint our nails, but Grandma Clara slapped my fingers and put poison on them to stop me from biting them down to the quick. I would wash it off in the night so I could suck my thumb, one of few comforts I could find at that time. I stopped biting my nails years ago, but they never grew strong and thick like hers or my mother's. Another sign of my shortcomings as a woman. I shredded my fingertips with my teeth, pulling little strips away at the cuticle until they throbbed and bled. I was just as nervous and careless with Max's feelings. I feared he might kill himself, but I had no idea how to help him without giving in.

When I worked nights and Lainey was at home, she would log into my chat room to let me know if Max was hanging around outside the apartment. At those times I stayed on shift a few extra hours, until it was 4 or 5 a.m. and I could barely keep my eyes open. If she didn't see him for a few nights, I'd stay on late just in case. I was executing a newfound self and being playful, but when she forewarned me that he was lingering I couldn't relax myself into the mood the job required. I moved half-heartedly when I thought he was circling the apartment. I would smoke and ask the chatters what they thought love meant. Sometimes I would turn off my camera and stop and stare.

I'd bundle and walk home, save for the odd scrape of a shovel, or the pigeons waking up in the gutters, it felt like I was the last girl alive. It was so cold that my legs would sting and burn. I don't know how Max could stay outside that long, some totally human things didn't seem to affect him. When I would finally get home and peel off my jeans, my thighs were red, but still I walked and saved all my money. Movement was a reprieve. Being under the night sky gave me something to yearn for. The city lights were my stars to wish on. I would sleep most of the day while Lainey was at school. I stayed indoors until it was time to go back to the studio. I waited, biding my time, for my passport to arrive, pocketing all the money and craving a new self.

One night I got home just before dawn. An angry frost attached itself to our building, where Max was sitting on the stoop. His head hung low and I watched as he looked up at me while I fumbled with my keys. He took off his hood and hurried up to me and as I tried to open the door, Max held it closed.

"Where do you go at night, Ines?"

"None of your business. Let me in my house."

"Why are you wearing so much makeup?"

Max let go of the handle and I was propelled forward.

"Why do you keep hanging out here?"

"Ines, I love you. I thought you loved me too." He dropped his arms in surrender.

"This isn't love, Max, look at us!"

"How can you say that, Ines? I need you to stay, please."

"I did love you, I do love you. Max, I don't even know what love means."

He put his hand on the door. "Can I please come inside?"

I could hear Cedric growling as we kicked off our shoes in the foyer and made our way upstairs.

We went into my room and closed the door.

"Why won't you talk to me, Ines?"

"I can't answer that."

"Why?"

"Because I don't know the answer," I snapped. I could not formulate words and since I didn't believe we were capable of healing ourselves now, what was the point? We were worlds apart, both isolated by our own fucked-up issues. I was ashamed of the commodity I had let myself become and my focus became breaking out of that hiding place first. I had to go at it alone. I couldn't let him use me up. I so deeply wanted to help him, but I also wasn't ready to forgive. Forgiveness was a wretched thing, my Christian parents preaching it but not practising it. Letting their daughter suffer the guilt of her sister's drowning. I pulled my knuckles through my eyes, taking cheap eyeliner with them. I thought I wanted to be sexy and in control, but I knew I wanted, more than anything else, connection and care.

"I just don't like myself," I managed.

"Ha, I don't like myself either. Ines, look at me."

"Stop saying my name. I hate my name."

"You are beautiful." Max reached his hand for my chin.

"I don't believe you."

"You must believe me."

"How can I, when you won't accept anything about yourself? You left *me*. You cheated on *me*, remember? Now you just hang out outside our place at all hours of the night, stoned or drunk."

Max sat on the edge of the bed sighing into his hands and sobbing. He didn't remember the elaborate plans that held a future for us. He did not remember the Labelle he had met in the observation room. He did not remember the incident at the hockey game. He cried because the people he loved the most, he pushed the furthest away. His mom had stopped calling. I was leaving. There was no one left and it was too late.

"I don't remember what I did. Do you know how lonely that is?"

"We're not all that different, Max."

We lay together on the futon. His breathing was slow and I listened to the rhythm and stared at the wall, unable to sleep, remembering how Clara called them *heart-beeps* when she was little. I heard the mailman drop papers through the slot downstairs and then the little hinges of the flap going back and forth. The tile floor was stained with salt and there were rocks and pebbles all over amongst the boots and shoes. I ran downstairs and in a pile with the flyers, I saw my passport.

✤ ✤ ✤

Lainey and Seb planned a going-away dinner, but Marie and Felix
couldn't, or didn't, come, so it was just them, April and me. Max
didn't show. They promised they'd invited him. They gave me an
MP3 player as a going away present with a bunch of preloaded
music. Seb winked at me and said there were some surprises. I'd
never been given something so expensive, but they cast it off as no
big deal. We ate Thai food downtown and shared different plates of
curries and meats. I went outside for a cigarette and leaned against
the cement wall in the dank alley and saw the guy I used to buy my
drugs off of.

"You wanna pick up?" he asked me.

"Nah I'm good, thanks, man."

"You gotta try this," he said and pushed a baggie into my free
hand and walked away. I looked down at it and laughed. The baggie
had Nike swooshes all over it. An athletic company logo on a bag
of drugs. It made me think of Max, of Nike trying to get involved in
skateboarding, how they at first were shunned, but then started taking riders from the small companies because they were able to pay
them more, and the smaller companies eventually shut down. It was
a money game. Skateboarding as a business, a sport. I smoked my
cigarette down to the filter, went inside to the bathroom and used
my keys to do a couple bumps. It was strong cocaine. I inspected
my nostrils and went back out to our table. I stopped the waitress
and ordered a Fin du Monde: a big bottle of strong French beer. It
was refreshing and masked the cocaine sliding down the back of
my throat. Through the numbness I couldn't wait to leave town.

April bought my dinner and kissed me on both cheeks. I told her I would come by the studio later, but I convinced everyone I was just going for a walk first. Lainey and Seb were going to a movie.

"Just taking in the city for the last time," I told them.

"This isn't the last time. You'll be back!" they insisted as they got into a cab. They didn't know I never travel backwards. I hated that people always said that.

I walked down Sainte-Catherine and knew that this city was more than I'd bargained for. In the summer it buzzed, and I with it, but in the winter, I saw through it and into its cracks. Every person on the street had a cloud of freezing breath attached to them and it was impossible to imagine what they looked like under the fur-lined hoods and big, dark parkas. They were shadows of themselves. I went to Le Sainte-Élisabeth, a pub hidden in a decrepit and oily alley, its brick walls lined with angry and incendiary murals. Dead vines cascaded down the walls of the empty outdoor patio, a spot that in warmer months filled with greenery and glee. The inside gave a warm and humble welcome. Wooden tables and chairs crowded the dark space, old beer signs decked the walls and a brass banister lined the bar, where I sat and ordered a pint. I was back to drinking alone and wanted it that way.

I was sad to not say goodbye to Marie and Felix, they were such good people, but they distanced themselves from me slowly after I met April and Lainey and distanced themselves from Max when he wasn't well. I understood. Their life was established: they had each other and a calm, peaceful existence.

I had bought my ticket, got my passport and strapped my skateboard to my bag. No amount of pleading from my mother could make me return home. I could see in an objective way how my transience could make her feel childless, but what she didn't understand was that this was about my survival. I had to go, if I could ever think of coming back. I was beginning to miss the trees at home, how they dwindled in the fall and hung on as long as they could.

The plane would be a perfect place to begin a new journal. I planned to spend time with my aunt in London and then, when I had my bearings, I would buy a train ticket to Paris. I could find a hostel and explore on my board, starting from the Arc de Triomphe all the way to the Louvre. I grew sad as I smoked, wondering what would come of Max. I finished my beer and went into the bathroom and did another bump; the coke would have to be finished before the night was through. Max and I both could not stop altering our consciousness, attempting to screen ourselves away from our own internal struggles. I walked by Foufounes on the way home and stood in the spot where Max and I had first kissed. Right from the get-go we were infused by disorder. I looked up and stared at the lumbering bar, a place people go to forget. I decided not to go inside. When I got a few blocks up Saint-Laurent I passed a group of sex workers and I stared, unable to control my curiosity about their stories. I came out at rue Prince Arthur and eventually cut into Carré Saint-Louis and backtracked for home. The bare trees cradled the park and in the quiet night, it felt like a cemetery. I was burying myself. I had to see it one last time. The resting place where I wished for love to heal me, and then it was granted ten-fold.

When I rounded the corner to my apartment the door was open. My nerves jolted as I peeked inside and up the stairs. I heard nothing and no footwear crowded the floor. I found Max standing barefoot in the middle of Lainey's room. Coming in from the cold, gusting wind, I was disoriented and there he was: flaccid and stark naked, holding the top half of a Styrofoam burger container with a toothpick flag stabbed into that read TIPS in blue ink. There was small change strewn about the floor. My adrenaline rushed and I tasted the copper pennies in my mouth. The pupils of his eyes were as big as the quarters.

"This is for you," he said, handing me the stolen goods, shaking. "The door was open. I was guided here. The chairs in the park facing your house, I have been sitting there watching you sleep. Then I came to your sleep."

I was high and my plan of keeling over onto my futon face-first until the taxi came to take me to the airport was going to have to wait.

"What are you doing here, Max?"

"I tell you, the door was open. Why do you look at me like that? You know I would not break in. It was open. I had to come to you."

"Okay. I know, but you're in Lainey's room."

"I am? But where is she?"

"She is with Seb."

His clothes lay in a pile on the floor. His Nikes were tucked beside the bed. He looked embarrassed; the high energy of his mission simmered as he came back into himself and realized what he had done.

"It was so dark, I was lost, I could not see. I needed to find you."

"This is crazy!" I knocked the container from his outstretched hands. Loose change sprinkled to the hardwood floor and landed in his clothes. He looked petrified. "I don't want this, Max! I don't want any of this. This is the tip jar from Lafleur!" I cried, the money spinning like a game of jacks.

"I wanted to give you something special, before you left."

"This is not *special*! You stole this!"

It was all too familiar. His rationality was rolled up like a love letter in a corked bottle chucked into the ocean, the seductive idea of rescue keeping him afloat, bobbing up and down with no explanation. I looked at his body, so skinny and hairless. For a moment I let my eyes trace the way his hips dipped down at the sides, his orange stubble and his brick-red hair that was growing back erratically. He was the man who roused my intimacy, but now he was a scared boy, and I did not know how to help him. His face creased in frustration as though if he could just get me to understand, everything would be right again.

"I just want to go from point A to point B, like I did before, my mind clear. I wish I could make you eat some snow for fun! A real Claude Lemieux."

He reached his hand out towards my face and leaned in, in his old natural gesture to kiss me, but I turned away. I stood cold and stumbled on my breath, which tasted awful, like old beer and cigarettes. I swallowed hard and the cocaine drip of my spit tingled.

He moved closer. I got more still, until I was shaking slightly. I told myself I still trusted him. I told myself he wouldn't hurt me, but he looked tangled in uncontrollable urges and thoughts and, possibly provoked by my lack of emotion, he grabbed at me. I slipped out of his reach. He grabbed at me again and I struggled away, but this time his fingers caught my Grandma Clara's necklace and the chain broke, sending beads of garnet rock pelting to the floor like drops of bloody rain.

Outside the wind blew in strong, angry whispers. I heard the downstairs door whip open and felt the breeze carry upstairs. Max must have felt it too, because he grabbed for his clothes, looking at me the entire time with those eyes that scared me and were scared of their own inflated delusions of power.

"I had to come. Something was making me. I had to see you. Désolé," he said. "I am so sorry." But he did not move to leave.

"You have to leave, Max, I want you to go." My voice sounded whiney, which was disheartening.

"Can I just stay here, please? I can't go home. I have no home. Je m'excuse. I cannot go there."

Holding his shirt over his stomach with one hand, he began to pick up the beads, collecting them in his palm as an apology and an offering. He reached down at my feet and picked up what was left of the chain and the delicate glass pendant. He sighed deeply, and I knew that this was my window into his reason.

"Max, just go, please. Look what you've done."

There were so many words, so many sorrows, so many songs, so many snowflakes. I could see them all out the window, blowing fiercely.

"I don't know what anything is anymore. I wanted to help you, but you weren't ready to help yourself and there is nothing else I can do."

We gathered the beads and the clasp and the line, and I put them all in a Ziploc bag from the kitchen and then into my bag.

"You can stay the night with me, but I am leaving in the morning."

"Please don't go, Ines."

"I have to."

"Why is this happening to me?"

"I don't know." I passed him his jeans.

"The lithium makes me lazy."

Max dressed and I watched him.

"I have no life in me no more."

"Of course you do. Why are you still smoking pot and drinking? You know what the doctors said."

"I felt so much greater than this."

We went into my room. My backpack was ready to go by the door, with my skateboard strapped to it, and inside, a few clothes, a dog-eared journal and my first passport. In the room, the desk was empty and the closet barren, anticipating a subletter who would arrive the following afternoon—someone new to the city like I had once been, with bottomless hopes and dreams. Maybe they would work at the studio with Lainey and April. I lay on the futon, feeling for the first time how low to the ground it was. I thought of having an adult bed, with matching sheets, a good quality duvet and a headboard. I wondered, when sleep becomes important to me what kind of person will I be?

Max lay down beside me and we looked up at the ceiling together. I could feel him vibrating. The poster of Matisse's *Blue*

*Nude IV* was still on the wall behind us. It was hard for him to remain still, so I grabbed his hand and squeezed it tight. I saw a single tear slide from the corner of his eye down his creamy cheek, where it stayed for a moment before it fell onto the blanket.

"Ines, I am sorry for all of this. I never meant to hurt you."

"Je sais," I told him. *I know.*

"I feel like when I'm with you, it's all right. Thank you for that. You have helped me. I love you."

"I love you too, Max, thank you for awakening me."

It felt like only five minutes had passed, but I must have slept. I blinked into the dark as the alarm sounded. I sat up and Max was gone. It was 5:03 a.m. I called a cab. I went to Lainey's room and she and Seb were asleep in her bed. I kissed the top of her head like she was my child. She made a sigh and smiled but said nothing. I knew she was awake, but it was easier to say nothing and have me go than to say goodbye or ask what had happened. I took the baggie of cocaine out of my wallet and flushed it down the toilet. I should have said a better goodbye to April, but I knew we'd stay in touch online.

The taxi was waiting, puffing eerie clouds of exhaust into the dreary morning. The frozen street was melted by traffic already and shone wet and slick like oil and I felt like I had been transported to another time. The driver opened the door for me and I shoved my pack into the seat and got in behind it, closing the door. The silent drive was restorative. Sleep would have to wait. I didn't brush my teeth. I was in a rush to make the cut-off time. I would have watery, black coffee for breakfast and after sipping its bitter grind-filled finish I would suppress the tears in my eyes with the palms of my hands, my elbows planted firmly on a plastic, foldable dinner tray, hearing the clear beep of the seatbelt sign and having trouble swallowing.

For now, we glided across overpasses looking out on the

glaring lights and brown brick of the city. The Farine Five Roses sign receded and I let my heart montage all the moments where April and Max helped make me feel alive. Near-frozen raindrops fell down the windows of the cab like Max's tears. It all plodded behind me, and I wanted to cry but couldn't. I'd used up all my tears. It was time to move on.

# Printemps

*Begin again*

⚛ ⚛ ⚛

The airport felt like an alien planet: grey carpets, tunnels and hallways, television screens and foreign beeps. Everything was subdued by the feeling in my head. I boarded the plane. I turned off the air dial that was blasting above me and turned on the lamp. Beside me a fat man pulled a duty-free bottle of vodka out of his bag and added it to his cup of cranberry juice. He put his finger to his lips and winked at me. I never knew planes were so big. A very tall woman with big hair sat in the seat right in front of me, blocking any chance of seeing a TV screen. I checked my belongings multiple times. My journal, *The Lion, the Witch and the Wardrobe*, my passport. I took the bag of broken necklace out of my pack and poured the beads into an empty plastic cup I got from the stewardess. One at a time, I rethreaded the garnet back onto its line, picking each one up with all the delicacy I could muster and sliding it down to the next one. Time passed, the plane took off and eventually the necklace was strung together. I tied the clasp on, pulled the knots tight with my teeth and though I couldn't cut the leftover ends, I put the necklace back on anyhow. I held onto the pendant and Clara's ring tightly for some time, and when I awoke it was to a female voice with a smile in it saying, "If London is your home then welcome back! And if not, we wish you safe and happy travels."

At Gatwick Airport my aunt was waiting for me at the arrivals gate. We hugged and then drove two hours on the motorway, speeding on the wrong side of the road. She didn't ask me how I was, and I didn't give up the details. I knew Mom would have told her everything. I anticipated a city skyline in the distance, but it never came. I waited for her questions, but she let me stare and watch. England was colder than I expected but it was lush and green. We drove down a muddy street past a slew of row houses lined up along a riverbank and pulled up to her small flat, so condensed against the others it looked like they had been comically squished together. It was not in the heart of London at all, but it was quaint and quiet and welcoming.

She had a bed made up for me in a small room at the back of the house, with a wooden futon on the floor, just like my old one. I unhooked my skateboard from my bag and spun the wheels and watched them whiz around until the bearings slowed. A wooden toy, like a compass, was the nexus of my heart. I unpacked my clothes and stacked them in a corner. I took the hottest shower of my life. It stung and made my eyes turn red. I counted on my fingers how long ago the first day of my last period was. I was four days late. When I got out, I killed a spider that waltzed its way across the carpet.

She had to work until dinnertime, and I was grateful for the chance to unwind alone. I got dressed and took a walk to a bench beside the local pub. There were robins flying around, landing in the meadows and plucking worms from the wet ground. The sky was a sheet of grey. I flicked on the new MP3 player, put it on shuffle and blindly waited for a song to play, to make me feel a certain way. It landed on an intro of old-world strings and a smoky French woman's voice: "Boulevard de la Chapelle. Où passe le métro aérien." The French record from the dinner party. I pulled out my journal and thumbed around through the pages, looking for a fresh place to write. I needed to rest a while, to get back to me. I started writing in the leftover spaces. Adding to all the stories of Clara and Max. Planning my next adventure of skateboarding over long, curved bridges, to second-hand bookstores and fresh flower stands. Gazing at maps, not worried about being lost, or this time, found. I started writing a letter to my parents, one I knew I would this time send. This one, not meant to be a burning remnant of grief, but a way forward in hope.

At low tide the riverbed smelled of clay and cold earth, and little wooden boats that lost their moorings looked abandoned, tilted in waterless time. Outstretched and rickety, the docks narrowed at the grass landings. The exposed bollards, holding everything up, showed years and years of wear. Now that Max and I were continents apart, I knew that we had love. It was raw, chaotic and vulnerable, it had hurt me, but it was a kind of love. Love is not an innocent word. I got what I wished for in my letter to the universe. *À la belle étoile.* I knew the expression from the song, and it was me, I was: *out in the open, under the stars.* The final verse of it quieted my soul, and I accepted the dissonance. It was time for me to be strong and beautiful, for Clara.

# Acknowledgements

When I was growing up, my sarcastic mother responded to my nosiness by saying, "What? Are you writing a book?" "Yes!" I would say. "I am." In fact, it's the only thing I've ever truly wanted to do. To never stop being curious or creating. I am driven by story and connection. Writing this novel has healed me from the reverie of grief and love experienced in my life and I hope it can do that for someone else.

*Late September* would not be what it is today without the encouragement, skills and vision of Karlene Nicolajsen, Janine Young, Karine Hack and the team at Nightwood Editions. Thank you, Silas White, for believing in this project. This story brewed inside me, sometimes painfully, for a decade. You have brought this dream to life. Angela Yen, I thank you for the sublime cover design.

To Chelene Knight, you opened doors for me, but you also taught me that there are other ways in, ways which are about authenticity, discipline and courage. To Kate Juniper of Juniper Editing & Creative, an Instagram contest serendipitously brought us together. You were the first person to read draft one. You found the themes in the mess, and never compromised the heart— thank you from the depths of my soul for understanding the intentions of *Late September* and taking me to the next level with your honest, brilliant critiques. I am proud to call you my friend.

Editors are truly miraculous people. On that note, I am grateful for the opportunities I had to decolonize my language in this text. May we keep unlearning and changing. It matters.

I want to thank my agent Carolyn Forde from Transatlantic Agency. I am so honoured to be among this cohort and am thrilled for future ideas. Allyson Latta, from our first conversation about starting this book, in a pool in Costa Rica in 2012, and to all the other regulars of your writing retreats that I've attended. Those are moments when I truly felt like I was in the right company. Christine Barbetta, and the craft books you sent to my doorstep. I miss you and may we all be together again sharing our writing and memories over food and beverage.

To Deb Wandler. Never underestimate how a teacher can positively change the course of your life forever. And well, vice versa, no thanks given to the ones who set you back and make you feel insignificant. To anyone struggling with their sexual identity, addiction or mental health, you are not alone and it can get better. I've been there. I am still there. When I say you are welcome to reach out to me anytime, I sincerely mean it and I will respond. To my earliest readers, Alex for always believing in me and my great friend Brando. My skateboard family past and present, you have always been my safe home.

And lastly to my son River, may you flow peacefully and be a part of something bigger than yourself. I love you.

# About the Author

PHOTO CREDIT: MATT MACLEOD

Amy Mattes holds an Anti-Oppressive Social Work degree from the University of Victoria and is currently enrolled in the Bachelor of Arts at Vancouver Island University's School of Creative Writing. She is writing a second novel, poetry and raising a child. She won second place in the Islands Short Fiction Review Contest in 2023 and has been previously published in *The Globe and Mail* and *Portal Magazine*. *Late September* is her first novel.